PRAISE FOR DELUXE DARKNESS

"Collective Darkness will draw you into the shadows and make them your home!"

- Angela Hartley, Author of Copper Reign

"If you love creepy things that go bump in the dark, you'll get a kick out of these spooky stories that tug at the gossamer threads of fear in your head."

- Dr. Trina Boice, bestselling author of 31 books and author coach

FREE GIFT

Thank you for your purchase. To claim your free gift
please visit www.CTPFiction.com

DELUXE DARKNESS

Three Horror Anthologies in One

A Collective Tales Publishing Anthology

Deluxe Darkness
Three Horror Anthologies in One

Cover design © 2021 by Editing Mee
Cover designed by Natasha MacKenzie
Edited by Elizabeth Suggs, Jonathan Reddoch, Alex Child, and Brandon Prows

Disclaimer:

Some stories contain descriptive violence.

CONTENTS

Book II
Little Darkness

Book III
The Darkness Between

Bonus Content

FOREWORD

I have known Elizabeth Suggs for several years through our local classics book club I run. She was always excited and ready to contribute as a reader to even the most difficult of literary texts that I pulled from the crypts of literature. We talked one day after a meeting, and she brought up to me that she was interested in publishing. I myself just published a few projects of my own, *Monster Brain: Conversations with OCD* and *Putrescent Poems: Horror Poetry Vol. 1.*

Like any author and fellow editor, I knew that, for the most part, she would be heading a great new enterprise—I welcomed her to the publishing side of the craft. Not all authors have interest or are able to transition from pounding out stories and poetry, to thinking up and executing entire book projects. My experience told me that unless you hit the ground and do the work, it never gets done—and Elizabeth soared!

I have watched her rise to be a fine author and fellow publisher in Utah, along with her publishing partner Jonathan Reddoch. They create exciting new content, generating original work, culture, and storytelling from the variety of work they have collected for publication and the people pulled into Collective Tales Publishing.

In these volumes, the reader can expect fresh, frightening, and hilarious haunting stories from new and returning authors. This mix of veteran and new voices keeps the storytelling unique while pushing the boundary of fiction, cementing the reader firmly in the darkness.

Daniel Cureton, MA
www.danielcureton.com
Forty-Two Books LLC.

INTRODUCTION

What exactly makes *Deluxe Darkness* so deluxe? Is it that it combines our bestselling anthology *Collective Darkness* with the lesser-known but fun companion book *Little Darkness* as well as *The Darkness Between,* AKA our brand new collection of horror poetry, flash fiction, and very short stories? Or that we made some small tweaks and edits to the existing tales in this updated edition? Or because it's the only way to read our ebooks *Little Darkness* and *The Darkness Between* printed upon the corpse of a sliced-up tree? Or that we included exclusive bonus content from the dark minds of Elizabeth Suggs and Jonathan Reddoch?

All of this makes it deluxe!

Deluxe Darkness is packed with our trademark spooky stories and beautiful poetry that you will be dying to read. We have returning favorites like Karyn Patterson ("Red Flag," "Ghost Train," and "A New Life") and Alex Child ("Pond Scum," "Backroads," and "Selena's Eyes") as well as incredible new voices such as Sophie Queen ("The Green Window") and DA Butcher ("In the Shadows").

We have stories about serial killers, malevolent trees, vampires, and gruesome oddities of all kinds. So, lock the front door and enjoy tonight!

BOOK I
Collective Darkness

Feast

Edward Suggs

Under a reflection of dark ale, a pair of foolish eyes peered
into mine. No matter how much I whisked the mug around,
her face always resurfaced. Seeing her was a grotesque
reminder of what I was: a foul vermin that could only be
described in some hellish poem. For this reason, I drank; with
every sip, those thoughts slipped deeper inward. But regardless of how deep into the pits I was, there was no escape from
my daughter's shrill and agitated voice.

"Mother?" she said, to which I ignored.

Though my nose was dipped into my drink, and my
ears were clogged by the thick banter of the inn, her cold hand
forced my attention on her. Reluctantly, I sat upright and glared
blindly into her flapping lips.

"Wonderful. You're back here again?" Alice sighed and
sat next to me. Her racy tavern-wench skirt narrowly kept splinters from the decrepit bench off of her. She stretched it down
her pale, round thighs and continued, "It's freezing outside,
so the patrons are only going to keep coming. You know these

men aren't going to drink themselves to death, and one girl can only do so much."

I sucked on my teeth, the faint taste of alcohol echoing off my tongue. Taking in a breath, I spewed out the words, "I'm tired."

"Of course, you're tired. What else could you be? It's not like you're always back here getting drunk, right? Come off it. You've left me this whole damn place to run for years, and how have you helped out? By getting drunk?"

"Alice, I..."

"Forget it," she spat, adjusting her dark hair behind her ear. "Just go make yourself useful and mop up the vomit at the bar."

I swiped her away from me and stumbled out of my seat. Facing away from her, I muttered, "You always have to ruin things, don't you?"

I was up and had gathered some cleaning supplies before she could reply. Her now-distant voice let out a sigh. I hesitated, regretting my aggressive remark. I watched as she collected my mug and went about with her work, quickly being enveloped in a crowd of customers.

Closing my eyes, I began to scrub. It was easier to keep myself blind so that I could do my job. In my mind, I found comfort in an inky void. A void which was only disturbed by the incessant shouts of the patrons around me.

Alice's voice pierced through the inn's common rabble and threatened my peace. She took orders and ordered others around. She played the part of the queen as if this inn were hers. I had owned this place for decades; she hadn't the slightest idea how exhausting it could become.

I pushed away from the sticky, stringy thoughts in my brain and followed the dried river of bile around the counter. I got down onto my knees before the vomit as if it were my very own god; then, I began to scrub again.

However, a new distraction whistled my way. A solitary voice coming from the window pulled at my strings, muttering words that I couldn't understand. I had gotten my fair share of interruptions throughout the night and was fed up with this nonsense. I turned my back to the noise, but it only seemed to grow louder.

2

I set down my scrub brush and scooted over to the window, wiping away the fog which clung to the glass. Behind the panes and quick-falling snow, was a white face, awfully close to the windows.

I flinched and pushed myself back, but the man's expression was unchanged by my shock. He just continued to idly smile, exposing his pink, toothless gums. Strings of his saliva spun from the top to the bottom of his jaw like spider webs, and his thick spongy tongue gently throbbed in his mouth.

In contrast to his red insides, his face radiated as white as the full moon. His skin showed no sign of blood, even in this life-sapping cold weather. His eyes were weighed down by black bags, and in his glossy blue eyes, I could find no emotion. They simply retained their stillness, peering into a part of me, which I thought I only found in my ale. His presence unnerved me. He had to leave at once.

I crawled a bit closer to the window, though still keeping some distance. The strange figure made no reaction to this as he watched me in what seemed an oddly patient manner.

There was something in those icy eyes that made me ill, so I avoided staring at them for too long. I spoke from the side of my mouth, saying, "Sir, if you would, please move away from there. It's warm inside, and there's plenty to drink!"

The stranger made no reply.

"Well, you don't need to come in, but you can't stay there."

After a few uncomfortable seconds, I was just about to give up and walk away from this experience, when he did something I hadn't expected.

Muffled from behind the glass, I heard his gentle voice speak my name, "Wilhelmina," though nothing more.

"Do I know you?" I gawked.

The face kept his lips sealed, though he stayed there for a while longer, watching me. As if he wasn't really looking, yet he saw me. Those eyes daydreamed the dreams of my own. My thoughts were an open casket laid out before him, and he simply observed.

Then all at once, he faded into the snowstorm.

I was alone. That wretched face burned into my mind and haunted corners that once were dark. It stood between what was sane and what was unknown. There was something wrong with that thing, something terribly wrong. No amount of scrubbing would make the face disappear from my memory. I grasped the countertop and lifted myself up. I purposely put my back to the window, in case the face returned. Yet, a part of me wished it returned—wished to see that white, hollow face once again.

So, why did I leave that spot? Why was I committed to expelling myself as far from the window as possible? I'm not sure, but I knew I needed to find my daughter. She could always bring me back to reality.

I walked where the customers spoke and laughed. Despite the died-down fires, the all-round-commotion of the place had lightened up. During these moments, Alice usually danced around conversations, laughing and drinking with the customers. Tonight, however, she sat in the back of the inn, near the staircase to our personal rooms, lost in thought.

"The floor's clean. Are you thinking about finishing up for the night?" I said, wearing a smile on my face. It was the kind that wasn't too convincing, yet still polite.

She blinked rapidly, slowly widening her eyes, then nodded. "I... Yes. Would you be able to handle things?"

"Obviously," I took a shallow breath and averted my eyes, continuing, "Get some sleep."

Alice looked at me with an emotion that I didn't understand. But after a few seconds, she turned around and walked to the stairs.

She stopped at the bottom step, with her back to me. "Goodnight, Mother. I love you."

Alice stood there for a fleeting moment as if waiting for something in reply. However, I was speechless. Her maiden "I love you" was enough to imprison any other words I had.

And after a moment of piercing silence, Alice cried out weakly and marched up the stairs.

I felt some sort of rash growing inside me, infecting my organs, and wringing out my lungs. I had made a fool of myself, that much was clear.

I fumbled after her, my feet walking over rotten, wooden steps. I kept replaying her words in my head, thinking something might change, or some other clue would give out, but I found nothing. Instead, my thoughts circled me like vultures, waiting to land. I was unsure if they were mine, or rather demons cackling at my stupidity. I shook my head and ignored them the best I could. Tears welled up in my eyes, and my vision became obscured. The weaving halls carried me to the ajar door of Alice's room. It was a lonely, little sanctuary that didn't often receive visitors.

And there she was, a silhouette sitting atop her dark covers.

"Do you hate me, Mother?" she asked, turning toward me. The light of the stars swam gently through the room and illuminated her flushed, red face.

Tears silently poured down my cheeks, dripping into my opened mouth. The suffocating taste of salt was a familiar friend. This time, I did not try to wipe the streams away. I did not try to snort up the snot, which mingled with my tears. Not this time.

"I'm… Alice, please forgive me. I'm sorry."

"I don't understand," she choked. Her cries were masked by the darkness.

"I never knew what love was," I whispered. "I always wrote stories of it when I was a little girl, and described it as if it were as fantastical as dragons. When I met your father, he spoke of love. And for that one night, I thought I finally understood it. You were always a reminder of him. You were a reminder that everyone leaves. That there was no love."

Alice was sobbing now. Her voice cracked and broke as she screamed into her pillow.

"Though, since you said what you did, I've felt this thing in my stomach. It's like I'm sick now," I said, the words going unnoticed by Alice.

"It's not my fault that I'm here! I just wanted a mama. I wanted someone to read to me, and play with my hair, and… and…"

"I know, I know. I'm sorry."

"Why can't you just be my mama?" Alice threw her tear-stained pillow, and it hit me limply on my chest.

I walked over to the side of her bed and returned it to her. She looked at me with defeat and pawed at my arm, and with every failed punch, her weeping swelled and burst anew. I sat down next to her. Being so close, I was able to make out the details of her face. She was beautiful. I never realized until then that she was absolutely gorgeous. It had been nineteen years, and I hadn't even stopped to notice that. I held my hand to her cheek, but she pushed it away.

"Don't," she whimpered. "Don't play with my feelings."

"No, Alice, listen. I'm sorry."

"You said that already."

"Seriously, I am. You're so strong, stronger than I ever was. I wish I had been better to you. I wasn't made out for this life. But you... you handle anything the world throws your way. I've always been so jealous of that."

"What are you talking like that for?" Alice said wearily.

The moonless night kissed both of our glistening eyes, and I felt something strange. It felt just like when she wished me a good night. I smiled, although this time, the smile wasn't false.

"Alice, the things you said... I want to be your mother. Can I try it again?" I reached for her hand, and she didn't move away. In fact, she was as still as stone. "If... that's okay with you."

The corners of her mouth twitched ever so slightly. Her jaw muscles clenched while she processed what I had said. Her eyes met mine, and she muttered, "Just don't hurt me again. I'm tired of worrying about what you'll say next."

"Okay. I'll do my best."

Alice shifted her gaze to the side. She straightened her posture and slid off the bed. Glancing over her shoulder, she said, "I'm going to get a drink," and left me alone.

Though she left, the tension grew thicker. The room was tight, and it clawed at my neck. If this was how she coped with her issues, then she definitely took after me. What a sick idea.

I backed up against the headboard and looked at the ceiling. The aged wood didn't quite cover the attic, so beams of dim light pressed between the boards and streamed down upon me. If she was anything like me, then perhaps she stayed awake at night and stared at the ceiling, thinking of a different life. Maybe thinking of love, or of a mother who took better care of her.

While I thought to myself, I heard a rat start to scratch at the wood above me. I frowned. They often found their way up there and kept me awake at night. I waited to see if it would give up on its little mission, although to my frustration, it persisted. I clambered out of bed and stood under the vermin. I searched for a broom or anything long. I found nothing.

Something dropped down from a hole in the ceiling. Whatever it was, it landed in my hair, freezing me in place. I picked it off and inspected it. It was small, wet, and pliable. I couldn't quite make out what it was, so I squinted, and then it hit me. It was a fingernail. A human fingernail. My face sank from disgust to horror. I gagged and flicked it away. But no sooner was I rid of the nail, did another one fall in its place, drenched in a warm liquid.

I looked up to the ceiling, expecting another to fall. But rather than a nail, a thick liquid seeped from the cracks and drenched my body. I opened my mouth, horror-struck, and tasted blood.

I shrieked and clawed at my tongue to get rid of the metallic taste.

The… thing from above only scraped its mangled fingers more vigorously as the stream of blood dribbled down. I backed up against the wall, my mind struggling to grasp what was playing out.

My feet moved swiftly across the floor, pressing me against the door. I tried the knob, but my fingers shook and slipped. I drew in a breath, steadied my hand, and twisted the knob. It opened, and I flung myself out into the hall, slamming the door behind me.

The muffled sounds from inside gnawed on my sense of understanding. I stumbled back, keeping my eye on the door as I traversed the halls.

Once I turned the corner, I broke into a sprint, nearly falling down the stairs. In my head, I could still hear the thing's nails digging deep into the wood.

I ran downstairs, skipping steps as I did. And as my feet touched the floor, I dropped, falling onto my knees. There I caught my breath, muttering to myself that I was alright. I knew I wasn't, yet I hoped I would be soon.

I stood back up and shook away lightheadedness.

Things were much too calm down here, and it made me nervous. Somehow, all the customers managed to leave at once, leaving only me and a slim figure at a table.

Alice.

I thanked the gods above for a familiar face.

As I approached her, she didn't react. Her face was low to the table and hovering over a mug of something strong.

"Alice? I think there's something upstairs," I said.

She stayed unmoved by my words. I grabbed her shoulder, hoping she'd notice my existence. After a moment, she turned over to me, glaring into my flapping lips.

"Did you hear me?" I said. "I think there's something upstairs. Something dangerous."

"Not something," she said, and as if in a nightmare, her eyes drifted to opposite sides of her face. "Someone."

The splintering of wood crashed from upstairs, followed by a thump.

"And he's been wanting inside all night."

A bitter chill crawled down my spine and wrung out my lungs. I looked at Alice, then to the stairs. The husk of my daughter grinned, waiting for me to meet our new guest. I opened my mouth to speak, to ask what had gotten into her, but it didn't matter, not really. I knew who was upstairs. And the anticipation was too much. I rushed past Alice, and back to the stairs—curse me for it.

I saw him—that little white face peeking out at me from the top of the stairs. I etched forward, then withdrew. A part of my mind knew the insanity of this. It tried to pull me back, to force me to scream, but the other part of me, the stronger part, caged the scream behind my teeth and moved closer.

He smiled wider than before, and suddenly, all rational thoughts vanished. The longer he stared at me, the less I feared him. Something else gnawed at my heart then. It was a feeling I hadn't experienced in years—not since Alice's father. I relaxed my muscles and smiled back.

I reached my hand out to him, the eater of my heart. And as I did so, he crept out from the corner, revealing his glorious full form. He stood on four legs, with the body of a wolf. No ordinary wolf, however, for he appeared to be taller than I was. His moon of a head protruded out from a mane of gray fur, and where paws or hooves would've been were humanoid hands—all the better to caress my soft skin.

All at once, I loved him. And I knew he wouldn't leave me like Alice's father. He'd never leave me.

His arms—surprisingly flexible—clasped the walls on each side of him, and he pushed his body up onto his hind legs.

Smiling, he gestured with his hand to come forward. I mindlessly did what I was told, and shuffled upward.

He dropped back down and retreated into the corridor. Without a second's notice, I bounded after him, my eyes set in tunnel vision. Nothing else mattered, and his eyes had told me so. In my glee, I believed that I had cornered him in Alice's room. But as I searched around, he was nowhere to be seen. I dug in the piles of debris from the fallen attic until I saw him, to which I shouted in joy. He was just outside the window, whispering for me to follow. But as I drew near, he scuttled downward, out of sight. I grunted impatiently, diving headfirst into the window.

Thunk!

I stumbled backward, clutching my skull. Again, I rammed the window.

Crack!

Shards of glass impaled my scalp. I rolled onto my feet, my vision in a haze. I took in a breath, charging it once more. The window shattered under my weight, and glass daggers tore through my skin like paper. One deep laceration in my stomach, one through my thigh, one through my breast. But I didn't feel a thing. I flew through the air like a beautiful bird and smiled, knowing that I was so close. I was so close to pure bliss.

I landed with a snap onto the snow. A lightning sensation nagged at me, forcing me to give it my attention. My right arm dangled lifelessly from a snapped bone jutting out of my skin. Scarlet blood gushed out from the wound with every beat of my heart.

My head throbbed, but I pushed up on my quivering knees and stood. I started running again, my eyes set to the forest ahead of me. I swore I could see movements in the trees, so it must've been him. I ignored my mangled arm, which screamed for my recognition. It was worthless anyway for giving up so easily.

The snow picked up, and my world was blurred. It was terribly cold, but my heart pumped warm blood through me. I was wheezing, but I could go a bit further, I knew it. He couldn't have gotten too far away.

Agony burned at my arm, but I continued on. The pain trickled down into my legs, knocking them together. I dug my fingers into my palm on my left hand in an attempt to diverge my body's focus away from the pain. But it was more than I could handle. My knees gave out, and I crumpled into a cushion of stinging snow. It couldn't be over. I hadn't even reached him yet.

The corners of my eyes blotched with black dots, and a buzzing from my ears swelled until it was impossible to ignore. I tried to punch my head and wake it up, but I was slipping away. Even the snow felt hot on my body.

The buzzing morphed into voices, the kind one gets right before passing into a dream. Nonsensical ones that say things, which don't make sense. I could hear the congealed rabble of crowds. Then I heard his honeyed-words. They had been so promising. When he called out my name, I thought it meant that he loved me. The bond we shared—I believed it to be special. Instead, he left me here to die. It was all a game to him. Worse than that, he left me with Alice, the daughter, who did not deserve her fate.

A blood-curdling scream resounded from the inn. The buzzing stopped, and I lifted my head. I knew that voice. It was Alice. My motherly instincts were enough to raise me from my deathbed, but not enough to hold me steady. I shambled toward the inn and ripped open the front door. To my great surprise, I beheld my lover once again.

Behind the ashy remains of the hearth, I spotted him. His jaw was dislocated like a snake, and Alice's lower half laid limp out from his mouth.

He gazed upon me with great pride, but deep in my throat, I fought back my horror. Likely noticing my reaction, he swallowed up the rest of my daughter. A wide toothless smile curled onto his lips. My mouth moved to ask why, but only dust came out.

"Wilhelmina, don't worry yourself."

I was taken aback, as I hadn't expected a word from him.

"This was all for the best. She will now nourish any children to come and live through them. Live through us," he

10

prowled toward me until we were face-to-face. His eyes bur-
rowed into mine, dominating any doubts which hid under my
skin. "You will now leave this unwanted life to live for me."

I closed my eyes as the joy found its way back. I didn't
need my daughter's love, for, after all, I had him. It made
complete sense why he did it; I understood that now. I wanted
nothing more than to take him up on his offer.

His warm breath lingered, just a movement away. I
parted my lips and met his with mine. The sweet taste of his
saliva swam about in my mouth, and everything grew light.
As my teeth slid out from their sockets, I was ready to become
beautiful, just like him.

Padua's Eyes

Jonathan Reddoch

Three miles outside the tiny hamlet of Croppenhaus, a lanky figure lurked in the shadow of a tall oak, stalking his nearing prey. The pale moon rested behind the treetops; the hunter was guided through the darkness by unnatural providence. The prey smelled spectacularly succulent to his acute senses, so potent, so alluring. The hunter chose to remain hidden and let the blood come to him. He felt it approach, felt it advance through the dense black thicket.

The dark figure's hunger intensified the closer his prey neared.

The figure watched his quarry emerge from the thick brush and stop beside a fallen tree. The hunter stepped forward. The howling wind disguised his footfall as he approached.

The wild boar sharpened its yellow and brown tusks against a lifeless trunk. The hunter's tattered cloak flew back in the brisk air. A lumbering shape haunted the boar's shadow. He stepped closer, and yet again, closer. A cold silhouette, merely resembling the shape of a man, loomed clandestinely over the boar, inching forward, ever eager, ever hungry.

The moon moved out of hiding, revealing the towering mountain range to the west. He was even closer to them than he predicted. The hunter carefully veiled his withered hood over his pallid face against the moonlight.

His garments stunk of death and decay, but he was careful to approach from downwind. With a blistered and blackened tongue, he licked his parched, anxious lips in anticipation. He was within grasp. His teeth extended in preparation. His eyes grew bright red. He raised his hands high for the kill, his sharp claws and fangs extending even further, glinting in the soft starlight. The wind settled. The only sounds were the whispering breeze slipping between leaves and the many tiny legs scattering from the hallowed trunk. He watched as the boar snatched a mouthful of escaping crawlers.

Muffled cries in the distance suddenly broke the stillness. Faint human shouts were heard. *The townspeople.* Since the early evening, their bloodhounds had tracked his lingering scent after he was caught in the company of several tender prize porkers. He had not even had a taste; his fangs had not yet broken skin. He had only caught a fragrance, a wisp of delightful indulgences before the angry pig farmer had seized him by the neck and tore him from the pigpen. There was a brief struggle. A bell was struck, and the town was up in arms. The pig farmer's arm was shattered while it swung into the encircling mob.

"Vampire!" an elderly woman had cried, seeing his skin shine like dark crystal in the moonlight.

The vampire had burst through the furious crowd and made his way into the woods. After an hour of restless wandering, he had assumed they had given up on him.

He was wrong, and they were now almost upon him again. The lights of torches shone through the glade. The boar, disturbed by the lights, then seeing the shadowy hunter, sped off through the trees. The heads of the townspeople were coming into view as they emerged from behind a lifeless knoll. The dark figure looked to the mountain. *So close.*

Though hungered, and tortured night and day for want of food, weakly and feebly, the vampire flew as fast his spidery legs would take him. He reached a gentle brook and turned to follow it, hoping the hounds would lose his scent.

They would not.

He ran upstream for about two miles until he reached a small farmhouse. The lights were out; it was late. The residents would be asleep in their beds. He spied a barn and adjacent stable. An open window drew his keen eye to the most delicious looking stallion leg, shaking off flies in its sleep. He knew he had to keep moving, but could not keep up his pace for long without precious sustenance, precious blood. He had gone so long without flesh. Maybe weeks—he could not remember.

He crept up to the stable and pushed open the creaky door. He admired the magnificent and extremely durable German lock and chain. It was of the finest craftsmanship. Unbreakable. *But someone forgot to lock it*, he thought to himself, *someone very foolish.*

He entered. The horses were all asleep. The stable presented a banquet of fresh meat. He salivated from the bouquet of well-circulated blood, the healthy kind that hungry vampires crave. Drool dribbled down his cheek, which he wiped with a ragged sleeve. His tattered cuff was stained scarlet from prior feasts.

He did not have time for sampling, so which was it to be? The beautiful mare, the handsome stallion, or the giant hulking Clydesdale? Then something frisky caught his eye, a small white horse danced spastically, trying to free itself. Panic-stricken, it managed to break some of its cords. It was a spirited little fighter.

A prancing pony, how sweet. He was lured toward it by that intoxicating aroma of fear. When he neared the tiny paddock, the pony turned around and kicked him hard with its short hind legs. The night stalker growled but soon calmed, knowing he was to blame for the blunder.

The sound of the frantic hoof stomping by now woke the other animals, which began demonstrating their own trepidation. The tumult was heard in the farmhouse, stirring the residents from their beds. Lamps were lit.

The bloodsucker cooed its victim into a hypnotic slumber then sank his fangs deep into the pony's back leg; he knew where to find the rush of life-giving blood.

The proprietor of the farm came out of the house half-dressed. He carried an old lantern, hastily trimmed. "Not another wolf," he said to his young daughter, "Cordelia, get back in there before he carries you off by the neck." He had dealt with wolves in the past. It was a nasty business but a necessary one.

Cordelia shuffled her feet on the veranda. She had never seen a wolf before. She only knew what she read in stories. They didn't seem too much trouble for Peter in "Peter and the Wolf." Then she remembered she had forgotten to secure the stable after riding.

As the bloodsucker purged the pony of its essential fluids, the farmer entered the stable, pitchfork in hand. The vampire did not notice as he continued suckling at the pony's hindquarters. He did not have time to relish the moment, but the taste was delectable if not fully savored. The farmer raised the pitchfork high as he neared for the strike. Then his daughter, watching her beloved pony collapse to the floor, cried out from the stable door, "Padua!"

The dark intruder turned to see the approaching farmer as he stabbed down into his unprotected chest, causing a shriek audible for miles. The farmer removed the tool to strike again. The vampire grappled with him for the weapon, holding the sharp end, and swinging the pitchfork. The farmer would not release his grip and was flung into a crate of oats.

Cordelia ran to her father. The crate had burst open, and he lay on it, blood soaking into the feed. His chest was heaving.

She was only fourteen. She had lost her mother to pneumonia the previous winter. She had lost her brother to war. She saw her beloved pony, Padua, lying lifeless in the corner. Now she was losing her father to a fiend of the night. His side was impaled on a wooden splinter.

She took his hand, freckled with cherry-stained oats. Blood flooded the farmer's chin as he tried to speak. He tried to call her name, but he could not. Yet, his eyes told her all she needed to hear. He loved her.

In an apparent state of bloodlust, the dark stranger rushed to the old farmer, knocking the girl aside. She scrambled to her feet in search of a weapon. When she found a sledgehammer heavy enough to smash a skull like a lemon, she dragged it across the floor.

The predator was now missing a sleeve, now tied to her father, the sight of this enraged her even further. She tried lifting the hammer, but the imbalance of it made it too difficult to manage. *Too heavy.*

She discarded the huge hammer and found a scythe, which was far too unwieldy. *Too long.*

She dropped the scythe and reached for a short sickle off the wall. *Just right.*

She crept up behind the kneeling figure as her father had done. The crate shard had been removed from the farmer and lay beside him. She overheard him mumbling gravely, "Sorry... the only way," before sinking his teeth into her father's shoulder.

She was too late. His fangs penetrated his flesh.

Cordelia sliced the sickle down the vampire's back, cutting him, ripping his cloak, and staining his back with the darkest shade of blood she had ever seen. It was too black to be blood, too rich, too soiled with evil. He wailed. His tattered rags were now drenched in the sordid fluid. He rolled into an empty stall.

New light filled the stable entry, as a young farmhand entered with an astonished look. "Cordie!"

"Billy!" She was not expecting him. She turned back to her father, whose lifeless face had yielded its last tear.

A man from the search party ran in with a pack of dogs, seeing the scene and the creature hiding in the corner. He shouted to the throng of townspeople making their way up from the brook, "Hallo, the devil is in here!"

Billy ran to the frightened Cordelia. She would not relinquish the sickle. Her face was as pale as the vampire's, as pale as her father's. She sobbed into Billy; tears trickled down his shirt. She began to tell Billy about her father while he kept a watchful eye on the creature crawling toward the rear door.

The rest of the mob quickly made its way inside. The vampire, though fed, was weak and wounded, but still dangerous. He stammered to his feet and jumped through the open window, fleeing westward, leaving a dark wet trail across the dirt. Most of the crowd followed.

The few who stayed tried to comfort the poor girl with their talk of vengeance. "Murderous creature will pay!" one promised. It was all talk, and she knew it. But it was cathartic to hear.

Billy heard the buzzing of insects as they crashed into his dim lantern by his feet. He didn't hear the mosquitoes as they sucked the blood from his uncovered ankles. He held Cordelia as tight as she held her sickle.

The doctor tended to the dying man before turning his back on him. There was little he could do medically. As they talked of revenge, the farmer's body began to stir, unnoticed by most except by old Rudiger, who stood up and said, "Billy, take young Cordelia to her room, will ya? She don't need to see this."

Assuming the man only meant she shouldn't be seeing her father looking so grim, Billy began to lead her out the door. As he did so, the reddened eyes of the old farmer reopened. Through a crack in the wall, a glimmer of light shone on his face, which glowed faintly in the moonlight.

The blacksmith grabbed the blood-soaked splinter beside the old farmer. "I am sorry, John."

"Father! He's alive!" shouted Cordelia. She ran to him, but before she could reach him and take his hand in hers, the blacksmith plunged the stake deep into the old farmer's unbeating heart. The living corpse screeched and sputtered blood. The dark light was put out. The same wooden shard that ended his first life, ended his second.

"No. No!" Cordelia cried when she reached his lifeless body. "What have you done? You killed him!"

"Cordie, you don't know what he was. Didn't ya see his eyes, his terrible, red eyes?" Rudiger tried to reason with her, tried to explain. She wouldn't hear any of it. She placed the sharp wooden fragment in her front pocket to keep it from again desecrating his remains. She screamed as she held her father's body, rocking back and forth with him. They let her carry on this way until the group returned an hour later, empty-handed and defeated.

"The hounds lost his scent near the caves," commented one. "They won't go in 'em."

Another agreed, adding, "Those caves are nothing but death; don't take a bloodhound to know hell on earth."

They all gathered around the splattered scene. One said, "Better call for the priest."

"He is on his way now," uttered the blacksmith, looking away in shame.

One said, "Let the girl have time to grieve alone."

As they made their way out, each shared their own wisdom on the situation. Billy sat by Cordelia, largely ignored by her. Then he saw Padua shaking his mane. "At least you have Padua; he won't ever leave you."

She looked up at him bitterly. "Why would you say that? Why!"

"Well, you do. It's not as if he is gone or nothing." He was confused by her sudden agitation.

Her tears turned to anger at his words. She began swatting him forcefully, belting him with knuckles, shouting, "He's dead! Padua's dead!"

Finally, after he had absorbed all the blows she could muster, some of the lingering townspeople returned to the stable from outside to see about the commotion. "Look!" she said pointing to the corner, "See, he's de—"

A lantern revealed Padua standing upright, proud as ever. She ran to him, squeezing him in her arms. Billy came too, followed by others whose attention had been piqued by the commotion. One of the men asked about the pony's defect. Another answered that it was an unusual condition.

"What defect!" asked Cordelia.

"Why, this pony is an albino."

An older man agreed, "Yes, why else would he have such a shiny white coat, and those eyes, those blazing red eyes."

Cordelia hadn't noticed in her excitement, but his eyes were bright scarlet, and his coat was much paler than before, even glowing where the moonlight hit his skin from the cracks in the wall.

The priest was busy attending to the farmer's body when one of the lingering men asked him to come have a look. The priest gasped. He hoarsely sought for the words of prayer.

Old Rudiger knew what was happening and stated, "This is an unholy creature, and must be destroyed." While the priest muttered prayers against evil, the men held Padua still as the carpenter fashioned a wooden stake to end the cursed beast.

Billy's father commanded him to hold back Cordelia, and Billy reluctantly complied. She pleaded with them to spare Padua's life. Her voice was mute to them but not to Padua. She commanded him to fight, to flee. He obeyed. He flailed, kicked, and jumped.

Cordelia elbowed Billy in the stomach. He fell to the ground then refused to get up. She picked up her sickle and threatened the men with it, swinging wildly in their faces. She came to the stall and loosened the tangled ropes. A man tried to grab her but was kicked in the knee by the erratic pony.

"What are you doing?" yelled the priest, too stricken with age to physically intervene. "Where will you take this unholy creature?"

"Away!" She jumped on Padua's back, and they rode past the bewildered men. Billy waved, but she did not see. She did not dare look back.

With miles behind them, they stopped. She had brought nothing. No food, no provisions of any kind. Just her and her pony. And the wooden shard in her pocket.

Padua was brighter in the starlight, much brighter. She led him into a clearing. His coat was vaguely luminous in the moonlight, glittered with speckles, dusted with diamond dust. His eyes were flooded with bright red hues, which swirled over his glazed stare. His demeanor was different now. He was still the same sweet pony, only more. More stoic, more austere, more regal.

She examined the inside of his mouth, revealing new teeth: fangs. She knew why the men wanted to kill him. He was vampiric, like the man, or what used to be a man, who bit her father.

She gently stroked Padua and stared up at the mountains where night stalkers were feared to dwell. Despite her pony's new condition, he was still her faithful companion. Together they would find a way to make it in the world and eventually slay the vampire that killed her father.

* * *

After several years of training and searching, she uncovered the name of her father's killer: *Touchstone*. She and Padua had been tracking him ever since.

The sun had passed over the mountain, but the fading light still blanketed the evening sky to the west. Cordelia removed her hood to view her quarry. Her brown hair was cut short now. Her eyes shimmered in the soft light. She carried her rusting sickle on her back, her only childhood artifact. She was tall and strong. Years of living on her own, brutally hunting and slaughtering vampires, had made her convincingly fearsome. Yet a boy like Billy would still admire her.

She had tracked her prey from Widower's Tavern on the outskirts of Croppenhaus. After entering the tavern for an ale, she found the hall empty. She recognized a subtle but familiar stench: *vampiric scum.* She checked the backroom for the proprietor, where the creature was feasting on the owner and his family in the storeroom. She attacked, clipping off his right ear before he crashed through the window.

She knew the region. It was once her home. She knew the rolling fields to the edge of the forest, rising to the Urights mountains. She knew where he was headed, the vampire sanctuary, the deep caves entrenched within the high slopes. The natural caverns had been widened and deepened by gold miners. Now their tools lay wasted and unused at the foot of the mountain, along with their bones as a warning.

Cordelia was not sure how he had gotten so far ahead, but now she saw. He was leaping straight up the center of the switchback. "He's taking a shortcut!" If he reached the caves before she reached him, he would be safe. She would not. A single vampire, with an ear missing, she could handle. An entire horde, who knew her by reputation, she could not.

She caught her breath before reminding herself what would happen if she failed to capture him. She could not follow him in there: the caves meant death. It was too late to turn back; once he reached the caves, he would send others after her. Then she would be the quarry.

The vampire laughed as he looked back, his pursuer a half-mile down the steep ridge. He pulled himself up a craggy ledge. He was startled to see a single white pony on the path. The vampire saw the mirror reflection of his ragged cloak in the horse's scarlet eyes. Padua rose into the air and struck the enemy's skull forcefully with his hoof. The vampire fell backward and tumbled over, down the craggy mountainside.

Cordelia double-timed it to the fallen vampire. A bramble bush had finally stopped his rolling. He crawled out of the spiky mass; his body was stapled with thorns. His arm and neck were contorted. His head was upside down and backward. It took him a moment to get right-side up. His ribs were protruding and needed to be reordered, and his insides rearranged. He lay against a rock to right himself. It was a slow, agonizing process. Bone met bone again until he was restored to near-perfect order. Out of convenience, a few small pieces were simply torn out, then eaten. *Waste not.*

No sooner was he able to stand before he discovered the razor end of a sickle kissing his throat from behind. Cordelia snatched the back of the vampire's head by the strands of his bloody, tousled hair.

"Good evening, Touchstone," greeted Cordelia with polite command.

"You must be a little touched in the head, wench."

She pulled hard on his hair to meet his uncouth salutation. He hissed disapprovingly. She tugged even harder.

She was sure it was him. His thinning hair, his swirling deepening red eyes, his wretched ebony tongue, and, of course, his token pale skin.

"You are—"

"My name is Fabian. I was once a man of fame and fortune from the high country. I have relatives, no doubt that would vouch for this much at least."

"As soon as they denounce you as a specter of hell?" she retorted.

"That they would also." She could not see his angelic smile. "I assure you, I am not Touchstone. You have wasted your time racing me up this hillside for nothing." He feigned an injured laugh in his discomfort.

She slowly rotated around to face him, careful not to lift the blade from his neck. She investigated his cheeks, his lack of wrinkles, his nose line. It wasn't him. "You all look alike, don't you?" She lowered her weapon.

He calmed. By now, he was wondering if he could take her with her guard lowered. But the approach of Padua galloping down the path tabled that secret mental debate.

"That's good," he said, laying back. "I better be on my way then."

22

She smiled for the first time. "Just one more thing. Where is Touchstone?"

He propped himself up with a tree branch. He eyed the road. He eyed the horse blocking the road. *I might be able to speed up the hill before she gets her claws into me.* "I don't know. He might be in the furthest cave up the trail."

Her smile was short-lived, replaced by a furrowed brow. "He *might* be?"

"I don't really know." Fabian jumped up and ran break-neck for the steepest incline. Padua cut him off. The pony displayed his distended fangs with discrete pleasure.

Fabian turned back. He would take his chances with the non-vampire.

She said, "I believe you, Fabian." Then she drew the sickle across his gullet. His neck became a coursing crimson fountain. He fell to his knees. This was not a fatal wound, not for a vampire. He was not doomed to die by a mere metallic incision. Not until she forced her wooden stake into his cold non-undulating inhuman heart. In a blaze, the deed was done, and he collapsed lifeless, deathless.

She wiped the stake clean of blood then placed it back into her satchel.

She stepped over Fabian to her beloved pony. She cuddled up to Padua. "You knew we were chasing the wrong one, didn't you?" She scratched his ears and patted his side. "We must have lost Touchstone's scent again in the woods outside... outside our old farm. He might still be in the area." The thought of returning to the old homestead was almost too much. She used to wonder at night what had become of it in her absence. Who had taken up residence, or had it gone unkempt? She imagined an undergrowth of weeds, briars, and tares all cramping the wide space between the Sunstone Brook and Waverly Hallow, whisking away the life of the green vegetables, the beautiful ripe fruit. And what became of their horses? The old cows? The livestock? Who was feeding them?

She imagined some new family living there. A ma and pa, a brother, a sister. Little baby. Billy would come over to help with the harvest. Maybe he'd married the daughter. Moved in, started his own little household next door.

With a few tears in her eyes, she took her sparkly vampiric pony by the reigns and tried leading him back down the way they came. She tugged gently, but he would not budge. Instead, he drew her toward the summit. "What is it, boy? Are you hungry? We will find you something. Maybe a nice cat?"

He pulled again. Then she realized he had never lost the scent. Touchstone had gone up this way, probably recently. She was closer than ever to avenging her father.

Up, up, up, they climbed to the summit. There they followed a concealed path past several false entrances. Padua's keen eyes and sense of smell led the way through the labyrinthine rock pillars. When they reached the proper entrance, Padua breached the doorway without hesitation.

Cordelia paused. *This is it. The end.* She did not see herself passing that threshold again. *I will find Touchstone and stake him before the undead horde rips me limb from limb.*

Nothing would keep her vengeance from her. With one step into the encompassing darkness, she declared her resolution to this end. "For father," she whispered and took the end of Padua's swinging tail.

Down, down, down, they went where the narrowing tunnels zigged, zagged, and collided into a rock surface. Cordelia straddled the cold wall, careful to keep one hand always on Padua's tail. The other hand reluctantly caressed the damp texture. *This is water*, she kept telling herself, *it's only water.*

Her fingers felt grooves that could only have been dug out by tortured hands, with broken nails that clung tightly. Her dizzying hand felt a fossilized fingernail embedded in the soft clay. The marks raced up the sides of the wall then were dragged back down into pits unknown. Cordelia shuddered as images filled her mind with tormented souls failing to escape. She wondered if such resistance, though entirely feeble, was pathetic or if there was something noble in the struggle that could only end in death. Maybe they had a chance of escape. Maybe even she had a glimmer of hope.

In the dark, anything is possible.

She stumbled blindly into a placid pool, stirring a malevolent odor from its grimy bottom. The stench was too great to keep her from choking. Her feet sank deeper and deeper into the muck as she rushed for the edge. She felt an arm and disjointed fingers reaching for her. In a moment of desperation, she called for Padua, who pulled her out of the quagmire.

She muttered to herself about the futility of her situation, as she sat on the bank and stared into the maw of unknown terrors. Was it too late to retreat?

She would go on.

The tunnels were thick with death, with the undead. She could feel them all around her. She could feel them mocking her in silence. *They must have heard me cry for Padua like a frightened infant.* She imagined them haunting her footsteps. They whispered calculated threats under their breath. She reminded herself this was only imagined, but she already accepted that her life became forfeit the minute she stepped into the vampire's realm.

A warm glow emanated from a leaky alcove, drawing Cordelia to a cavity illuminated by a hundred golden candlesticks. A stockpile of unpolished gold lined the walls of the forsaken storehouse. Stagnate air filled Cordelia's lungs with the decaying stench of rotten oats. Bound by thick German-made chains to a large crate, was Touchstone, dead to the world in quiet slumber.

Cordelia fell to her knees before her treasure. "Such great mercy that has delivered him into our hands, Padua. Good boy!" She hugged her pony and whispered promises of fresh squirrel blood and sugared gopher hearts into his perked ears.

A lumbering shape stumbled blindly into the room, cowering from the intense light. "Still here, Touch—" He saw Cordelia then shouted, "Help, she has come!" He turned to run, but her sickle caught the fringe of his cloak. She pulled hard and lifted his legs into the air. His head planted into the stony ground. She plunged a stake into his heart to his spine.

He squealed like a pig under the butcher's knife. He writhed, twitched uncontrollably, sputtered blood-soaked obscenities, and then became as petrified as a headstone.

Touchstone stirred from his nightmarish trance and soon relinquished the terror in his dumbfounded eyes. He was unsheltered from the deluge of painful light. She looked into his ragged face: she knew him. "How could I ever have mistaken anyone for you!"

25

"I know you," he said pensively. "So you have come. I was searching for you."

"I am sure of that. Perhaps in my home. Perhaps in my sleep." She waved her sickle artfully in the air.

"I am ready to give you what you want. I was once a farmer's son... I was taking cabbage and carrots to market. I was ambushed on the highway. I did not want to be this—"

"But this is what you are, aren't you?"

"I am. So let's be over with this. You should be quick if you hope to live."

She brandished her sickle smoothly as she spoke, "I have waited this long. But tell me, why did your blood brothers lock you up like this? Such a nice package wrapped in gold for me?"

His scarlet eyes were not as she recalled. She chose to remember them as fires of unquenchable evil. But there was something familiar about them. Now they appeared less severe, rosier. "I was seeking you. I returned to your farm but you—"

"I do not own a farm," she interrupted harshly. "Why did you seek me?"

He laughed. She noticed now how weak his voice was, even weaker than the first time they met. "Solace. To end your suffering. Our... suffering."

She laughed too, but mordantly. "Yes, I am sure you want that. And your brethren, what do they desire?"

"You."

"Me?" she asked. She quit fiddling with her weapon to give full attention.

Padua stammered his hooves. He knew something was happening; his sharp ears sensed activity down the gauntlet of barren tunnels, the slightest echo of numb fingers and wild toes crawling their way to the golden chamber. His sensitive nostrils flared as a stench filled hollow spaces, which told the history of putrid stained exploits and cruelty unmeasured.

"They knew you would come. You've swept through their ranks. They want blood. Blood for blood. That is their law." He coughed. He did not look well, even for the undead. He was starving.

"They would sacrifice one of their own as bait?"

"I am not one of their own."

"Then, what are you?" She looked at Padua. She looked at his gentle but disheveled face

"I am just a dead man, like everyone else."

Touchstone had her father's eyes. He had Padua's eyes.

She looked back into Padua's beautiful rose-tinted pupils. She tightened her grip and swung her sickle at the thick German chains, merely scratching the chain but shattering the blade.

She used the thin shards to pick the lock. She removed the heavy-weight from Touchstone's neck. He gestured that they should take the tunnel behind him, "Leads to the southern mountain pass."

She complied. By now, even she could hear the hurried preparation for the hunt. They were scrambling for the entrance. It would not take them long to overtake her. She turned from the sound of shuffling feet and led her vampiric pony out. The sun would rise soon, and they would be safe.

"Wait," called Touchstone weakly as she was leaving, "release me."

She walked back to him, and again in a flash, withdrew a familiar wooden stake and plunged it deep into his heart. She removed it slowly from his lifeless body and placed the crate splinter beside Touchstone. It would never take another life.

She witnessed Padua's eyes close on Touchstone's sullen face.

Pond Scum

Alex Child

Isaac tugged at the No Trespassing sign that hung from the broken fence. He watched as Corey slipped through the peeled-back wire and called for him to follow. When he didn't move, Corey grabbed his arm and tugged him through.

The two boys followed the forbidden path until it led them into a clearing. They stood at a small knoll overlooking a sickle-shaped pond. Thick ebony algae nearly concealed the dark water. A whiff of neglected decay drifted in the air.

Isaac rubbed his nose at the smell, "We have a fountain at my house. It gets mold in it sometimes, but nothing like this."

"Could be for retention from the old mines," Corey said.

He arched his back and walked down the steep embankment with his knees bent sharply. "Maybe there are some fish we can catch," he said, dropping his feet into the water. It was surprisingly cool.

Isaac followed and examined the area around them. There was no vegetation growing along the bank. It was as if all the plants were trying to run away from the pond. Perhaps it wasn't the best idea to get close.

Corey examined the pond with wide eyes. A clear layer of liquid rested above a bed of gray wisps that swayed with the currents of the pool. Just past the wisps, the clear liquid turned murky with splotches of black swirling in circular patterns.

"This water is weird, man," Corey said under his breath.

Isaac crouched at the pool's edge on all fours. The imagery was somehow enchanting. "I've never seen water like this before," he agreed.

"It might not be water. Maybe it's pond scum?" Corey suggested.

Isaac laughed, "That seems unlikely. Pond scum doesn't look like this."

"What do you think then?" Corey splashed water at Isaac.

"I think that's probably not a good idea," said Isaac. "My mom told me some of these old mining ponds have chemicals in them that can give you cancer."

Corey shrugged. "My grandma had cancer and kicked its ass. Plus, I'm way stronger than her, so I'll be fine." He smashed his feet through the liquid like an old-time grape stomper. The scum in the pond temporarily moved away from his legs before snapping back into place. "That's where you gotta be careful," Corey said with a smile. He took a few more steps in, "It's not too deep."

"Well, it probably gets deeper in the middle," Isaac said. "Maybe you should get out?"

"Nah, I can swim," Corey said with a dismissive wave. He quickly changed the subject, "Wanna sandwich?"

Isaac smiled and nodded.

"Catch," Corey said, tossing a sandwich that he kept in his fanny pack.

Isaac's hands flailed helplessly over his head as the sandwich hit him in the stomach and dropped toward the circular pool. He picked it up before it fell in the water and unzipped the bag.

"I'll be back, gonna make a raft," Corey said as he got out of the pond. He climbed the small hill in search of wood.

Isaac replied by lifting a hand with a half-raised thumb. He scratched his nose as the strange scent wafted through the air. He couldn't quite put his finger on what it smelled like, but it somehow reminded him of mildew in laundry. Puzzled, he looked around. There was nothing but trees, dirt, and the polluted water in his surroundings. He didn't think the trees or dirt made this smell, so it had to be the pond. "I still don't like this water," he mumbled between mouthfuls of his sandwich.

Isaac continued to eat in silence. He took another bite when he realized that it was too quiet. There was no sound. The birds that flew by uttered no notes. The wind was silent. His chewing created no audible noise.

The pond bubbled loudly, making Isaac jump. He stared into the water in a trance. Something about it felt off.

The sound of snapping branches careened down the pit, breaking Isaac from his daze. "Catch!" Corey yelled. He threw another sandwich down the hill. Isaac jolted to catch it, but it sailed through the air and fell into the pond. A small circular wake appeared, bubbled, then hissed. The plastic-wrapped meal failed to appear.

Corey skidded down the incline like an Olympic skier and kicked up a wave of dirt and gravel as he went. But when he stopped, the hissing was still there—teasing them, although Corey failed to notice it.

"Feast your eyes, young one," Corey said as he walked ankle-deep into the pool.

Isaac saw the small gray hairs in the liquid stiffen. They tilted in unison, pointing in his direction. It looked like a million tiny fingers stretching outward.

Corey raised his hand high over his head. He held a combination of several small twigs and branches bent over and around each other in the shape of a rough square. "I hereby christen thee the USS Scum, in honor of our pond, here," Corey said with a spit to his side, not caring that the spit and dirt cocktail landed on his forearm.

"Looks like shit—it's gonna sink," Isaac laughed.

"Go to hell," Corey said. "Prepare yourself to witness the maiden voyage of the US Navy's greatest ship."

He stooped over, his hands at each side of the crude raft, and gently lowered it into the water. When its balance was ensured, he released his grip.

Tsunamis instantly formed at each of the raft's sides. It dropped beneath the surface like a lead cannonball. The drab wisps entangled around the branches and twigs, dragging the humble raft helplessly into the abyss.

"Shit, shit, shit!" Corey cried. He violently shoved the dark wisps aside. The ashen tendrils coiled around his limbs. With panicked vigor, Corey stooped onto his knees and plunged his arms deep into the pond.

Isaac watched as a mixture of horror and laughter worked its way through his features. The laughter won. "Wow, that was sad."

"Shut up."

Corey paid little mind to his now soaked clothes. On his hands and knees, he scoured the bottom of the pond for any sign of his lost ship. The gray broth circled the base of his neck as he spent several long minutes searching. His extremities were all but covered by the dreary grasping tufts. He sighed and stood. The gray threads slid from his body and wobbled as he left their reach. Fluid spilled down his dripping clothes. He turned toward Isaac and saluted, "God bless those brave sailors."

"Their families are gonna be pissed that they died fighting some water," Isaac said with a smile.

Corey rocketed his hands to his sides. "They died defending the world from this evil water. Their sacrifice will not be in vain." Corey pointed at the unsettled gray water and said, "I hereby declare this pond an enemy of the people."

"You really can't find it?" Isaac asked.

"Nope, it's gone. Blown up, most likely. Maybe someone hid a bomb in the engine room, or a terrorist blew it up." Corey exited and plopped down next to Isaac. "Oh well. Where's my sandwich?" Corey asked.

"It's gone," Isaac said, shrugging. "It fell in."

"And you didn't grab it?" Corey said in disbelief.

"It sank before I could." Isaac kept the mood light, but he wondered if it was normal for water to behave this way. First, the sandwich and now the raft had vanished into the pond? It unsettled him, yet it was almost impossible to pry Corey from whatever activity he was focused on, so he decided to wait this out. At least for a little while longer.

"That was my only food, you know. The next meal is coming out of your paycheck, soldier." Corey said as he tossed Isaac a handful of smooth stones from his pocket.

"I'm sure we can afford it," Isaac said while examining the collection. He set it down, selecting a particularly smooth stone. He arched his hand back, carefully calibrating the angle it would strike, and flung.

It rode through the air, parallel to the pool's surface, and seemed to speed up as it approached. The stone struck the liquid's surface and unceremoniously dropped like a bowling ball.

Corey snickered.

Isaac examined the small pile of round stones before selecting a sleek circular one. He wrapped his fingers around the rock's smooth edges, then swung his arm out several times and examined the angle. The stone remained tucked between his fingers.

"You're not pitching for the Yankees; just chuck it," Corey said.

Isaac slung the round pebble. His arm sailed in a perfect arc and channeled his full strength. It glided beautifully through the air. At the stone's first contact with the pond, it vanished below the gray threads.

Corey cackled, his volume notably increased. "You got twigs for arms or what?"

"At least my balls have dropped."

Isaac tossed random stones from the pile in quick succession. Each stone was immediately consumed by the water and left large reverberating wakes as fluid splashed onto the shoreline.

Corey stood up. "Well, we can't sail in it, and we can't skip rocks in it. I got an idea." He sloshed out of the water and searched the nearby earth. Finally, he picked up a lizard.

Isaac frowned. Corey wasn't the most reliable person when it came to animals. "You're gonna drown him, man; lizards can't swim."

"Don't be silly. This is a pocket lizard. They're awesome swimmers. Besides, he's got the world's greatest swimming coach here to help him figure it out." Corey held the lizard in an open palm and stepped into the liquid. "You should help. This is going to be a big moment for the little guy, and he needs all the support he can get."

Isaac remained seated. "I don't wanna get my pants all wet."

"You're wearing shorts and got two boney legs. They're holding you up just fine right now."

Isaac sighed. He reluctantly removed his socks and shoes. He stood and stared at the murky fingers hiding just beneath the pond's surface. They were somehow intimidating.

"Don't make me pull you in."

Isaac hesitantly dropped one foot into the pool, ready to yank it back out in an instant. The chilled water, gleefully wrapped around his foot, providing frigid relief from the summer heat. A small undercurrent swelled along the swampy bottom, but it somehow failed to move the dull-colored threads. They continued aiming directly at Corey.

Corey cupped the small lizard in his hands and said, "Come on, man; he wants to swim."

Isaac dropped his other foot into the gray broth. Mud oozed between his toes as the unsettled wisps of darkness stagnated around his lower leg. He slid close to Corey.

Corey bent carefully, holding the lizard just above the surface. "Okay, boy, I'm gonna hold you while you get your sea legs. Don't you worry." He gently lowered his hands until the fluid seeped between his fingers and pooled around the creature's legs. "Attaboy."

Isaac looked down. The wisps had grown. They were now just a few inches beneath the surface and had begun to form a thin circle around his ankles. He raced back to the shoreline.

"Dude, those things were wrapping around my leg," Isaac said.

"Don't be such a baby. Seaweed just wraps shit up. Besides, you're scaring the lizard, man."

Isaac could see the creature supported over the water. The wisps were touching the surface now. The poor thing turned its head sporadically, its chest expanding and contracting rapidly.

Isaac looked at Corey's ankles and saw the wisps slowly surrounding the base of his legs from the calves down.

"Dude, you should get out! It's wrapping around your legs, man!" Isaac cried while pointing.

Corey remained focused on his little friend. "And I told you, seaweed and shit does that. Quit whining."

Isaac fidgeted. He paced and decided on another approach."I... I don't think he likes it, better bring him out," Isaac said.

"Nah, he's fine. He's just getting used to it."

The lizard suddenly sprung from Corey's hand. "No!" he cried.

His hands flew through the water in front of him. The lizard left a small wake as he plopped into the gray broth and disappeared. Corey erupted into a mass of thrashing limbs.

All at once, the hissing had stopped. Isaac glanced around him, concentrating. The only sound echoing in the small embankment came from Corey's increasingly frantic search. He shielded his eyes from the splashing water with his hands, only catching small stills of Corey pummeling the liquid around him.

The water calmed, and Isaac lowered his hands. Corey propped himself on his knees with his back nearly parallel to the liquid, arms outstretched beneath the surface.

"Just let him go; it's not your fault he jumped!" Isaac shouted.

"I can't just leave him!"

Isaac helplessly looked on. The gray threads around Corey's legs thickened into an encompassing lasso.

"Dude, we can find another one. It's no bi—"

The water cracked. Corey suddenly lost his footing, and his body twisted onto its side. He let out a shrill cry, temporarily paralyzing Isaac in place.

Isaac ran toward his friend as time slowed. He came to the water's edge, daring to touch the surface, but his knees gave out and dropped him on the ground.

Corey's head audibly slapped sideways against the water, submerging quickly. At first, he didn't move, but then his hand broke the surface, reaching for Isaac. He forced his head above the water, screaming. The tendrils whipped around his head, piercing his eyes, then his nose and mouth.

His screams became the dull hissing in the pond. His body went limp as he stared at Isaac with punctured eyes, slowly sinking below the surface. His last look of horror forever carved on his face as he was swallowed whole.

A moment later, the pond was still.

Brisket, Please

Becca Rose

Bright red blood pooled from the wound on Vanessa's stomach.
She grabbed the hole, trying to keep her insides from falling to
the floor. Her attacker watched as she fell to her knees, a sick
smile on his face as he raised the blade. She closed her eyes.
Tears flowed.

"Cut."

The camera crew put down their equipment to get
snacks. Chad Murphy, director, made his way over as Don knelt
by Nessa, careful not to get blood on parts of his costume that
were supposed to be clean.

"That was beautiful," Don said, his cruel grin traded
for a soft smile. Nessa blushed. Don Winters played the perfect
villain, but damn he was attractive. His light brown hair worn
shaggy, crystal blue eyes, and a killer body. This was Nessa's
third time working with him on their specialties: horror flicks.

"Ness!" Chad approached, waving his hand to get her
attention as Don slipped away. Nessa could just make out the
scar on Chad's wrist under the lights, barely noticeable if you

didn't know it was there. "That was great, but I think I want some sound. I know your guts are spilling out, death is coming, but give us one big scream as the knife comes down. Sell your last shot."

Nessa nodded, irritated that she was still on the floor while everyone was taking a break. Couldn't someone help her with the guts?

Chad patted her hair, which made her freeze. "I'll have someone bring you a drink," he said absently. "Then, we'll reset the innards and reshoot." He walked away to find help.

Nessa resembled her father, Chad, with his whitish blond hair and deep green eyes. He'd shoved her into the film business as soon as he'd won full custody, saying her adorable looks were perfect on screen. Her child chub turned to curves as she aged, giving her more opportunities. Nessa stuck with acting but moved out at fifteen for a little freedom.

"Miss Murphy!" Her assistant Hannah came rushing over, a water bottle with a straw in hand. She held it out so Vanessa could rehydrate. "I've got a meal in your trailer for when you're done." Hannah Green, an aspiring actress, was eager to please. She was as cute as a button with wide brown eyes, a spatter of freckles and curly red hair. She did anything Vanessa said, as long as Chad didn't get in the way. "Do you want me to call the crew to reset the guts?" Hannah asked.

"Yes, please," Vanessa said gratefully. She was exhausted. She hadn't been sleeping well recently. Add that to the long days of shooting, and she was always running on empty. Caffeine and concealer could only get her so far. Luckily, this was her last day shooting for *Horrific Hotel*.

The crew descended in a flurry, getting her up. The guts went back in the fake stomach, and the blood around them was reloaded. The makeup team freshened up her cuts. Someone put more congealed blood on the head wound she had gotten in the scene before. Her character was the last survivor in a hotel full of guests. No happy ending here.

Horrific Hotel was highly anticipated. Nessa hated to admit that Chad was a great director. The fans came out in droves. Nessa even had a small following. It was a tightrope to walk, keeping the fans in love but not obsessed. She was lucky to never have been in danger, but Don had some scary incidents. The girls who loved him weren't violent, but they were determined to invade his life. It was a wonder how he stayed so sweet to everyone. Don got back into place, giving Vanessa a wink.

"Action."

Nessa backed into a corner, looking wildly around as Don approached her, knife raised. She gave a guttural sound when he slashed her stomach—the guts spilled. She fell to her knees, eyes wide as he smiled and brought the knife down. Nessa closed her eyes, let out a terrified scream, and the retractable knife hit her neck. The blood contraption on her shirt went off, spurting blood past the fake blade. She fell to her side, and Don pulled the knife away. Some twitching and crying, then holding her breath with eyes wide open, and she was done.

"Cut. That's a wrap on this scene. Ness, you're free to go."

The crew clapped politely for Nessa as she sat up and let the guts fall away. No need to keep them on her. Don came to help her up.

"Hey," he said softly. "That was really good."

"Thanks, Don," Nessa said appreciatively. She wiped some blood before it dripped into her eyes, looking up at him. She was very aware that he hadn't let go of her hand.

"Hey…" He glanced around nervously. "I know I've still got a few scenes, but when I'm done, do you want to get a bite to eat?"

Nessa's heart stopped. Don. Don Winters was asking her out. Wait, was he really? Don was more famous, older at just over thirty, and mature.

"Like, just the two of us?" she asked.

"If you wouldn't mind," he said with a sheepish smile. "I've wanted to spend time with you since our first job together."

Vanessa's mouth went dry. Was this happening? She didn't date much; it was hard to find the time. Dating another actor was nice because you understood the busy schedule, but time together was hard to get unless you wanted to fly all over to maybe get a full day together. Dating co-stars was easier but not a good idea if you wanted to keep working together after the breakup. Dating anyone who didn't act could be more relaxing, but they didn't like the long hours or any romantic scenes. In short, that led to only a few guys in Nessa's life. She wondered if she should risk it with Don. He seemed like he was mature enough to handle an actor/actress relationship.

"Sure," she croaked out. "That sounds like fun." He beamed down, then glanced at her lips. Vanessa gave an inner squeal. She might actually get to kiss Don Winters tonight.

"Perfect," he said. He reached up and dabbed a bit of blood away from her cheek, which was useless by the amount of blood she was covered in, but Vanessa was grateful for the contact. "I bet we'll be done by eight. See you then." He squeezed her hand before leaving to get fixed up for the next scene.

Vanessa almost floated out of the sound stage. Hannah trailed behind. "Miss Murphy?" she asked when they got outside. "Are you alright?"

"Just great," Vanessa responded with an airy laugh.

They entered her trailer, and Vanessa's senses freaked out at the scent of food. There was a burger. Not a burger. THE burger. Urban Skillet's brisket burger with an order of onion rings stuffed inside. All Vanessa had eaten since she got to set at six was some yogurt and berries. Now it was after three. Her stomach rumbled.

"Hannah," she breathed. "Why are you the best person in existence?" The girl giggled, blushing. "Did you bring the liquid gold as well?" Hannah crossed to the mini-fridge and pulled out a small container. Vanessa's stomach growled even louder as she stared at the white sauce. Hannah's cream and wine-based sauce was a secret recipe and Vanessa's drug. Hannah was too busy to make it all the time, but when Vanessa could get it, she freaked out. That sauce paired with the burger... her mouth watered.

"Clean up while I warm the sauce," Hannah suggested. "You can eat before we go." Reality hit, Nessa had about five hours until her date. She'd be hungry again, but she had gotten to set in pajamas. The exhaustion was hitting as well. With traffic, it would take over an hour to get to her home in Beverly Hills, an hour to get ready, and an hour to get back. Add the time it took to eat and clean up here…

"Hannah," Vanessa moaned. She covered her face with her hands. "I know you do way too much, but can I ask you for something else?"

"Of course," Hannah chirped, as happy as ever.

"I have a date with Don after the shoot."

"What?" Hannah yelped. Vanessa peered from between her fingers. Hannah's face shifted through emotion: shock, confusion, and excitement. "That's great! I have to say, the chemistry between you two is undeniable." Vanessa dropped her hands, grinning like a schoolgirl.

"Really? Oh, Hannah, that means a lot. The problem is that we think they'll wrap up around eight."

"Ah," Hannah sighed. "I see the problem. Okay. Here's what we do. Clean up as best as you can. Eat and get a nap in. I'll get some supplies. Do you need some makeup and an outfit?"

"Yes," Vanessa gasped. "Hannah, you are literally the best person." She reached to hug the girl, then remembered the blood just in time. "Are you going to go all the way back to my house?"

"I can. Your makeup is there. Is there a specific outfit you wanted?"

Nessa pondered the contents of her closet. She had a lot of options… where was Don planning on taking her? She wanted to look good, but not too casual. He'd only seen her in sweats or in costume. She couldn't wait till he saw what she looked like when she tried to look nice.

"Grab that mini dress Versace sent over," she instructed. "That should look great. Thanks again, Hannah." The girl nodded, and Vanessa went to wash off in the trailer's shower. It took way too much time to clean up. The blood in her hair was caked and dried. She had to rub her skin raw to go back to her pale shade, but she finally emerged fresh and happy, ready to devour her food. The burger was absolute heaven. The cream sauce complimented it nicely. Nessa had suggested that Hannah mass-produce the sauce, but the girl seemed content to give it to the people she liked. Nessa got most of it, but other cast and crew members were occasionally lucky as well.

Nessa savored each bite, licking her fingers clean when she was done and lapping the leftover sauce from the plate. No one was around to judge. Then, wrapped in a nice soft robe, she went to her bedroom and collapsed on the mattress, out like a light.

* * *

Her frantically beating heart and the urge to scream jolted Nessa awake. She glanced around wildly, trying to shove the nightmare she'd had from her mind. Screams, blood, and tears. It had been a while since she'd dreamed of murder—she'd gotten used to the insane scenes she took part in. This one had seemed intense, though. She shivered as she crawled from bed. Emerging into the living area of the trailer, she was pleased Hannah had dropped off her stuff and even cleaned up lunch. Nessa grabbed the cosmetic bag, heading for the bathroom to get ready. She needed to give that girl a raise.

Blood-stained the shower. Nessa rinsed more off, sending red down the drain, and noticed blood under her nails. She scrubbed them clean before starting on her look. Natural appearing skin, lips a seductive dark red, and her hair in a loose bun were done effortlessly. "Eat your heart out, Don," she murmured to her reflection. She slipped into the dress, sleeveless, short, and formfitting, and put on a simple pair of flats for comfort.

Stepping outside, a chill came over her. Most film crews were inside their sound stages or done for the day, but the heavy silence was eerie, especially after her nightmare. She paused outside the stage door. A prop leaned against the wall, a machete covered in blood. She rolled her eyes, grabbing the handle to take it back inside. Extras never really understood how expensive realistic props were.

The lights were on inside, but she didn't see any crew members or hear a sound. There were still things scattered around, and food was still out on the table. Had everyone taken a break at the same time?

"Hello?" Vanessa shouted. "Guys?"

No answer. She walked toward the fake alleyway.

"Chad? Don? Hannah? Are you here?" Approaching the set, she saw a guy and girl on the ground with their arms around each other. She laughed. "Caught you guys. It really isn't appropriate to fool around on set." She walked closer, but they didn't move. "Not a great hiding place, either." They still didn't move even as she got closer. Maybe they were sleeping?

Napping on set wasn't ideal, but everyone had been putting in long hours. She set down the prop and reached a hand for the girl, giving her a shake. "Hey, wake up." The girl was still—too still. Vanessa rolled the girl onto her back.

Dead. The young girl was stiff, going cold, and stared with wide, startled eyes. Nessa knelt at the side of the body, not comprehending. She moved over to shift the boy. He was in the same state. Both had their throats slashed. They weren't moving, weren't breathing. She swallowed hard as she checked their pulses. There was nothing. She shoved herself backward, scrambling to her feet. "Hello!" she yelled again. "Is this a closing day prank? These are really good dummies. We should use them for the next movie." Her pounding heart was the only reply. "Come on, this isn't funny."

She spun on her heel, determined to leave, and not give them the satisfaction of seeing her discomfort. She froze, and a small giggle escaped her throat.

Chad was in his director's chair. He was slumped, so she'd been able to gloss over him when she approached the couple on the floor. His throat was cut, blood soaking his front. His skin was pale, eyes unseeing, and mouth hanging open.

"Chad?" she breathed. "I didn't know you'd gotten into acting. Looking good."

When he didn't respond, she inched closer. "Is everyone in on this? Are there cameras to watch me freak out?" She glanced around, then back at her dad. Taking a wrist, she was met with no pulse. "Okay," she whispered. "That is a good dummy. These all are. The skin feels very real." As she moved her hand away from the wrist, her fingers grazed a scar. The scar on his wrist, slightly raised. The scar he typically tried to keep hidden. He'd tried to take his own life when he was younger. She stared into his familiar eyes, flecked with amber. Nessa fell to her knees and threw up the burger.

When she was done retching, she heard movement to her right, somewhere in the dark. Whoever had done this was still here. She turned to run, grabbing the machete to have some protection.

Her heart raced as she heard the footsteps. They were getting closer. As she ran through the sound stage, she saw more bodies. Each had their throats cut and were still. Whoever had done this had no mercy. Her coworkers, her family, her friends. The monster. She started to sob as she ran, trying frantically to find a place to hide. Finally, she yanked open one of the storage closets. There were people there—some unknown extras. They screamed when they saw her.

"Shh," she hushed. "Let me in. Whoever did this is still out here."

The few people just kept screaming. Nessa stepped away and shut the door. They were in shock. She didn't want to lead a murderer toward such helpless people. She looked around for another place to hide, her heart in her throat. Then she saw Hannah. The girl sat against the wall, a deep slash in her shoulder.

"Hannah," she gasped as she ran to the girl whose eyes fluttered open. "Oh my gosh, Hannah, what happened?"

"You did."

Hannah smiled at Vanessa's puzzled look.

"You're a selfish idiot," Hannah snarled. "Do you think you deserve all you have? The fame, the money? Even Don? Hell no. Anyone can take your job. Surviving a murderous rampage will turn all eyes to me." Hannah's eyes glinted madly.

"What?" Nessa gasped. "What are you talking about? I think you've lost too much blood. You're not thinking clearly."

"You didn't think clearly," Hannah hissed. "Which was the point, of course. I'm just lucky you ate every drop of my sauce. LSD has mixed effects, but I got the results I wanted, plus a wound to show off."

Nessa dropped to her butt, her insides turning ice cold. She stared at the girl, at the wound, and her wicked smile. "You... you drugged me? You made me kill all these people?"

"Just helped you along, Ness," Hannah said with an arch of her brow. "And lucky for me, the cameras were still rolling." She glanced over Nessa's shoulder, her expression changed to one of terror. "Don! Don, help me." Vanessa turned just in time to see Don, his own wounds fresh and real. He had a knife. It glinted, looking very sharp. His eyes were tear-filled and wild as he brought the blade down on Vanessa's neck with no warning.

The blood was real this time. The pain in her throat was searing. Vanessa fell on her back, shocked as she looked up at Don.

44

"I'm so sorry," he wept. "I don't know why you did this. I wish I could've known you were struggling. We all would have helped you. Nessa, it didn't have to be like this."

Damn Hannah, Vanessa wanted to yell. Her vision blurred, memories of the people she'd cut down flitted over her gaze as she lost consciousness. Hannah's smug face looked down at her. Nessa should have cut her throat when she had the chance.

The Figure in the Mirror

Brandon Prows

"My son's eyes are blue. Look at them; you've never seen eyes so blue."

The man inside the gas station gestured to the flyer in his hand. A child's face was printed on the paper with "MISS-ING" written in bold red letters below it.

Asher was distracted. The air conditioning was not working, leaving the building stuffy and humid. On top of that, he was late. The last thing he wanted to think about was this stranger's missing son. He had made what was supposed to be a quick pit stop when the man began pleading with him at the sales counter. Although, to his credit, the child's eyes were quite blue. Though not the bluest Asher had seen.

"If you see my son, please do something." The distraught man gripped Asher's hand, preventing him from walking away. "He's special. He can't take care of himself." The father was tall and burly with oily skin, dark brown eyes, and a thick mustache. Tears formed in the corners of his eyes.

Asher was in a rush to reach his destination, but the sight of a father crying over his son stung him. He pitied the man. "Look, I'm just traveling through the area, but if I see your son, I promise I'll contact the authorities."

The father's face lit up at the proposition. "Thank you, sir! Here, there's a number here. Please, take a flyer. You're a kind person. No, a hero, sir," he said.

Shuffling his feet uncomfortably, Asher took the flyer, paid for his gas, and left. The father was beaming when Asher walked away from him. Perhaps, no one else had accepted one of his missing child posters. There were probably not many customers in this part of the Uinta mountains.

I guess every little bit helps. I hope they find the kid, Asher thought.

He wanted to believe that the child could be found alive and well. But out in the middle of nowhere like this, he found himself doubting it was possible. The thought disturbed him, but he pushed it from his mind and drove away.

* * *

Hornwood was smaller than Asher remembered. The town consisted of a single dirt road that ran for a mile and ended with his grandpa Clint's home. An enormous white tree that marked the start of the property was considered the town treasure. More than an hour away from the closest city, it was an isolated place to live, but Asher had loved that growing up.

The initial drive through town should have been nostalgic, but Asher was confused. A variety of homes and small stores lined either side of the main road with charming disorganization. However, it looked as though many of the shops were now permanently closed, with boarded-up windows and sealed doors. Asher always remembered the place popping with flowers and blossoming trees around this time of year, but the plants and grass still looked gray from the winter.

What was more, there was barely a soul in sight and not a single child. When he was young, there were always other kids to play with. They'd all run up and down the main street in the open daylight, but now he could see no sign of any youth. He passed the playground where he'd spent so many summers, but it looked unused and overgrown with weeds. It was possible that the families with children all moved away. He supposed there would be no reason to stay in a small town like Hornwood.

Still, something in the air didn't feel right for a place that had once been so welcoming. He'd barely been here for ten minutes, and he was already starting to regret coming back.

Something felt damp on Asher's left eyebrow. He pressed a finger against it and was surprised to find that it was bleeding. Strange, the cut there had been a scar for years.

Did I hit it without noticing? he wondered. He drove on, dabbing the scar with a tissue until the light bleeding subsided.

On the other side of town, Asher parked a few feet from the white tree that marked the start of his grandpa's old lot. Like the rest of the town, it looked lackluster compared to his memories from childhood. The tree had been a favorite spot for Asher and his friends. It always had full boughs of golden leaves, regardless of the season. Now there were none. The bark looked more gray than white, and the branches stood bare and skeletal against the sky.

The home itself was still somewhat of a mansion, but the paint on the wooden siding was faded and cracked. At least there was no graffiti. Still, a tinge of disappointment tugged at Asher's heart. He'd known that the house would likely be in a poor state. No one in his family had taken care of it since his grandmother's passing. He supposed he was as guilty as anyone, but he hoped to make up for it by visiting after all this time. The estate was up for grabs, after all, and it didn't mean much to anyone but Asher. It's not like the land was worth much out here.

He went slowly up the yard to the front door, noting how much smaller the porch seemed now that he was older. He was just about to fit the key into the knob when a voice called out to him.

"Asher Bryne, I presume?"

Asher jumped at the sudden greeting. He hadn't noticed anyone approaching.

Standing at the bottom of the porch was an elderly man with a gnarled wooden cane and thick dark goggles that covered his eyes. He smiled with thin pale lips.

Asher returned the smile and approached the newcomer. "Yes, sir," he said, extending his hand forward. The old man accepted the gesture. His grip was weak.

"My name is Mr. Elon. I'm the mayor of Hornwood. You might not remember me from when you last came here. I was much younger then, and you were quite small," he spoke with a quivering voice. He looked older than dirt and talked like it too. He rambled on through formalities, noting it was rude of the town not to come and greet their first visitor in years, especially when that visitor was old Clint's favorite grandson.

"I reckon you've come to inherit Clint's old mansion," continued Mr. Elon with a gesture to the summer home.

Asher nodded. Before he could say anything, the old mayor continued to prattle in a wistful drawl. "You know, Mr. Bryne, the people of this town, truly loved your grandfather. He was a good man. A man of the town."

"I loved him too," said Asher in a surprisingly affected manner. He had not actually spoken about his grandfather to anyone in years.

Mr. Elon scratched his gristly chin and sighed, "It's a shame what happened to Clint, you know. He was like a brother to me. Loved him, I truly did. It touches me to know that one of his kin cares enough about this place to come care for it."

"I'm happy to be back, Mr. Mayor," Asher said.

Mr. Elon cackled. His voice wheezed with every breath he took, "Please, just call me Elon. Any family of ole' Clint is family to me, you know."

Asher forced a smile. This conversation was running longer than he wanted.

Perhaps the old mayor noticed his discomfort. He became serious when he spoke. "I'm not sure if this the right time to tell you this, but everyone in this town has fond memories of this manor. We all loved your granddaddy."

"Yes, sir, I know he was well-loved," said Asher.

"Yes, well. You know, should you not desire the home," the mayor continued slowly, "We, as a town, would be happy to purchase it from you."

Taken aback by the offer, Asher answered hastily, "That won't be necessary, Mr. Elon. I would never think of knocking this place down."

The mayor smiled. His grin was nearly too big for his face. "Thank you kindly, son," he said. "We would love to have this place remain a part of our town forever. That and the old tree, here. And of course, Clint's own flesh and blood just completes the picture. Oh, and I hope you don't mind that we've been keeping the interior in order. Didn't feel right to let Clint and Jewell's place go to rot. Took the liberty of getting the water and electricity running too when we heard you was coming. Anyhow, I'll let you get settled. Please keep us in your thoughts, we'll do the same and keep you in ours."

Asher thanked the old man and wished him a good day.

Mr. Elon turned to leave, leaning heavily on his cane. As he went, he called over his shoulder, "You know, you've grown a lot, Mr. Bryne. I remember you being quite the crybaby when you were little."

The words were spoken like an afterthought, but Asher was surprised by how much the remark stung him. He felt reluctant to raise his hand in a final farewell to the old mayor, and found himself standing alone on the empty porch with a bitter feeling.

A small group of the townsfolk had gathered around the property. Asher hadn't noticed them coming, but at least he now knew people still lived here. However, now wasn't a good time. Everyone looked old, and he didn't have the energy for more endless chatter. He was exhausted, and the mayor's words had soured his mood.

Asher mustered a pleasant smile and waved at the people before turning inside. Mr. Elon shooed the onlookers away from the lawn and walked away with them. Asher heard the mayor's gentle prompts to the folk, "Move along, everyone. Move along," as he closed the door at last.

* * *

As the mayor promised, the interior of the home was in decent condition. A thin layer of dust coated most of the fixtures, but Asher reckoned a simple dusting was all the place needed. A flip of a switch revealed that the lights were still in working order. All in all, Asher was relieved at the state of things.

He wandered into the kitchen. It was a little empty, but he could still almost smell the aroma of sausages and coffee. He smiled fondly. His grandfather would cook for him and his grandma every morning during the summer.

Asher continued to explore the home. Most of the furniture was covered in white sheets, but the living room was different. Everything was spotless right down to his grandma's pink reading chair, which stood uncovered and still had a book on the cushion. He passed countless summer evenings in that chair on her lap as she read to him.

Asher considered sitting in the seat, but there was more to do.

He went back outside to fetch his things. He had not packed heavily for the trip. From his trunk, he brought in some hygiene supplies, a few changes of clothes, a cooler of food, and his own pillow, just in case.

Aside from the potential creepiness of staying alone in an old home, Asher felt a childish excitement. He headed straight upstairs. His old bedroom was the last door on the left.

The room looked largely the same as he remembered. Surprisingly, there was no dust here either. Perhaps the towns-folk really had been expecting him. The bed was already made with the same checkered sheets he remembered. The sight was instantly inviting.

Outside his window, it was getting dark. The sun was setting somewhere behind the house, and the white tree cast a long shadow down the length of the town. Without wasting another moment, he plopped face down onto the mattress.

"What a day," he muttered to himself.

It was good to be back. However, laying in his old bed and knowing his grandparents were not here undercut the nostalgia with a stroke of longing. Still, his mind wandered as he lay in the old bed. It was impossible to be here without remembering who had made this his home.

* * *

He could not remember why he had been crying that day. He did remember that it was hot, and he had been hiding in the backyard. He hadn't wanted anyone to see him cry.

52

It was grandpa Clint who found him behind the toolshed.

"What are you doing out here by yourself? Don't you know it's bad luck to cry alone?" he asked while propping the young boy on his knee.

Sobbing and embarrassed, Asher tried his best to hide his face. After a few moments, Clint tried to coax him with a deal. "If you promise not to tell your grandma, we can sit here and cry together. How does that sound?"

Asher remembered looking up, surprised that his grandpa would be crying too. But there were no tears in his grandpa's eyes. At first, Asher was confused, but then he smiled a little.

Grandpa Clint's eyes were special. They were a deep blue, like the sapphires Asher's grandmother wore. Tiny flecks of purple that almost seemed to glow dotted his irises. Asher always thought they looked like the universe. They sparkled with laughter.

"Gotcha!" Clint teased while tickling Asher under his arms. Asher tried not to smile, but all his worries were melted away.

The old man held the boy in his arms until his tears were dry. In the end, Asher hugged his grandpa tight and let himself be carried to his bed upstairs.

Before that day, Asher had not been so close with his grandpa. It was just after that that Clint suggested to Asher's parents that he visit for the long summers.

Those summers were the best of his life, and there hadn't been enough of them. Even in his teens, Asher had looked forward to his weeks in Hornwood, but then came the year that Grandpa Clint was transferred out of town to a hospital in Salt Lake City. The doctor at home was unable to identify the disease that plagued him, and the new medical staff was supposed to be better equipped to treat him.

A fungal infection that fed on his eyes set in soon after, slowly making him blind. His eyes grew cloudy and gray. The sparkle was gone. Before long, they began to dry out and shrivel, but even after the removal of his eyes, the infection spread and consumed his body.

Asher could still remember the stink of the hospital room. It smelled like death. His grandfather looked weak and pale on the bed. He must have been connected to a dozen different machines.

On that day, Clint told his grandson that he was ready to die.

"How could you want to die?!" Asher had shouted at him before bursting out of the room, tears running down his face. He'd hidden quickly.

He wouldn't let anyone see him crying, not even his grandpa this time.

Clint died shortly after, and his body was quickly cremated. After his outburst, Asher never saw his grandfather again. A burden of guilt had weighed on his heart since that day. He never said a proper goodbye.

In the years since his grandfather's death, he usually pushed away most of the memories from those days. He wasn't ready for them as they flooded back to him now. He turned his face farther into the pillowcase when tears started forming in his eyes.

I remember you being quite the crybaby when you were little.

Why did the mayor say that? Back then, he only let his grandfather see him cry. Did Grandpa Clint tell the town about how Asher cried often? No, he would never have done something like that.

"I miss you, grandpa," Asher murmured. His voice was heavy with exhaustion.

Eventually, his mind calmed down, but he didn't move from where he was.

His final thoughts before sleep were of the man with the missing son. He still had the leaflet of the child in his car.

That poor kid. I wonder if they'll find him.

* * *

Gentle rays of sunshine woke Asher. He scratched his face. It felt small—his hands felt small. Too small. He sprang up from his bed, looking down at himself. He had the body of a young boy dressed in bright blue teddy bear pajamas.

"I must be dreaming," he said to the empty room.

Taking the dream in stride, he went to the window in his room. Outside there was the white tree. Its leaves were bright gold and glistened against the warmth of the sun. It was just as it should be.

Asher excitedly ran from the room toward the stairs.

He paused on his way down to stare at the canvas that was mounted above the stairwell. It was a large portrait of him and his grandparents. He was painted between the two of them. All three were smiling. His grandfather's eyes were incandescent.

The familiar tune of his Grandpa Clint's morning whistles drifted up from the kitchen, along with the smell of sausage and coffee. Asher's heart leaped. He raced down the stairs, but a tinkling laugh caught his attention before he could make it to the kitchen.

Asher turned around. From where he stood, he could see straight into the living room.

Grandmother Jewell was there reading in her favorite chair. She looked normal, still dressed in her pink nightgown with green rollers in her plump white hair. Her eyes were fixated on the romance novel in her hand. The cover depicted a broad and handsome man with flowing brown hair. He was holding a sword in one hand and a scantily clad damsel in the other.

The little Asher blushed at the book cover but rushed in to give his grandmother a quick kiss on the cheek. After all, he'd missed her dearly as well. But his lips never met her skin. He'd closed his eyes for the kiss, but when he opened them, there was only darkness.

He could not see; he could not hear; he could not breathe. It was as if the shadow surrounding him was a physical blanket, suffocating him. He tried to move, but the concrete blackness kept him in place.

He began to panic, but an instant later, a source of light returned. Through the living room window, Asher saw the white tree outside wrapped in flames.

A harsh sigh ripped the air. His grandmother reappeared before him. She coughed loudly with raspy, wet breaths. Aghast, Asher took a step back. Grandmother Jewell's figure no longer resembled the sweet old lady that Asher loved. She was naked and disformed. Her eyes were missing, leaving two gaping holes set in beds of swollen purple skin. A steady flow of black blood oozed out of the sockets.

Vicious scratch marks covered her entire face. Her cheeks were so torn up that Asher could see her teeth through the skin. The infected flesh boiled out white and yellow pus that dripped down over her body, where maggots writhed in great open wounds.

Asher was horrified. He tried to run away but stumbled to the floor. Grandma Jewell turned her head and looked directly at him. Her ruined lips moved in obscure speech patterns. At first, she spoke slowly in a corrupt hissing voice. Then she erupted into yelling so foul that her mouth appeared to rot with every syllable.

The language she spoke did not sound human. It was evil. Her words hurt his ears. With great effort, he pressed his hands against them to block the noise. But the words pierced through in a way he could not escape.

Asher could not take his eyes off of his grandmother. Her body writhed in strange directions. He could hear her bones breaking. The tendons in her neck twisted and snapped as her head turned unnaturally. It was terrible.

Then, without warning, she collapsed. In a heap upon the floor by his feet, she finally spoke to her grandson in English. Her voice was so deep that Asher could barely understand her.

"The pilgrim returns to the shrine of worship. The lamb has left its flock. Recompense and salvation await. Venerate the eternal glory."

She laughed an abhorrent cackle, like a choir of children screaming. It was the worst sound he had ever heard. Asher screamed to try and drown out the sound, but the cachinnation violently shook the house. The walls and floors crumbled around them until a ceiling beam crashed down onto his grandmother's body. It cut her in half, and she was silenced.

* * *

Asher woke. His heart raced faster than he thought possible. He placed a hand over his chest and breathed heavily. His face was wet when he touched his forehead, but it didn't feel like sweat. When he looked at his hand, there was blood. Had the scar on his eyebrow opened again?

56

He groaned when he discovered that he had also wet himself. It must have been out of fear from the nightmare. He was embarrassed, but no one was around to see his shame.

It must have been truly horrible, though the dream was already fading from his memory. He struggled to remember what occurred. No matter how hard he tried, he could not imagine what frightened him so deeply.

At any rate, he supposed he should shower. The water was working just as Mr. Elon said it would, but it took several minutes to heat up.

Asher was nearly finished by the time it started to feel warm, but that was no matter. The brisk temperature helped clear his head. He changed into clean clothes back in his room before stripping the bedsheets and throwing them in the old laundry room. As he did, he thought how strange it was that he had wet the bed at such a mature age. It hadn't happened since he was a child when he used to have nightmares.

The sun was rising by the time he finished. Seeing as there wasn't any point in going back to bed, he decided to walk around the property. Some fresh mountain air would be good for him, he thought. Besides, his memories of the toolshed last night made him wonder what in it might still be of use.

The shed was in the backyard. It took some work to pry the door open due to the lock having rusted. The interior was a disorganized mess with tools of all sorts scattered across the workbenches. Asher recognized many of the items from when he and grandpa would do garden work.

Mounted on the wall were larger tools like the old orange rake, a shovel, and a rusty sledgehammer. Standing in the dusty doorway, Asher decided against touching anything. He had just bathed, and he had no need for anything in here at the moment.

Asher went back inside and made his way up the stairs. He paused at the empty wall above the stairwell. Something was missing, but he could not put his finger on what. Maybe it would come to him later.

One of the only rooms Asher hadn't visited yet was the library. It was long with tall bookshelves that spanned the lengths of the walls and created thin aisles to walk down. As a child, he used to play hide and seek with other children in here.

He never bothered to read any of the books when he was growing up since none of them had any pictures.

Now as an adult, Asher was genuinely interested in what his grandfather had in his collection. He wandered through the aisles, taking any book that caught his eye from the shelves and flipped through their contents. His grandfather had been a well-read man. He never knew that Clint had an interest in so many subjects. An entire shelf was dedicated to eyesight and anatomy, while another was full to the brim with religious histories. There were even a couple volumes on botany. Asher created a small reading pile and settled down next to it.

He had only meant to lightly browse, but when he stood up for a stretch and looked through the window, he saw that it was already late afternoon.

How did I lose track of time like that? he thought.

At the very least, he should eat something. Asher began to put the books back in their places. When he shoved the last one in, he pushed too hard, and something clattered on the other side of the shelf. Wincing, he went around to see what had fallen. On the floor were a few loose books and another object that didn't quite belong. It looked like a large picture frame.

Curious, Asher lifted it up. It was surprisingly heavy. His face beamed when he recognized the painting that had once hung above the stairs. How could he have forgotten?

It seemed to have been stored in here for a while as most of the canvas was covered in dust. He ran a careful hand over the surface and was pleased to see the image of him and his grandparents were still clear.

But his joy dissipated as quickly as it had come. The eyes of all three figures in the painting had been burnt out, leaving the surrounding areas on their faces charred black and malformed with holes through the canvas.

Asher stared with wide eyes. It took him a moment to process the sight, but he broke from the stupor and hastily put the painting down.

He left the library, and went to his grandfather's personal office, where there had always been family photos. Any one of those happier scenes would be a welcome sight after what he had just seen. He approached the desk and turned one frame around to look, but froze. He seized up the other photos that were on the desk, then fled the room. Heart racing, he ran down the stairs and checked the hallways where pictures lined the walls. He smeared the dust off the glass off each one, revealing the faces of friends and loved ones. Hands shaking, he stepped back in horror. They were all the same. Whether it was a painting or photograph, all of the eyes on every face had been burnt out.

He went back outside, heading straight for the toolshed. He took the sledgehammer from the wall and returned to the house with it gripped tight in his hands. He had no idea how the pictures had come to be in that state, but he was unsettled by the thought of someone else having access to the house to vandalize them. Knowing that something like this was possible in Hornwood shook Asher. Maybe he would leave town and come back when he could upgrade the security. For tonight, at least, having the hammer close gave him a sense of comfort.

His stomach grumbled loudly.

That's right; I still haven't eaten today.

There were ingredients to make basic sandwiches in his cooler. He made a simple roast beef but felt more at ease in his car, where no disturbing pictures could haunt him. He ate in his front seat while listening to the radio. The news ran a story on that missing kid. The reporter interviewed the father that Asher met yesterday. He recognized the man's voice as he pleaded with listeners to take action if anyone found his son.

"My son's eyes are blue," the man grieved.

After everything, Asher went to bed early. He fetched the clean sheets and blankets from the laundry and tossed them onto the bed, not bothering to make it. He lay down on top of the rumpled mess and fell asleep the moment his head touched the pillow.

* * *

A loud crash of thunder shook Asher awake. He yelped in a high pitched voice that he did not recognize. He looked at his hands. They were small. He was in his familiar blue teddy bear pajamas.

The forgotten memories of his last dream filled his mind. The image of his grandmother's torn body and her de-

59

monic voice haunted him. He tried pinching and slapping himself to wake up from what was sure to be another nightmare. But the dream would not end.

A steady rain pitter-pattered against his bedroom window. A flash of lightning lit up the sky outside, followed by a powerful wave of thunder. Covering his ears, Asher left the room and shut the door behind him. He had to escape the terrible shaking sound.

Outside of his room, the house was dark and silent. He faced a chasm of blackness. It was so quiet that Asher thought if he focused his hearing hard enough, he might be able to hear his own rapid heartbeat. He made his way toward the stairs, moving slowly with his arms extended forward to prevent himself from walking into a wall.

He was nearly at the stairs when he heard something.

"Help... me..." a barely audible voice whispered.

The young Asher jumped from surprise. He looked around, but the darkness was so thick that he had no way of knowing if anyone was near him.

"Is someone there?" he whimpered.

No one responded.

Asher called out again, louder this time, "Is someone here?"

Again, there was no response.

Did I imagine the voice? No, he definitely heard someone call out to him. *Was it just part of the dream?* It somehow did not feel that way.

The stairs were not as troublesome as he had anticipated. He made his way down them by crawling backward, holding onto each step for support. When he made it to the ground floor, moonlight poured through the window in the door. He crept forward and peered through. The rain was no longer falling, and the white tree was unburned, unaffected by the previous nightmare.

He moved to open the door but stopped. Something was wrong. Until this moment, the home was filled with a disturbing silence. But now something else began to penetrate the stillness.

The sensation was barely perceptible—a gentle hum that came in pulses. With his hand still on the doorknob, he could feel it slowly vibrating through everything, but he sensed its source was strongest behind him.

He turned his head and looked down the stairs that led to the basement. There was a faint glow that emanated from the crack beneath the door at the bottom. The longer he stared at the thin sliver of light, the more fascinated he became with it. He could not place what color the light was radiating. *Was it blue? Could it possibly be maroon?*

Asher did not know when he started to go down the stairs. He could not remember taking the first step. All he knew was that the hum became clearer as he descended toward the basement. By the time he reached the door, it had evolved into a choir chanting in a foreign language that he did not recognize. The voices of the chanters sounded like those of children.

You should turn around. Leave this place. Wake up. But he could not. His body would not listen to what he told it to do, and instead, against his wishes, he opened the door that led into the basement.

The size of the basement was impossibly vast. There were enormous heaps of boxes and belongings piled high like pillars from floor to ceiling. It was an ominous cavern that was made even more off-putting by the presence of the uncolored light.

"Help me… please…" The unknown voice that had spoken to him earlier appeared once again. This time, though, he was not startled by the sound. The eerie tune of the children chanting had him transfixed. It drew him deeper into the depths of the basement like the song of a siren.

The mysterious light shrouded everything around him. He could not place where it was coming from, and he did not care to. He followed only the sound of the choir.

As he ventured farther, the voices of the choir distorted and changed. It was not long before they sounded like grown men, rather than children.

He did not know how long he wandered, and he did not bother to remember the way back. He pressed forward until he found what resembled a furnace room. The heat from the coal-powered fire was oppressive. Inside, the choir sang louder than ever. It made his ears ring, and his head feel like it was spinning. Asher searched for a source of the music. The only possibility was a small iron door with a golden knob nestled behind the furnace.

He gently touched the knob. It was hot but did not burn him. Taking a deep breath, he twisted it firmly and opened the door.

The room behind the furnace was large and round. The floor was made out of dirt, and the walls were carved from black rock, similar to obsidian. Long gashes ran from the ceiling to the floor. At the center of the room sat a tall mirror with a frame made out of white wood. The non-color light that permeated through the basement poured out through cracks in the wood.

The surface of the mirror did not reflect anything. Where there should have been a glass pane, there was instead a material that resembled a half-frozen lake. A thin fog delicately puffed out from the surface, creating willowed branches of mist that slowly fell to the floor. Some wisps resembled hands that beckoned Asher to come closer. Their fingers reached seductively toward him and quickly faded from existence.

Never before had he seen something so beautiful and ethereal. But in that moment, he was petrified. The mirror had a presence as if it were living and somehow conscious. Asher felt as if he was meeting someone for the first time. But it was someone he didn't want to meet.

His mind started to go blank as if he were going to lose consciousness. The ceaseless chanting of the invisible choir and the sight of the mirror overcrowded his senses. Together they were a force like a hook lodged into his mind. He could not look away. Without realizing it, he took a step forward. His feet moved without his consent.

His mind woke up in alarm over the loss of control. This was not right. He should be able to walk away freely or wake up, but he could not.

The choir's chanting grew louder with each step that he took. The language they spoke became harsh and painful to hear. Each word pierced him like it was made with jagged edges.

A milky visage was forming from the fog at the center of the mirror. It was long and thin with high cheekbones and enormous black holes where its eyes should have been. The hollows bore directly into Asher, filling him with dread.

Get out of here! Run away! Leave! His inner voice pleaded with him to flee, but he could not stop moving forward. It was as if he were under a spell, and he could not find a way to break the enchantment. Hot tears streamed down his face as the invisible force pulled him closer.

The visage wore a pained expression on its face as if it were putting an enormous effort into its actions.

"O, Undaunted One, the Pilgrim... grant me thine eyes, so that I may become whole again."

Never before had Asher heard such an unholy sound. Even the voice of his grandmother had been more bearable than what he heard from this being. "Willst thou concede thine own vision for salvation?"

Asher wept. Fear gnawed through his entire body, tearing at his insides. The longer that he stared at the face, the greater the horror inside him became. He shook his head, trembling. He fought with all of his being to stop, but he barely slowed his approach.

The pale face groaned in anger, sensing Asher's resistance. "DO NOT DENY ME, FOOL." Its voice shook the entire room. Bits of the ceiling and walls crumbled at its undeniable strength. The fog cascaded from all sides of the mirror, converging beneath the head, shaping a twisted, writhing body.

With a crude carcass formed, the figure fought to break free of the mirror. Without substance, its arms perished on contact with the world outside of its misty prison. The creature screamed in agony as its body let out bellows of steam while it dissipated. Ignoring its own anguish, the figure in the mirror pressed forward. With each attempt to break free, it became more corporeal. Asher watched helplessly as the white fingers stretched closer and closer to his face.

The choir was deafening, with voices so deep they no longer sounded human. Asher couldn't tell if the voices were chanting, singing, or screaming. His ears felt like they were splitting. He tried to cover them, but he could not move his arms.

Now inches from him, the hand of the creature was no longer made of fog. It had skin that was sickly and wet, oozing a strange purple liquid that evaporated upon impact with the floor. The flesh was rotting, and broken black fingernails jutted from the bloody fingertips.

"HELP ME!!!" the voice from earlier cried again, louder than ever.

The voice snapped Asher from his trance. He could move freely again! The young boy pulled his head back as the diseased hand lashed at his face. Though Asher escaped its grasp, its fingertip grazed his brow.

A deep, potent burn engulfed Asher's entire face. He fell backward to the ground, clinging to his left eye. He screamed in torment as thick spurts of molten blood poured from the wound, burning his hands, face, and body.

* * *

The sound of Asher's own wailing woke him from the nightmare. His hands were on his face, clawing at his burning skin. He was sweating profusely, but something else wet his shaking fingers. They came away from his forehead covered in red. His scar was bleeding again.

He paid it no mind.

The mirror. The basement.

The figure in the mirror!

Asher scrambled from his room and sprinted down the stairs to the ground floor. Without a pause, he headed for the basement.

Unlike in his dream, it was just a cluttered old storage space. The furnace room at the back was dim and silent. No voices. No door in the corner. Just the furnace and broken plaster.

He should have been relieved to know that the mirror was not real. But he was not. He was only confused.

His mind was racing in all directions. Too much had happened in such a short time. Something was wrong with him. No sane person should ever want to see such a thing again. But he did. He wanted to see the mirror with his own eyes, not just in a dream.

Asher sank slowly onto his knees. He was rapidly forgetting what the mirror looked like. He closed his eyes and thought, but the dream was fading. He'd had a nightmare last night too, hadn't he? He knew he would soon forget them both.

Despairing, he gave a futile look around the furnace room. But there was nothing.

Unless...

Unlike the plastered walls that made up the rest of the basement, the wall behind the furnace was made out of burnt clay bricks. The mortar between them was uneven, spilling out in some places. It was as if someone had rushed to complete the project.

Asher crept toward the wall and put a hand on the brick. A strong vibration shocked him. His heart dropped. Whether it was from dread or relief, he did not know. Tripping over his feet, he ran back up the stairs.

The sledgehammer was still in the kitchen. He grasped the tool with white knuckles and bolted toward the stairs. Before he could set his hand on the banister, a frantic knocking erupted at the front door.

* * *

"HELP ME!" a child's voice cried from outside.

Help me...

help me...

HELP ME...

A flash of pain darted through Asher's skull. That voice, he had heard it before.

"Please, help me!" the voice barked.

Asher pulled open the front door. A small boy ran into the home and clung to him tightly.

The child was shaking and covered in sweat. His skin was dirty, and his shirt torn. He looked up at Asher. He was eerily familiar as if the two had met before. The child's eyes glittered with the porch light. They were blue.

"You're the kid that's been on the news," he said.

The child continued to hysterically sob, "They're after me! Please, you have to take me home!"

Still gripping the sledgehammer, Asher looked outside."I don't see anyone there," he said.

"They're out there! They're watching us right now! Please, let's go," the boy was inconsolable.

Asher stared at the child blankly. "You want to leave?" he asked.

"Yes! We have to go right now. They're out there!"

"I... I can't." Asher said. There was something that he was looking for, but he forgot what. *The mirror.* "I can't leave without it."

The child looked at him in disbelief. "But you're supposed to help me," he said.

Asher winced as another bolt of pain split his head. It was like a chasm had formed in his mind. On one side, the mirror and his dreams called him. The other side shouted reason. At the center of the fissure, the child's voice pleaded for help.

Something's wrong with me, he thought, but the call from below was too great. He pulled the child inside the home and locked the door.

"What are you doing?!" exclaimed the boy.

Asher said nothing as he dragged the child down the stairs with him.

"We're going the wrong way!"

But Asher held tighter onto his wrist. Nothing mattered but the mirror. Where was the choir chanting their hymn? Would he hear it again if he broke down the brick wall?

"Please! Let me go! Let me go!" the child screamed as he beat his fist against Asher's arm. Asher did not notice.

At the entrance to the furnace room, Asher released the child. He moved forward, not heeding the pleas. He took the sledgehammer in both hands and, without hesitation, bashed the tool into the brick wall.

The tool smashed through the brick. The mortar crumbled, and dust filled the air. The beating rhythm momentarily drowned out the crying child.

Asher's eyes widened. There, behind the brick, was a gold plated handle. The door was here. He dropped the hammer and pulled the rest down with his bare hands. The broken pieces fell away with ease until the way was fully opened. He pushed inside.

Beyond the door was the round room, and in its center stood the mirror. Its veil of mist puffed and danced calmly across the surface.

Asher stared. It was smaller than before—not even as tall as one man—but it was as beautiful and terrifying as it had been in his dream. He was possessed with a bittersweet catharsis. Now that he was here, he could remember the despair that had consumed him in its presence, but he had no will to turn away from it.

"O pilgrim, thou hast returned to me," said a decrepit voice that came from the mirror. "Partake in communion with me."

Asher shuddered at the sound of that voice but wanted nothing more than to obey. Tears rolled down his cheeks as he stepped closer, his hand outstretched.

"Help me!"

Asher froze. *That voice. The child weeping.*

Don't you know it's bad luck to cry alone?

The memory of that day behind the toolshed shook Asher to his core. His grandfather's words rang through him as if they were in his soul, chasing away a thread of the mirror's trance. His grandfather had comforted him then, and for an instant, he thought he could feel those protecting arms still around him.

Who would protect the blue-eyed child if not Asher? He'd heard the boy's voice in his dream. That had to mean something. What would his grandfather say if he saw him now? Clint would have helped the boy. Remembering the tenderness in his grandpa's galaxy eyes, Asher knew that much in his bones.

He shuddered. This wasn't like him. The mirror warped his willpower and made him lose control. When he tried to pull his hand back, he could feel a crackle of anger from beyond the misty glass. The thought of disappointing the figure inside made him tremble.

But the thought of his grandfather and the sound of the child's cries reawakened Asher's mind. It was a moment that defied what he perceived to be possible. He turned his back on the mirror and ran out of the room.

The little boy was crumbled just outside the furnace room with his face buried in his hands. Shaking from the grief of leaving the mirror and filled with shame, Asher placed a cautious hand upon the boy's shoulder.

The child looked up. Asher was taken aback at what he saw. The boy had a cut on his right eyebrow that hadn't been there before. It was nearly identical to Asher's scar. Blood trickled from it.

"What happened to your face?" asked Asher.

The child did not answer him. "Please," he whimpered, "take me home."

Asher pushed other questions from his mind and helped the child stand up. He was weak but stood with Asher's support. "What's your name, kid?" he asked.

"It's Connor," the child replied.

"I think we should get the hell out of here, Connor."

Connor nodded.

As if to say goodbye, Asher cast one final glance back toward the mirror's room. But there was no doorway. There was nothing but smashed brick revealing only a wall of dirt. Claw marks cut through the soil as if from digging. Asher noted the black soil under his fingernails before tightening his grip on Connor's shoulder.

"Let's go," he said as they hurried toward the stairs.

The stairway to the front door was illuminated with a ghostly crimson light. The distant chanting of voices drifted toward them from above. The choir had returned.

"Do you hear that?" Asher asked aloud.

"Hear what?" Connor whispered.

A chill crept up Asher's spine, but he had no choice but to go forward. Holding Connor close, he ascended through the panic that crawled through his body. At the top of the stairs, he could see the source of the light through the opaque glass panels in the door. It was flickering as if it were aflame.

Asher opened the door.

* * *

The townsfolk of Hornwood stood in a ring around the yard, blocking the way. The men were dressed in deep crimson robes, and the women wore immaculate white. They lifted their voices in dissonance and harmony as they brought the song of his nightmares to life.

Beyond them towered the white tree. On either side of it, two fires burned in large black urns that gave off the crimson light. Their luminescence was so deep that Asher could not tell if it was creating light or taking it away.

Mr. Elon, the town's old mayor, stood in the center of the ring. He wore a holy garb of red, white, and black. Eyes of varying colors were sewn into the garment. His dark, goggled lenses gleaned in the ethereal light of the flames.

With a wave of his hand, Elon silenced the choir. The deep crimson fires returned to a natural color. The old man licked his chapped lips and smiled at Asher, revealing thick, crooked teeth. They were grossly yellow and sharp at the end as if they had been filed to points.

Asher gripped Connor's shoulder. "I won't let them hurt you," he whispered.

Elon let out a laugh that echoed in the night. "Asher Bryne! Congratulations on fulfilling your destiny!" The audience let out a single clap of applause.

Two robed men seized Asher from behind, prying his arms away from Connor. He flung himself, trying to break free, but their grips were iron.

"Get out of here, kid! Run! Go!" Asher shouted at Connor.

The child did not move.

"Run, Connor!" Asher cried in disbelief.

Connor stood still with a blank expression on his face. His right eyebrow bled into his eye, but he did not wipe it away.

Elon took in a deep breath and sighed. "Ah, a hero unto the end. You are truly worthy of the title, Mr. Bryne."

Asher's face contorted in frustration at the words, "What are you talking about?" he demanded.

The old mayor laughed again. "I understand that you're confused, but be comforted that the boy was never in real danger. At first, we thought that you might be another failure, but at the last you proved yourself worthy of our faith. Praise Mitris, the long wait is over."

"Praise Mitris, O Hallowed One," the choir echoed.

"But I didn't prove anything," Asher said.

Elon slapped him across the face. The force of the blow was blinding. "You must never say that," the mayor scolded. "To do what you did is something countless before you have failed to accomplish. The mirror is inexorable. Its grasp almighty. No ordinary man can withstand its call. When you fled with the boy, you became greater than you were."

"But, there was no mirror," Asher said. His thoughts reeled. None of this made sense.

Elon flung his head backward and cackled. The bones and joints in his neck cracked loudly. "Your eyes are not yet open. You have your sight, but you cannot see." The old man turned around and shouted to the crowd, "Praise Asher Bryne, the Undaunted!"

"Praise Asher, O Undaunted One," they echoed.

"Now, Asher, the Hero, partake in communion with us," Elon said. Then, motioning to Connor, he said, "Come forth, akivara."

The crowd shuffled aside, opening a pathway to the white tree. The choir resumed their chanting. The flames in the urns gasped and regained their crimson pigment. Connor took a step forward.

"What are you doing? Run while you still have a chance!" Asher screamed. Tears welled in his eyes.

Connor ignored Asher's pleas. A man from the crowd stepped up to meet the boy at the foot of the white tree. He pushed back his hood, revealing his face.

Even in a dazed state, Asher was able to recognize the man. It was Connor's father. He held his son tightly and kissed his forehead. "I'm proud of you, boy. You're making the right choice."

"I love you, dad," Connor said with a quiver.

"And I you," the father said with a final squeeze.

Two men tied ropes around Connor's wrists while a woman stepped forward to place a strange eyepatch over his left eye. Connor showed no sign of a struggle even as they used the ropes to lift him off the ground and up to the naked boughs of the tree. Where the thickest parts of the wood diverged, the branches formed a grotesque cross. The men held Connor high while others waited above in the branches. Asher watched in horror as they drove thick nails into Connor's palms, pinning him against the tree.

Connor wailed in agony as dark blood poured out of the wounds in his hands. He kicked his legs, thrashed his head.

It didn't take long before his eyes rolled toward the back of his head as he passed out from the pain.

The two men that held onto Asher dragged forward toward the tree. Asher wanted to scream and resist, but no noise escaped him. He could only stare as the unholy scene unfolded before him.

As the blood from Conner's pierced hands dripped red onto the white tree, the bark of the trunk began to shimmer and warp. A light began to shine from within until it poured out like a doorway had opened. Wisps of fog cascaded to the ground as the length of the trunk up to Connor's feet transformed into the rippling surface of a grand mirror. Asher could not tell where the mirror ended, and the tree began as if the one had always been a part of the other. Inside of the veil, he thought he could see thousands of faces forming and disappearing in the mist. Their expressions looked dreadful.

This was the mirror of his nightmare.

A burning pain pierced Asher's scar more intensely than ever before. His mind went black from the shock. Fresh blood dripped down his face.

Elon stood before the mirror with opened arms. "Such beauty!" he gasped. "Let us rejoice in the blood."

The old man turned and knelt down in front of Asher, kissing his face. His lips were cold and dry. He smelled like death. He pulled back and smiled at Asher with his lips covered in blood.

The old mayor stood tall and smiled. He removed his goggles, revealing enormous empty sockets where his eyes should have been. The skin around the holes was gray, brittle, and cracked. With his face fully uncovered, Elon looked like a dead man walking.

"And now, akivara," Elon called, "You will grant us eyes so that we might become whole again."

"Akivara! A sacrifice!" the townsfolk echoed.

Elon wrapped a deep crimson bandana around his eyeless face. Elaborate depictions of eyes were embroidered across the fabric.

"The marriage is nearly complete. I invoke the blood bond!" Elon shouted with a powerful voice.

The white fog that enveloped the mirror surged forward, converging on the ground in front of it. The ghostly pale figure from Asher's nightmare slowly rose from the churning white. Unlike in the dream, it formed its physical body with ease. It was not long before it stood fully realized outside of the mirror, directly beneath Connor.

Elon took a deep breath and approached Asher, a black eye patch in his hand. He placed it over Asher's right eye.

Elon turned to face the crowd and spoke, "Now we shall unite the souls of the Innocent and of the Hero, taken on this consecrated ground."

With a thin rusty knife, Elon prodded the tip of his thumb until a thick glob of black blood was produced. He held out his hand and allowed the liquid to drip freely onto Asher's forehead.

Asher screamed as the fluid burned his skin. The smell of charred flesh filled the air.

Elon pressed his cut thumb against the molten wound. With a swift push, the tip punched directly into the skull.

Asher's eyes rolled into the back of his head.

* * *

Elon held his thumb firmly inside Asher's skull like a hook. He twisted it fiercely as if trying to make the hole larger. Asher's left eye erupted with an agony he could not describe. A loud, warbling sound filled the air with the chantings of the choir. Somewhere far away, Asher thought he could hear Connor shrieking.

Asher did not know if he was screaming anymore. The only thing he knew was the pain.

Then, abruptly, Elon stepped back.

A crackling pop filled the air, and with it came relief.

* * *

The men that held Asher loosened their grip. He fell forward, throwing his hands to his face. He ripped the patch from his right eye as he fiercely clutched his left. Something was wrong. The terrible pain was gone, but the area was inflamed and bleeding. A timid prod of the socket struck Asher with

72

horror. A mutilated hollow was left in his face where his eye should have been.

Asher cracked open his single eye. Through tears, he strained to lift his gaze to the tree where Connor still hanged. His head bobbed weakly as he muttered an unintelligible prayer to himself. Asher could see a darkened stream of blood flowing from the child's right eye.

Beneath the boy's feet, Elon stood in front of the mirror with outstretched arms. In each hand, he held an eye.

His face was tipped toward the sky, and Asher trembled as he saw what looked like streams of blood pouring through the bandana that covered the old man's hollow eyes. The blood drained forth from the wound that had been opened in Asher's forehead, and from Connor's crucified palms. Elon gently moaned as the final drops fell into him. He sighed in satisfaction and stretched his back.

The man who was the mayor no longer resembled himself. He stood taller with broad shoulders and thick black hair. Slowly, he lowered his head, and the bandana fell away. When he turned, Asher looked into the face of a man sixty years younger. Elon opened his eyes, revealing glowing blue irises with purple flecks speckled through them.

* * *

"Grandpa... Clint?" Asher whispered. It wasn't possible. Those eyes had disappeared with his grandfather's passing. But here they were in the face of someone younger and stronger than Asher barely recognized.

The man gave no answer. Instead, he turned back toward the white tree. Its golden leaves had returned in full as if touched by the same youth that transformed Elon. Each leaf gave off beams of light in every direction, illuminating the sky like a beacon. They were beautiful. Asher had never seen them glow like this before.

Hope filled him. He tried to crawl toward the man who resembled his grandfather, reaching a feeble hand toward him. "Grandpa... I missed you..." he said weakly.

The newly formed Clint ignored Asher. His luminous eyes rested on the figure that loomed outside of the mirror. "The pilgrimage is now complete. We offer unto thee the soul of the Innocent. Feast, my lord."

Connor was still praying to himself when he combusted into a monstrous ball of fire. He was only able to let out half of a scream before his body went completely limp. The smell of burning flesh and death filled the air. The white wood of the tree and mirror bled black blood through its cracks as the child died.

All of the blood left inside of Connor's body gushed from him and poured onto the ethereal figure in front of the mirror. It staggered to the ground, struggling to rise again as the blood painted its form.

The choir continued to chant in a language so foul that their mouths bled. But their voices gave the figure strength until it mustered the power to stand.

Its body was a churning tempest of blood and fog in the growing shape of a man. Bolts of lightning discharged inside of the storm followed by deep rumbles of thunder.

Clint knelt in reverence before the entity, holding up the eyes taken from Connor and Asher.

"We offer thee thine eyes, given of the akivara. Let them serve thee in this world."

The figure took the eyeballs with half-formed hands and brought them to its face. An explosion of energy surged from the body, knocking down many who stood by. The fires went out from the force. Everything fell silent.

With tears running down his face, Clint turned to the choir and rejoiced, "The matrimony is complete. He walks among us, the Great One reborn, Fultus!"

"Hail, Fultus, the Savior of Man," the choir echoed.

The figure, now glowing black, stooped and sank its hands into the earth, feeling the dirt with new fingers that were made of flesh. Then it stood tall, the naked visage of a man with features that appeared as though they were carved out of marble. With a regal air, he softly waved his hand.

A deep sigh escaped the people of Hornwood. Everyone, save for Asher and Clint, fell to the ground dead. Clint knelt before the powerful entity and kissed its hand. Fultus beckoned the man to stand.

"Arzhur, my friend, why is this akivara still breathing?" When Fultus spoke, there were two separate voices. One was the gentle whisper of a woman; the other was deep and shook the ground.

"Fultus, my Savior, I present to thee my true son, Asher Bryne. Raised from birth to be the hero that brings you into this world."

Fultus nodded. "No bond is more sacred than that of flesh and blood. The akivara is yours to partake of. But with haste. We have work to begin."

"Thank you, my liege," said Arzhur.

Asher trembled when he realized that they were speaking of him. But his body was numb, his mind broken from the terror of all he had witnessed. He looked into the eyes that had been his grandfather's for rescue. Clint—or Arzhur—came forward and cradled him in his arms. There were tears in his magnificent eyes.

"Look at me," Arzhur whispered. "I am the one with tears now… there may come a day in the afterlife when you understand what has happened here. On that day, I hope you can forgive me. I have loved you, Asher. I'm proud of you."

Asher was comfortable being held by Arzhur. He could not tell if the man truly was his grandfather, but he was warm and smelled like old summer memories. Asher felt like a child again in his arms. He was scared, but as everything turned to blackness around him, he held fast to the light in those blue eyes speckled with purple flecks.

They were like the universe.

Red Flag

K.R. Patterson

Shane told me he's going to kill somebody.

I fingered a page of the diary I started when my son, Shane, was born, paper stiff from dried tears. I penned the words almost two weeks ago, and I've read them at least two hundred times since.

I knelt on an old mattress in the attic as I read, springs poking at my knees, the fresh sheets at odds with the dusty, forgotten things. It was dark outside—not just with the oncoming night, but the storm, which was supposed to be a doozy. The electric tea lights flickered. A wall sconce provided a constant light that was dim, but sufficient. I cradled the diary like it was the newborn child. If I hoped hard enough, God might let me start over.

As a child, he was sweet. Special, even. When he played among other children, all the others were bullies, it seemed. If some kid tried to take his toy, Shane would give it to him, no complaints. It broke my heart, how tender he was.

The rain pounded on the dull, gray skylight, as if insisting my brain let the obvious sink in.

I flipped to one of the early pages, written twenty-four years ago.

> *Shane is barely one-year-old, and not only does he say hundreds of words, he's been starting to string them together! His first little sentence was "please come." He mispronounces please, and blends it together like one word: peas-come. Adorable! He always wants me near. To hold him, watch TV, or just to show me something. Peas-come.*

I refused to read the other entries, the ones I had flagged with Post-it yellow arrows. I started putting those in the journal when things didn't add up. Odd things he would say. The warnings. And then there were the red flags.

The happenings.

The first red sticker marked his fire in the park at age seven. All the fires got a red arrow, five or six total. Then there was the money he stole from my purse. The first phone call I got from the police. The drugs.

All the help I turned to—counselors, police, teachers— told me he was going through normal stages. He had problems, yes, but he'd make it through. He was a good boy, they all said.

I knew Shane was a good boy, but I also knew something was different about him.

I flipped back to the last yellow flag, the most recent one. The stiff-with-dried-tears one. I had read about our little picnic in the park again and again, hoping it would have a different ending if I simply read it enough times. But you know what they say about insanity. Doing something over and over, hoping for a different result.

But of course... the story never did change.

* * *

It was a typical Carolina summer. The air was heavy and ripe with the scent of magnolias. Toting a picnic lunch from Popeyes, I strode with a giant smile plastered on my face to our usual spot.

For the past two years, Shane had held a steady job, remained married to a wonderful woman, and now, they were even trying to have a baby.

Shane—clad in jeans and a black T-shirt—lolled with his limbs askew on a curvy wood-planked bench beneath a myrtle tree in full, flaming-red bloom.

I adjusted my sunglasses and waved hello. He jumped up, ran over, and gave me a tight hug. I wrapped my arms around his strong upper back, still clutching the bag of chicken. Scents of rosemary and paprika wafted out, beckoning. Other than the stifling heat, all was right in the world—for a few, final moments.

"Mama, how you been?" He gestured toward the bench. "Please, come sit."

I beamed with joy and pride as I placed the contents of the bag between us. *Please, come.* Still saying it. My boy. Everything had turned out alright after all.

Shane opened the box and chose a drumstick. I grabbed a breast, took a bite, and nearly swooned. Salty, greasy, moist, and crispy. Then, I asked about his job.

He was movin' up, he said with a wide grin.

I glanced at him, cockeyed. "Above funeral director? What... you going to own the whole mortuary?" I couldn't keep the stiffness out of my voice. I didn't like his obsession with death, for one. For another, he needed to take care of his future family, and morticians didn't rank too high on the monetary scale.

"I got a pay raise, ma. I'm making forty-thousand a year now." From the tone of his voice, you'd think he was talking about a million bucks.

"Well, I'm glad," I said. I looked him up and down, reminding myself how far he'd come. Clean cut, short hair, smooth face, nice clothes that didn't ride too low.

He wiped his hands on a napkin, opened a bottle of his favorite ginger ale, downed half of it, and reached for a second drumstick.

"Are you happy there?" I asked, trying to keep an open mind. "Do you get along with the people you work with?"

"Since most of them are dead, yes."

I forced a smile, hoping he was joking.

He didn't smile back, only sunk his teeth in the drumstick and tore.

After finishing the chicken, which only took a minute, he looked at me as he wiped his fingers on a napkin. "There is this one guy…" he said, and then trailed off, pressing his lips together, jawline hard and distinctive.

A rock formed in my gut. I knew that look, and it wasn't good.

Despite his faults, Shane was truthful. He could watch a deadly car crash with morbid fascination, and admit straight out he liked it. There was a detachment I'd noticed since age four (first yellow flag), like a wire that wasn't placed quite right. But in spite of all that, or maybe because of it, he could flat out tell me, "Yes, ma, I'm shootin' heroin," or "Yes, I took that five dollar bill from your purse."

I felt fainter than what the July heat had already made me, even before he said it.

"I think I'm gonna kill him."

* * *

Shane's father left when Shane was three and I'd never remarried, so my best friend Hilda was my go-to gal for all the what-should-I-dos. Setting down the iced tea she'd given me—afraid that between my trembling and the condensation, it might slip straight out of my hands—I told her what Shane had said.

"Honey, you gotta commit him before he kills that man."

My heart pounded, fit to burst. I looked down at my iced tea.

She lifted up my chin with her soft, sweaty fingers, the scent of jasmine lotion tranquilizing me. "What happens if he kills someone and you coulda stopped him? You want that death on you?"

I swallowed. "I can't just betray him like that."

She let go my chin and pitched both hands on her hips. "Don't give me no big ol' word like 'be-tray.'" She emphasized and drew out the word for effect. "You are helpin' your son when he needs you."

80

"What if he gets out?" I asked. "I'm afraid he'll—"

"If your boy got somethin' wrong upstairs—and we both know he does—they gonna medicate him, get him right in the head before they set him loose."

When I stayed silent, she finally said, "Do what you want. Mother knows best." She tightened her lips in an almost sardonic smile. Picking up her iced tea, she took a long gulp, after which she gave quite an exaggerated ahhh. "Just don't come to me when he's killed somebody."

A drop of sweat rolled down my spine. A moment later, with hands trembling, I called the police.

* * *

A week went by, and the silence was ominous. Finally, Shane called me. I jumped at the sound of my ringtone, which hardly ever chimed. My finger shook as I swiped the bar.

"Mama." A statement. I waited. "Why did you do that?" He laughed. "Do you really think I'm some kind of psychopath?"

"I'm sorry." I tried not to let my pounding heart be heard through my voice. "I… just…"

"It's fine, Ma. No big loss. But it did make Charlotte worry. She almost canceled her meditation classes and came home."

I knew I shouldn't have taken Hilda's advice. During the entire week after calling the police, I scoured through those flagged pages. And I remembered… he knew how to walk the walk and talk the talk. He said exactly what those psychiatrists wanted to hear, and they bought it hook, line, and sinker. But I knew better. They never saw his secret retaliations like I did.

He was capable of anything.

His next move would probably be to kill me.

That's why, a few nights ago, I started sleeping in the attic with the butcher knife. I closed the hatch and muscled a heavy box of books on top. That way, I would hear if Shane broke his way in, and have time to get ready. But tonight, with the storm, I wouldn't hear anything. I'd have to stay awake all night.

To kill time, I read the early pages of my diary about Shane. He was so innocent back then, before he turned four.

I remembered how right after he was born his tiny arms and legs flailed, helpless, in the cold. I could almost smell his sweet, newborn scent all over again. I recalled the way he'd gazed at me, his eyes so big and blue. So filled with wonder.

I wept. How could God let…

My face twitched. Then, a transformation happened. I quit being afraid for myself and started to be afraid for Shane.

He was an innocent. As his mother, I knew. He couldn't help whatever happened in his brain, some disease, uncontrollable, like Alzheimer's, eating away his four-year-old brain. It was only a matter of time that he would commit murder and go to Hell. I had no other option. I had to save his soul.

"Lord, help me. Forgive me."

Thunder crashed.

It was a sign. There was no other way.

I peeled one of the transparent red tabs out of the journal and held it in the palm of my hand, like a tiny fetus. It glowed in the light of the wall sconce behind me. The sconce had always reminded me of a man, peering through the wall. A bronze gentleman's top hat, the rounded bulb beneath it like a little head. I felt like he knew my thoughts, and he might tell. I had to hurry. The flickering lights agreed. The time was now.

I tucked the knife in my purse and got out of the attic. My heart wanted to explode, probably like Abraham felt with Isaac. I rushed down the hall and opened the door to the garage. Sweltering air engulfed me, smelling of petrol.

I climbed into the driver's seat, hands drenched with sweat. I tried to remain calm as I opened the garage, started the car, and veered out into the night. The streets were rivers, washing the world of its sin, overfilling the drains.

Twenty minutes later, I pulled up in front of my son's house, cut the engine, and shut the headlights off.

Rummaging through my purse, I pulled out the red flag from his journal and set it on the seat, reminding myself why this needed to be done. I pulled my knife up by its smooth, black handle and concealed it by my side.

This was it. Judgment Day. Better by my hand than God's.

I looked in the windows and found him still up, watching TV. I thought of knocking on the front door, but dismissed it. If I saw his face, happy to see me…

No matter. I had a key to the kitchen door on the backside of the house. I was grateful Charlotte was gone; grateful they'd had no children yet.

The thought almost stopped me. Shane's future babies. The only grandchildren I would ever have. But then I imagined what kind of future lay in store for them. They'd have their own red and yellow flags, if they even survived childhood. I tried to picture their little faces, but I only saw them staring in the darkness, begging me to save them, too.

Around the back, I knelt on the wet cement by the rear door and waited. I knew the noise from the TV would mask my entrance but I wasn't taking any chances. The thunder was my only true ally.

I grasped the key in my trembling hand until the sky blazed its crisp and silent illumination. I only had seconds before the thunder.

Swallowing against a dry, taut throat, I waited for the impending drum.

One, two, three…

Boom.

I jammed the key in the brass-plated lock. It wouldn't go in. Wrong way. I cursed. Turned it, jabbed here, there, and finally, blessedly, the key slid in with pleasant little clicks. I opened the door just as the rumbling died, then hurried to close it.

Tiptoeing across gray kitchen tiles, I pressed myself against the wall connecting to the living room. Taking in deep, silent gulps of air, I used my breath as a way to shut my mind off and inched toward the living room. I thought he would be watching some horrible, violent show, but that wasn't the case. It was a cooking show, telling him to "Scrape the browned bits from the pan as you add the wine." I almost faltered with this trivial aberration—but regained my composure.

With the next crash of thunder, I steeled myself and dashed into the room, knife raised.

Shane's eyes went wide and he said, "Ma?" just before I reached him. A question. He held out both arms to brace himself, like he did as a child when I insisted we were going somewhere he didn't want to go.

I closed my eyes and thrust. I would go through his hands. Get to his chest. Make it quick.

The knife stopped. I wondered if it had gone clean through, no resistance, when I felt his hands on my wrist.

They squeezed, hard.

"No," I cried, tears springing to my eyes. "No, no, no." My hold loosened. The knife made no sound as it hit the carpet; the silence juxtaposed the terror that raged between us.

I tried to pull free from his uninjured grip. We wrestled our way toward the bookshelf, crashing into it. Books rained down on us, accentuated by another boom from the livid sky. I tried to pull free of him, but the books encumbered my steps.

He managed to get both of my hands in his one, large hand. Using my legs as leverage, I tried again to escape. Seemingly unaffected by my efforts, he maneuvered his body to hold me with one hand and stretch with the other, intent on something in the bookshelf. I planted my feet with all my strength and tugged. The effort was futile.

Dear God, I prayed. *No.*

He would kill me now. He would kill me and go to Hell. I had failed.

Shane, finally retrieving what he sought, held it high. He straightened, towering over me with a heavy, bronze horse head bookend. I'd given the antique set to him as a housewarming gift, passed down from my parents.

There was a lunatic gleam in his eyes, made more intense by the bright flash of light that filled the room. He raised the relic in the air and swung it down in full, furious speed, like he was God and held the lightning.

* * *

I stood over my mama. I'd dropped the bloodied bookend and picked up the knife, examining the familiar, black wood handle. Tears streamed down my cheeks. I didn't try to stop them or wipe them away.

How could it be? The woman who put bandages on my knees after I fell, who let me sleep in her bed when I was scared there were monsters under mine. And once, while playing water balloons, she cried when she accidentally threw one that burst on my cheek.

The woman who gave me life, who cared for me when I was going through some difficult times, and not just the teenage years. The drug addiction. The trouble I'd had with the police. Everything.

I noticed she'd been anxious lately, but, calling the cops? She completely overreacted when I said there was a guy at work who drove me crazy. In retrospect, I shouldn't have said I felt like killing him, but didn't everyone say things they didn't mean sometimes?

When the cops came to my door, asking me if I'd said I wanted to kill someone, I laughed and said yes, but I didn't mean it. Still, they were dutifully concerned after Ma's embellished report, so they asked me if I would stay for a voluntary seventy-two-hour observation. I agreed, hoping it would ease Ma's mind.

Now, I kicked myself for not picking up on the signs. During my seventy-two observational hours, I'd met a few people with paranoid schizophrenia that showed striking similarities to my Ma's condition. When she started talking about a "best friend" named Hilda, a woman I'd never heard of in my life, that should have been the nail in the coffin. But it wasn't. I had to find out now, when it was almost too late.

I knelt beside her unconscious form and felt for breath by placing my cheek near her face. The air came out slow, but steady. She was alive.

Pulling my phone out of my pocket, I called 911.

"What is your emergency?"

"There's been an accident," I said, my throat tight with emotion. I gave them my address and squeezed Ma's hand, glad she was still breathing. Glad she would get the help she needed.

"Please come."

Crimson Snow

Austin Slade Perry

I pushed open the unlocked door to my grandparents' old farm-house. It had been years since I was last here, but it felt like no time had passed. The living room was full of furniture and assorted family pictures on the wall. I stepped away and into the kitchen.

"Home sweet home," I muttered to myself.

The sound of footsteps pulled my attention to the stair-case where a stocky older man with graying black hair descend-ed. He wore tan overalls over a red flannel shirt and a thick coat. He furrowed his brow.

"Are you Torryn, boy?" he asked in a gravelly voice. "You've got the same bright red hair like your grandma. Has anyone ever told you that?"

"Yes," I answered. "I take it that you're the caretaker, Mr. Richards?"

The man nodded and shook my hand.

"I made sure to restock the firewood," he explained. "Everything is up and running for you and your friends." He pulled out a long bony key from his pocket and handed it to me. "Here is your copy of the house key. Have a good weekend."

"Thank you, sir," I called out to him as he turned and walked out the open door. He carefully dodged to the side as a young woman emerged through the doorway.

"Torryn!" Becca called out. "I can't get over how beautiful it is up here. Matt, isn't this place perfect?"

Matt lugged his and Becca's suitcases into the house, brushing away strands of blonde hair that had fallen loose from his bun.

"Of course it is," he responded. "But I'm so tired—that drive nearly killed me. Hey, Torryn, maybe you could help Hayden with the rest of the stuff since you napped the whole way here."

"Sure," I said while walking outside. "If you two want to go ahead and get settled, maybe we can go sledding later."

I stepped outside. Hayden was by the truck admiring the surrounding area. I stood by for a moment, letting him enjoy the view. He wore a formfitting black sweater that showed off his strong build. He looked handsome.

He turned away from the view and retrieved his bags when he noticed me.

Cocking his head to the side, he gave me a flash of his crooked smile. "Are you just going to stand there or give me a hand?"

"Only if you say the magic word," I teased.

He chuckled. "Will you, pretty please, get down here and help me?"

"That's close enough," I said as I started down the steps. I gave him a playful wink. His cheeks reddened slightly.

He took another look around the clearing. "It's so beautiful up here. You must have had a blast as a kid."

I shrugged. "It was fun during the summers. I've never been up here during the winter," I explained.

I pulled out my suitcase from the back of the truck. Looking up, I glanced at the edge of the clearing. The bare branches looked like long boney fingers covered in ice. There was something about the imagery that was unsettling.

"What is it?" Hayden asked, eyeing my expression.

"Nothing, just admiring the view," I said. "Let's get this stuff inside so we can go sledding."

Back inside, I made my way to the master suite at the end of the upstairs hall. I paused at an open door as a cool breeze hit my face. This led up to the attic. Mr. Richards might have accidentally left a window open. I walked up the narrow, winding staircase. As a child, the attic had been off-limits. My siblings and I once dared one another to go up and see what it was like, though none of us made it past three steps. But the fear I had as a child was gone, and in its place was abject curiosity.

Rows of dusty trunks and cardboard boxes stacked up against the short walls. A light bulb hung in the center of the room, but it wouldn't turn on. The window at the end of the room was open. I closed it.

A loud crash from behind caused me to jump and turn. A thick book had fallen on the ground. I picked it up. It was *The Tales of the Crimson Prince* that my grandmother read to me as a child.

I opened it to the first brightly colored page and smiled as I began to read:

> *Long ago on a mountain top, so covered with summer's warmth, dwelled a mighty kingdom. In the castle, there lived a fair prince with hair so red it earned him the title* The Crimson Prince.

"Torryn," Hayden's voice called from the stairs. "I think Matt and Becca are about finished getting settled in, if you still want to go sledding?"

I nodded to myself and placed the book back on the shelf where it had fallen.

* * *

We spent most of the afternoon sledding down nearby hills. As the sun hid behind gray clouds, the wind picked up, becoming frigid and harsh.

"Was it supposed to snow this weekend?" Hayden asked.

I shook my head, "No, not according to my phone."

Becca and Matt climbed their way back up the hill, grinning from ear to ear. They handed the sleds off to us. Becca gave a quick countdown. On three, we took off. Hayden's screams of laughter filled the air as I zoomed past him.

We were going fast. Too fast. The cold had turned the snow into ice. Our speed, combined with the falling snow and the hard wind made it difficult to see. I struggled to maintain a straight path down the hill and accidentally steered into a large bump. I flew through the air and tumbled into a tree.

My eyes fluttered open, vision blurry as my head pulsed in pain. A shadowed figure moved amongst the trees, coming closer to me. I closed my eyes and opened them again. The figure was gone. There was nothing but the looming frosted trees. My body shaking, I rolled over and stood. Vibrant red wildflowers littered the surrounding area. They were beautiful but unfamiliar. During my summer trips, I had never seen anything like these. They were so red.

"Oh my god! Are you okay?" Hayden called out to me.

"I'm fine," I said.

Becca ran over and examined my head as my eyes remained fixed on the crimson flowers. "Thank goodness you're okay. There's no blood or anything," Becca said, relieved. "Why don't we call it a day and get some ice on Torryn's head?"

Hayden held me close. "I've never known flowers to bloom in winter," he muttered to himself on our way back.

* * *

We spent the rest of the evening inside. As everyone made themselves comfortable around the fireplace, I settled at the far end of the living room and flipped through the pages of *The Tales of the Crimson Prince*.

Each story was adorned with colorful patterns and images. These were my favorite tales. I knew all of the stories by heart. But there was a new one that I didn't recognize. Rather than the usual vibrant colors and images, its pages depicted gray and charcoal bare branches from an enormous dead tree, sprouting from stones and crusted earth. Behind the tree, lurked a dark cloaked figure with black eyes that seemed to glow off the page. Bright red wildflowers scarcely dotted the page, providing the only color.

The title of the story was handwritten in deep, scratched letters that read, "The Lair of the Mountain King." I started to read:

The Crimson Prince lived a life in a long summer. Never once had snow touched his cheek. Never once had he understood the winter night's chill until the horn of winter was blown. A fallen warrior, long-forgotten, woke deep below the mountain, and with him came winter.

The more I read the story, the more I struggled to focus. There was something about the art in this passage that pushed me. The dark colors were discomforting, and the Mountain King's image was somehow haunting, as if he were looking directly at me.

Perhaps I was just tired. A lot had happened today. Hoping to clear my mind, I shut the book and excused myself to take a bath.

* * *

The tub's pipes started with a rattle before a jet of hot water expelled from the faucet. Steam filled the room as I peeled off my clothes. I sunk myself into the water.

When I emerged, the bathroom was gone. I stood waist-deep in a hot spring next to a low hanging black tree with frost clinging to its naked branches.

The sky was dark, save for the faint blue light coming from the full moon. I was surrounded by a dense forest and crimson-colored flowers. I opened my mouth to speak but was interrupted by the sound of something stepping into the water.

The water shifted as it moved closer to me. My breathing became uneasy. I couldn't move. Whatever it was, touched the base of my spine. It was like ice, stinging my flesh. I held my breath as it traced its fingers up my back and around my neck. They tightened their grip and pulled me against them. I wanted to fight back, but they were much stronger than me. I shuddered as a cold breath brushed over my ear.

"Don't be afraid," an icy, low voice whispered.

I arched my head back to look up at their face. Staring down at me were black, eyeless sockets from a skull partially hidden by a dusty linen hood, spiked with seven long, bony horns.

I pried my head free and tried to scramble away, but the figure grabbed my wrist and spun me around.

"I have waited for you, Torryn," his voice boomed like cracking ice.

I fought until I was able to break free from the cold embrace. In the struggle, I found myself falling back into the water. When I broke the surface, I was back in the bathroom.

My eyes darted back and forth as I tried to slow the beat of my heart. Was he in here with me? I could still feel the monster's touch on my body. I wanted to convince myself that it had been just a dream, but there were fresh bruises on my wrist. Still trembling, I got out of the tub and dressed.

I headed downstairs, stopped by a wind sweeping through the living room. The front door was wide open, letting snow blow violently inside. I ran to close the door but found Becca standing on the porch with a blanket wrapped around her.

"Becca, what are you doing?" I asked. She didn't respond. She stared blankly into the vast darkness surrounding the house. I touched her shoulder. She felt like ice.

"Do you see them?" Becca whispered.

I looked outside but couldn't see anything. "Becca, there isn't anything out there."

Becca snapped back and looked around wildly before landing her eyes on me. "Torryn, what's going on?"

"You must have been sleepwalking."

Her eyes widened and scanned over the porch and yard. "I kept seeing dark faces in skull masks. They were out lurking in the trees. They wanted you to have this." She held out her hand. In her palm was a crimson wildflower.

My heart sank. I wrapped my arms around Becca and led her back inside. "It was only a dream," I said, trying to hide the terror in my voice.

She nodded, but I doubted she believed me. I wanted to say something, but I saw Hayden watching us outside his door and went silent.

"What was that all about?" he asked.

I recounted what happened while trying to hide my anxiety, but he must have noticed something was wrong. He kept frowning and shaking his head.

"Maybe just for tonight, if you would like, I can sleep in your room. I can even just crash on the loveseat. I want to make sure you're safe," he said.

I gave his offer some consideration before nodding. He smiled and grabbed his blankets before following me to my room. Once settled in, Hayden was snoring almost immediately, but I couldn't sleep.

* * *

The following morning, I woke early and quietly slipped out of the room. The events of last night still had me shaking with questions. I put on my jacket and went to the attic. I searched through old boxes and shelves until I stumbled upon *The Complete Encyclopedia of Flowers.* I thumbed through the entire volume without finding any trace of my red wildflower.

I set the book aside and continued searching. In another box, I picked up a worn-out journal. Inside was a black and white picture of a suited man with a thick mustache. This was Harold, my great grandfather.

Most of the pages were water-damaged, limiting my reading. In the first pages, Harold wrote about moving with his pregnant wife, Mary. They had been seeking isolation and bought a plot of land in the mountains. That plot of land was presumably where we were now.

I glanced through more pages of the book. Most passages detailed the construction of the house. They had started in early spring, and the home was completed by summer's end.

After that, the pages became less legible. His handwriting grew harsh, some of the words smeared. There was one passage clear enough to read, though it unsettled me:

> *Mary has been having frightful nightmares of late. She speaks of a phantasm in the woods. She claims that it has woken from a slumber and holds a grudge against us.*

She believes that she can see it walking in the woods at night. It appears as a pale man with an uncovered skull for his face. She has started to pray each night before bed. I pray to God to end her hysterics.

I scanned through the water-damaged pages until I found another readable passage:

The spirit has made himself known to us. He stands outside every night. I approached last night and entreated him to depart, but we received no answer.

The rest of the page was illegible. I went to the next clear passage:

Mary went into labor when they surrounded our home—he and his ghoulish horde. The creatures stood at attention as Mary gave birth to a girl. We named her Edith. After the birth, his horde retreated back into the woods. But he remained outside and alone. He stood at attention, waiting for us.

After Mary and Edith fell asleep, I went to him. He did not utter a word, despite how hard I begged him to leave us be. I promised him anything so long as he would leave my family in peace.

I turned the page and found only one legible passage left.

The following nights gave no signs of the spirit, nor his horde. We had peace for a time, until last night. I was haunted by worrisome visions.

In the dream, I stood in a mist-covered lake where an enormous dead tree towered over the center. Surrounding me were crimson wildflowers and strange men in skull-shaped masks. They sang and danced around the flowers. In the distance, I saw a shadowed figure move among the trees. It was him.

He came to me from behind. He wrapped a cold hand around my neck and squeezed. Here, he finally spoke to me in a dead tongue. Somehow, I understood the words that spewed from his mouth. He told me not to fear him, for he did not desire to harm Edith, Mary, or myself.

When I asked him what he desired, he gestured toward the crimson flowers. Sitting as though he had emerged from the flowers, was a boy adorned as a prince. His clothes were crimson. His hair was crimson. His freckles on his pale skin were crimson. Even his eyes were crimson. He was the striking image of Mary and I, had we been blessed with a male instead.

I pleaded with the man, the King of the Mountain, "Please, no."

But he only stared at the child.

I don't know how long I dreamed. But when I woke, I found my hands bloody and raw. I was surrounded by an enormous pile of papers illustrated with my own gore. The images were that of my visions. I could not bear to keep them in the home, but Mary insisted that we bind the pages into a book. She titled it, The Tales of the Crimson Prince *and said we had to keep it to remember. That he wouldn't let us forget. And as if she had forgotten where the stories came from, I later found Mary and Edith sitting by the fire reading the book.*

I had come seeking answers but only found more questions. I sat for a long while, struggling to process what I had read. The image of the spirit and the visions in the journal matched the man who had visited me in the tub. What did he want? I shivered. The cold was finally getting to me. I needed to get out of this attic. More than that, we needed to get as far away from this place as possible.

I made my way downstairs, holding the journal and photograph. Everyone was already in the kitchen, laughing and having breakfast. When they saw my face, their smiles dropped.

Matt walked over to me and placed a hand on my shoulder, "Dude, are you okay?"

I shook my head, "I know what I'm about to say is going to sound crazy, but I don't think it's safe for us to be here. I think we should leave."

"I don't understand," Matt said, frowning. He pulled his hand away.

I sighed and placed the journal on the table. As I showed them the passages, I told them about my dream. When Matt scoffed, I showed them my bruises.

"Where did these come from, then?" I demanded.

Matt paled. Shrugging, he said, "Those could be from anything. Remember how you fell off the sled yesterday and flew into a tree? You probably gave yourself a concussion. You probably got those bruises then."

I shook my head. "They're finger marks, Matt. How would I get them from crashing in the snow?"

Neither Matt nor Becca said anything. Becca looked over the journal. I let myself believe she would understand, but she shook her head and handed the journal back to me.

"Becca," I pleaded. "You told me you saw something last night on the porch."

"Torryn," she said. "That was just a dream."

I shook my head in disbelief. They weren't listening to me. "But what about the journal and the flowers and my bruises?" I asked, attempting to hold back just how afraid I was feeling. It wasn't working.

Hayden's hands came down on my shoulders. "Hey, it's okay," he said. He turned to Matt and Becca. "I think we should listen to Torryn."

"What?" Matt asked.

"Look, I know it sounds funny, but he's our friend, and he confided in us," Hayden defended. "Something is clearly off about this place, so maybe we should listen to him and head out."

Matt let out a frustrated sigh, "Even if we wanted to leave, it might be impossible with all this snow. It would be better and safer to wait."

He gestured toward the window; he was right. The snow piled high against the side of the house, and several of the trees bent under the weight of it. There was no way we'd make it safely down the side of the mountain.

"I'm sorry, Torryn," Becca said sympathetically, "But Matt's right, it's just too risky for us to even attempt the drive without chains or something."

"It's dangerous even with chains," Matt mumbled.

I stared blankly out the window as her words faded. I headed back upstairs with the journal in hand. If they didn't want to listen—fine, but I didn't need to be happy about it.

Hayden's footsteps echoed behind me but stopped at the base of the stairs. I waited for him to call out. If he had, I would have stopped. When he didn't, I continued onward and collapsed onto my bed. Maybe sleep would help.

Sleep didn't come, not really. I tossed and turned until past midday. By then, the sun had started its early winter decline, and the moon was coming out. I went to the window and placed my forehead against the cold glass. Matt and Becca were outside, playing in the snow. It looked like fun.

I was startled by a gentle knock on my bedroom door. I spun around to see Hayden with a bowl of soup.

"I thought you might be hungry," he said, setting the soup on the nightstand.

I hadn't eaten anything all day, but it was only with the food in front of me that I realized I was starving.

"Mr. Richards called," Hayden said. "He was worried about us being up here with the snow. He said he'll start plowing the road later tonight so we can get out of here after the weekend is over." He paused. "I also told him you wanted to leave. He offered to give us a ride back tonight."

"Us?" I asked.

He nodded, "I want to make sure you're safe. We can get a hotel in town, and then Matt and Becca can pick us up on their way down."

I gave him a faint smile, "Thank you." I sat for a moment with Hayden. "Why do you put up with me?" I asked. "I mean, you've always been there for me."

Hayden shrugged. "Well," he said, clearing his throat. "The thing is, Torryn, I've always cared about you. I guess what I'm trying to say is that I've always loved you." His words made everything stop. "I've just never really known how to express it till now, I guess."

I put my fingers to his lips, "It's okay, I guess in a way, I've always loved you too."

My fear gave way to his smile. He wrapped me in a tight embrace. I didn't want to let him go.

"Pack your things," he told me. "Let's get out of here."

He headed to his room to grab his bags while I started packing mine. My heart was racing, and for the first time in what felt like forever, I was smiling again.

I pulled back a blanket. *The Tales of the Crimson Prince* fell to the ground with a thud, opening to the last page. I went to pick it up and noticed the edge of the paper was peeling away. Hesitantly, I gripped the page and pulled it, breaking away the dried blood that outlined the edge of the page.

As the image behind the paper was revealed, my breathing grew heavy. Across the top, written in harsh red words was *The Promise of Crimson.* The first page depicted a charcoal forest. The background was littered with blurry red and black beasts.

> *Through a broken hinge, only crimson is seen. Where red wildflowers grow, blood freely screams. Bring us a Prince of Crimson, who has been betrothed. And give him to He who won, the king of the snow.*

The words echoed in my mind as my eyes drifted to the other page. The image made my heart sink to my stomach. The Mountain King stood in the center of the page, his cloak covering half of his body while he loomed over a pale naked figure at his feet. This was the Crimson Prince. In all these stories, the prince's face was hidden. Now I found myself staring face-to-face with him. His face, his lips, his nose, his eyes. All of his details were mine.

A violent howl burst out from the roof, pulling me away from the image.

Hayden ran into my room. "What the hell was that? It was right above us!"

"Let's get out of here," I said.

We rushed downstairs. Matt and Becca were in the kitchen huddled together. Becca held Matt's arm with a tight grip.

Another howl burst from above. Whatever creature the cries belonged to scraped at the roof and crawled along the side of the home until it reached the back entrance that the kitchen led to. Then there was silence.

"What was that?" Becca whispered.

The door began to shake. Whatever was behind it was scratching at the wood, trying to get in. The old door shifted from the force until the hinges on the side broke, and the door fell to the ground, revealing a porch shrouded in darkness with a looming form in its wake.

We were momentarily frozen, never taking our eyes away from the image. Finally, Matt mustered the courage to move. Removing Becca's hand and nudging her to stay back, he cautiously moved toward the door. Nearing it, he slowed his approach and stopped. The form in the darkness growled. The clouds moved away from the full moon outside, casting a blue light onto the porch. The form moved forward and entered the light.

It stood on hind legs bent backward like a canine. Its lean body was half-covered with black fur while the other side exposed rotting flesh. Its arms hung low at its side with long claws. Its head was that of a wolf with one half matted fur and the other bloody skin. Its thin lips curled around sharp teeth as it released a growl.

The creature dropped to all fours and lunged at Matt. As he screamed, the creature dug its claws into his legs—his blood splashed out across the white kitchen tiles.

The three of us reached to grab Matt's hands, but his fingers were slick from sweat and blood. The creature yanked on him, and he slipped from our grasp. Matt tried to grip the doorframe, but he couldn't find a hold and was dragged out into the darkness.

"You bastards!" Becca cried as she grabbed a kitchen knife from the counter. She made a charge for the monster, but Hayden grabbed her and pulled us away from the kitchen toward the front door.

From behind us, the creature snarled as it returned through the back doorway. Blood dripped from its mouth. Hayden threw open the front door and quickened our pace to the truck.

The sounds of other creatures growling in the darkness filled the air. It was hard to say how many there were. But I could hear them, crawling across the snow toward us.

"Come on," Hayden screamed.

He climbed into the driver's side and started up the engine. I ran toward the passenger's seat only to realize that Becca wasn't behind me. She walked slowly, dragging her feet through the snow. Her eyes were in a daze. She squeezed the knife's handle, her knuckles going white.

"Becca!" I screamed. "We need to go. Now!"

I pulled her into the truck behind me.

Hayden slammed his foot on the gas. The truck rampaged down the driveway. Becca struggled to close the door as we jostled over the snow. The movement of the truck made shutting the door impossible. One of the creatures ran up alongside the vehicle and lunged at the opening. It reached its arm inside and dug its claws into Becca's stomach.

She wailed as the creature dragged her from the truck. I reached out to catch her hand, but it was too late. She fell into a pile of those horrible creatures.

Tears streamed down my face as I struggled to process what I had witnessed. I had lost two of my closest friends.

"What the hell is that?" Hayden asked, squinting through the snow.

The car slowed to a stop as a new figure became clear.

A sharp gasp escaped my throat. He stood in front of the car. His skull mask glowed white in the headlight. His eyeless sockets stared at me, making my skin crawl. His black cloak whipped around in the harsh snowstorm. He raised his ash-colored arm, clenching his fist. I looked back up at the hillside we came from. I could see the dark silhouettes of the beasts that had attacked us. They stood still, waiting for his command.

Hayden studied my expression. He looked from me to the man in front of our truck. His eyes narrowed. He slammed his foot on the gas, narrowly missing the Mountain King.

I turned around. The Mountain King stood in the road. Both his arms were raised. He swung them hard to his sides. The storm immediately grew more intense. The wind blew in from the side, swerving the car.

"Watch out!" I cried.

Hayden tried to correct himself, but the gusts of wind and snow were too powerful. He lost control. The truck drove off the road and rolled down the hill throwing us into the side of a large tree.

Something wet was dripping down my face. I pressed my hand against my forehead, and when I pulled away, it was drenched in blood.

There was a sharp gasp next to me. I looked over and saw that Hayden's leg was badly wedged between the door and the tree. A thick branch from the trunk lodged into his side. Blood was coating the seat. Trying to steady my breath, I reached for the branch, but he quickly gripped my hand.

"Go," he said, hissing through the pain. "Get to safety."

"I'm not leaving you," I snapped.

"I'm not arguing with you." His eyes filled with tears. "I'm in no condition to move. I care about your safety."

I leaned in and kissed him. The taste of his blood in my mouth bittered the moment.

"I'll come back for you," I promised. "I'll get us help."

I jumped out of the vehicle and into the growing storm. I stumbled against the wind. I was losing so much blood from my head and was getting dizzy, but I couldn't stop. I needed to get help. Mr. Richards was supposed to be coming up to get us. Maybe I could find him.

"Where do you think you're going?" I heard his icy voice in the air.

An overwhelming gust of wind roared, knocking me to the ground. The snow was blinding, but I kept crawling forward.

"You cannot escape what has already been foretold," he said.

More wind came crashing down. I stumbled backward into a tree. My eyes adjusted to the storm. I could see him shifting toward me. I tried to move away, but he squeezed both my arms and held me in place.

"You are mine," he growled.

There was a loud howl in the distance. I could hear Hayden's agonizing screams.

My whole body shook. My breathing became difficult as tears burned my eyes. I narrowed my gaze to my captor and fought against his hold. He wouldn't budge. I reached out and pulled away the cloth covering the bottom half of his face. His lips were dried and cracked. He smiled with rotted black teeth.

I broke from his hold and fell to the ground. My head slammed against the tree.

"What do you want?" I cried as the dizziness took hold. I was bleeding even more. The blood dripped onto the fresh snow.

"You," he whispered.

He grabbed my legs and pulled me through the white powder, leaving behind a trail of crimson snow.

The Last Light

B. Todd Orgill

"Stay to the light!" Kraig ordered. Everyone huddled under the meager light of the wagon's lantern. "Light another lamp, Sherin."

All the color had drained from Sherin's skin as she rushed to grab two lanterns from the bed of her wagon, striking them alight with her flint. The added light did little to stop the crushing blackness that enveloped them.

Two of the guards, Draken and Baerd, walked over to help Sherin with the light.

"It's not enough," Kraig mumbled, wondering if he shouldn't let some of his light free to break through the growing gloom. He was an addition to four traditional guardsmen who were all muscle, scars, and false bravado. When the guards failed, and they would, he was meant to protect them from the creatures that lurked in the darkness, always seeking a body to inhabit. He could trap light within him, and release it in the night to protect from the creatures that were always lurking. He was the only one he knew of with this gift.

None of them would be out here if it wasn't necessary, and it always seemed to be these days. The towns were blinking out—becoming consumed. The town they traveled to was just one of many who were desperate for medicine and help.

When the night came, only Kraig would make any difference.

"It will have to do," Sherin said, fidgeting.

The forest air shifted. Rusting trees brought the smell of pines. The cloud hiding the moon soon continued on its way, and ambient light returned, just enough to settle the nerves.

"Oi, hate this," Grip, the third guard, muttered. He turned to another one of the guards and said, "Got me jumpin' this way an' that."

"As you should be," the last guard said. Kraig hadn't caught his name. "But, you know, they don't come all at once. The darkness has to push away the light three times to draw them out."

Kraig knew of the superstition, but in all of his experience, he'd never had the presence of mind to track the light to see if the myth were true.

This guard stared at Grip for a moment with dead eyes and a cold face. For the first time that night, Kraig felt a true sliver of fear himself. How had he not spotted that look sooner? Those were the eyes taken by the creatures that dwelled in the darkness. The eyes of the consumed.

Kraig swiftly pulled his sword out and swung for the man's neck. The consumed guard moved with inhuman speed and knocked the blade aside with his cudgel.

The guard stared back with cold, lifeless eyes. "You've spent too many nights in the dark, friend." The creature's voice was grating, like fingernails dragged over slate.

Kraig kept his sword outstretched as he grabbed a lantern from his supplies and used a spark from his mind to light it. He had trapped this light from the dawn of a cloudless day. It pulsed in his mind, waiting for release.

While it may protect them from the creatures lurking in the dark, one of the consumed was mere feet away. He cursed himself for not noticing sooner. A bead of sweat ran down his back. The grip on his sword was tight enough that a knuckle popped. "If I'm supposed to keep you safe, let me keep you safe. We need to kill it. Now."

"Put your sword away while you can, boy," the consumed guard said, his voice so close to human. The creature's face twisted into an unnaturally wide grin, and a sound like hollow thunder broke the night. A rolling wave of darkness tore across the forest, extinguishing the light of the lamps.

Kraig's breath caught in his chest, and his instincts told him to run, to duck, to hide. But there was no hiding from darkness. Through sheer will, he ignored his baser self and released the rein from the light he had storming around inside his mind. His brain burned as if on fire. His mind howled and ached and fought him as he released a torrent of pure morning's light. It shone from his eyes, brighter than a lamp or the moon above, bright as a hundred bonfires.

Baerd whispered under his breath, "It's true."

But to the side of the wagon stood the consumed guard, his face passive, collected, and measuring the situation with a turn of his head and a glance. "I've been waiting for you, you know." His voice came out like crushed gravel laced with brimstone, his deep grin set in his face like stone.

Without hesitation, Grip lunged toward the consumed. He was fast, but the man was faster. Before his strike could land, a dark and foul wind rushed from the consumed's mouth. Darkness filled the area, putting out all sources of light, even the light from Kraig's eyes.

A deep chill settled into Kraig's bones. For the first time ever, he struggled to set the light free. Normally, he had to restrain the light, but now, he had to coax the light, to fight for it. What was happening? This was more than the normal creatures watching from the dark. The consumed guard came closer, holding a bloody cudgel in hand. It hovered at ease above Grip's crushed head and lifeless body. He grated through an empty smile, "Your light won't hold us any longer. The time has come."

They've been looking for me.

Eyes stared at him from the darkness; he'd never seen them before. Now, they revealed their ugly visages. They were creatures out of sight, out of this realm, bound to the shadows. Their eyes shone with iridescent darkness, hundreds, no, thousands of pairs, staring with a hungry intent which couldn't be mistaken.

"Back, you unholy beasts," Kraig said, mustering more strength to his voice than he felt. Into his words, he imbued the light from inside so that another burst of sunshine came from his eyes.

The lustrous eyes dimmed and faded into the darkness, but he could still feel them out of sight. Waiting. He was burning through his trapped light too fast. He relit his lantern, hoping that the dark force that had stolen its light could not do so again.

The consumed had vanished. Sherin, Baerd, and Draken shot quick glances across the forest in a panic.

"What do we do?" Baerd asked. His voice quivered, though the sword in his hand didn't waver.

Kraig shook his head. "I... I don't know."

"You mean you can't help us?" Sherin said, her face blanching as her tone accused.

"That thing is washing away my light. I don't know how it controls the darkness. I'll keep a steady light, just in case the lamps go out again." He paused and threw force into his next words, "But I don't have an endless reservoir."

Someone audibly gulped. He couldn't tell whom.

"We need your help," said the consumed. The voice came like a whisper from just over Kraig's shoulder, but when he turned, all he saw was the silhouette of skeletal trees in the darkness.

"It wants you," Draken said, motioning to Kraig while still twitching and jerking erratically at every shifting shadow. "I say we leave him behind. We've got our lamps. Maybe they will leave us alone."

Kraig wanted to argue, but Draken had a good point. Maybe the others would fare better without him. "You might be right. Go. There's no need for anyone else to die on my account."

"That's that then," Baerd said, nodding to Draken and then turning to Kraig. "Sorry, mate. Hope we both find ourselves in the light when morning comes. Best of luck." He grabbed the horse's bridle and used it to urge the wagon onward. The others shared glances with Kraig but quickly moved to follow suit.

He didn't wait to watch them roll off into the night. Sherin had paid him half upfront. If they didn't want him anymore, then he'd best go back to town while he still could. They were probably safer if he was headed in the opposite direction.

The darkness of the night grew and waned as clouds made their way across the sky. The black of the forest felt oppressive, and he was keenly aware of how utterly unprepared he was for another encounter.

"We're coming," said the disembodied whisper.

The night turned into a blackness so thick Kraig could feel it crawling through his skin. The air tasted putrid and felt clammy in his lungs. It was as if a million infinitesimally small vermin had skittered between his lips and clawed deep inside him.

He screamed in defiance, imbuing his voice with the last of his light. Pure light poured from his mouth like a wild white wind, bright, and powerful. It pushed against the blackness. But despite the ferocity of his scream, he was losing the fight. The shroud of darkness before him was overwhelming and shoved back with a terrifying and enormous force.

The light wavered around him.

He grew desperate, and in his desperation found an untapped trickle of energy tickling the back of his mind. He didn't know what this energy was. It was not the light. This was an entirely different force in some primal part of him. An untapped well. A dam ready to be set free by removing one tenuously set stone.

He called upon it.

His scream was anguish and fear. He'd pulled loose the stone in his mind, and the unfamiliar energy surged into a guttural cry. The air left his lungs as if it had decayed into something unbreathable. His blood rushed through his veins, clawing and shredding his insides near where he stored his light. A part of him had broken, but in its breaking, an unrelenting force of light was unleashed. The light burst like an explosion. All around him, rolling like a wave through the night, a pure whiteness washed every inch of the forest, moving outward like ripples on a lake, blasting the blackness away.

And then there was a calm.

The forest slowly came back into view, lit by the ambient light of the night. The darkest of the shadows hidden under nearby trees held none of the watching eyes. They'd be back and he'd be ready.

The familiar creak of the wagon drew near. *Had they turned around?* If they had, that meant something might have happened. Kraig reversed his course, going deeper into the forest to meet Sherin and the others.

It was not long before their paths crossed, and only when he came close did he realize they no longer had any light. Their lamps were cold and dark, hanging uselessly from poles on the wagon.

"You turned back," Kraig said, waiting for an explanation. In the dark of the night, lit only by the moon, he could barely see Sherin's face, but her gaze stared at the ground.

Silence hung between them for too long. Draken and Baerd stared listlessly at the ground before them, as if unaware of Kraig's presence.

The consumed didn't act like this. This was something else. He stepped forward. "Why'd you turn back? What happened?"

Again, silence.

"Sherin? Draken? Baerd?"

The horse nickered in reply. The sheer quiet unnerved him. He didn't know what to do. Perhaps they were in shock, spooked from their encounter with the things that haunted the darkness.

He stood a safe distance away and watched as they dragged their feet along the dirt. They moved as if being pulled by an unseen force.

This was all wrong. He knew he should turn back and flee, but something kept him there, watching them. He needed to understand, and maybe that's why he followed behind the group, close enough to see and hear them, but far enough away that he could react should they suddenly manifest signs they'd been consumed.

108

The tension he felt didn't diminish as they broke the edge of the forest, and the town walls came into view. A heavy knot had grown in his back and head. The longer he watched Sherin and the others, the more anxious he became. But they weren't attacking him. This couldn't be the consumed, or at least, he hoped not.

A throbbing pain behind his eyes was growing in the back of his mind, like he had stared too long at the sun. The closer he drew to the lights of town, the worse the pain became. He squinted slowly and found the pain more tolerable, but only just.

Just ahead, Kraig could see the walls that fortified the town. Several guardsmen stood watch on parapets with brightly lit braziers. Kraig tried to pull the meager light to him, to use as he had done a thousand times before, but nothing happened.

"Finally, you will see," came a voice behind him, ephemeral and ethereal; it was gone as quickly as it had come. He knew it was the voice of the consumed guardsman, though less harsh and grating than earlier, almost sweet. "The aphotic tide rises. Join us lest you be washed away." The voice slipped under his skin like rancid oil, fouling him. A deep, brittle gloom settled in Kraig's bones.

Kraig searched but couldn't find the source of the voice. The night was empty. Even the forest behind him held nothing but mundane shadows. Where were the signs of the consumed? What had happened to the obsidian eyes of the watchers?

He was alone. His voice crumbled like burnt coals as he whispered, "I don't understand."

"Forget the light," the ethereal voice said. "The night is ours."

He meant to speak again, but the same force that had kept him close to his comrades had silenced him. The voice grew wide and long, like a body floating just above his mind. Sprouting tiny tendrils with claws, it slipped into his skull and chipped away at his mind. It removed all thought of light, of the powers he'd used to keep himself safe. They vanished from his mind without a trace. It stole everything of himself as if it was a distant memory, possibly never even existing.

The light in front of him burned his eyes. He turned his back to the town, facing the long shadows of the forest. They compelled him to return.

He was a void. A hollow vessel. His mind screamed to fill the emptiness, its voice an order he could no sooner explain than resist.

Lust.

He lusted after the darkness. His eyes and ears, the feel of his skin, all thoughtlessly sought shadows calling to him. A faint part of him wondered at the longing, but even that curiosity vanished like dust on the wind.

"Now!"

Kraig reached out to the shadows, not with his hand but his mind. Darkness rushed in, as surely as if he'd grabbed it.

The blackness oozed through him, twisting and turning, forcing its way into every corner of his mind. It even made its way into the place where he'd found the spark of energy earlier. And in that part of his mind, the night stayed, burrowing and clawing until it shaped the space into its new home.

When it was done, he greeted the darkness like a forbidden lover in the night.

"Now you can see. Look," said the voice.

Kraig turned back to the town and noticed them.

Eyes. Eyes liked he'd never seen. Hundreds of them. He could see every eye in town, even through the walls and wood and stone. They were burning like little fires in the night. They were beautiful.

But when he looked to Sherin, Baerd, and Draken, he found no light to their eyes. No darkness. Nothing. Whatever and whoever they had been had washed away during the chaos of the night.

With the barest thought for what he was doing, he breathed out some of the darkness within him, willing it into the bodies of his lifeless companions.

They shifted, standing straighter, almost on alert, and turned to him as one. "We follow," they said in haunting unison. Their voices matched the people they were before, but they were devoid of warmth. Hollow.

110

Kraig watched them stand with unnatural stillness. A fragment of him knew this was wrong, but he couldn't say why, and soon he stopped caring. "Come," he said, and they did.

Kraig took one last wistful look at the forest and the shadows it held and headed to town with a fetid darkness swirling in his mind, ready to be released.

Polter Geist

Jen Ellwyn

The inhospitable antique store could be easily mistaken for an indoor cemetery. It was deprived of light and cluttered with cold objects that only served as markers in memoriam of life. Very few mourners entered the store. More often, grave robbers slipped through the barred windows, passing through the panels that were as chilled and transparent as themselves.

One such thief ventured through the glass in this manner. He crept through the narrow aisles of the store while stepping carefully around corners and angling his shoulders to minimize their width in the crowded space. Vases, mirrors, and ornaments of the expensive sort were precariously perched on equally expensive glass shelving. They were each waiting for the slightest encouragement to fall and shatter. Wild-eyed and alert, the thief searched for his target. He also searched for those that would target him.

He was not alone. A girl named Mary stood in front of the clerk's desk, watching the thief with a cryogenic smile. "Have you come to try again?" she asked with a false innocence. "You are foolishly reckless, Polter."

Someone who didn't know any better would have thought of Mary as a child who believed many things—like the existence of the tooth fairy, or happy endings—yet who knew nothing of the grim, terrible reality of life. Such a person would be grimly, terribly wrong.

"This is dangerous for you," she reminded him, tilting her head and playing with the lace lining her nightgown.

Polter ignored her and continued straight for an artifact atop a display cabinet.

"You're going to regret thiiiiis," Mary chanted. She swayed in her nightgown to entertain herself, though her focus was locked on the older boy.

He paid her little attention, instead finding stable purchase upon the cabinet to reach up for the vase. "This is mine. It should be with my mother. I'm going to return it to her." Carefully hovering his hand around the stem of the vase, he began to close his weak grip.

"Be carrrreful," she crooned with little faith that he would heed her warning.

He ignored her. The vase was heavier than anything he'd ever imagined. It was also more delicate and fragile than spun glass. The boy's hand trembled, weary and hollow of nourishment.

He took a breath, winced, and decided to go for it. With a yank, he stepped off the shelf. The porcelain base scraped like stone as it teetered over the edge. Then, it fell.

Polter caught the vase against his chest and miraculously managed to prevent it from plummeting straight to the floor. He collapsed to his knees under its weight. Panting, he struggled to stand with the vase in his tight embrace.

"That was close," Mary grinned.

She glanced behind her as a shadow emerged from the backroom. Polter noticed the visitor too and dropped to a crouch. As if it were as volatile as a landmine, he gently set the vase on the floor and held his breath.

The shadow's vaporous mass assumed a towering shape. Leaning out from the door frame, it appeared as if it were looking around the shop. After a few moments, the shadow relaxed and abandoned the doorway, bobbing with the sway of its cloaked steps. It moved behind the counter and fussed over the register.

"They will hear you. They will see you. They will find you," Mary predicted, overwhelmed with delight at the young thief's impending doom.

"No, they won't," Polter whispered. His voice was masked by the clack and ching of the register. The boy hefted the vase up again, waddling carefully with it toward the front door.

She watched him intensely, grinning with anticipation. "You'll drop it."

While slowly maneuvering himself and the vase toward the door, he hissed at her, "I won't."

"You'll trip."

He took a broken step, dragging his foot against the floor. Still, he argued, "I won't."

"You'll fall."

He lost his balance and dropped to one knee. The vase teetered in his arms, but he stabilized it. Still, it rolled lightly on its base when he rested it on the ground. Glancing back at the register, whose sounds had now ceased, he saw the shadow look up and around the room once more. Entire minutes dragged over the distorted faces of the antique clocks, which no longer told time, but only idly spun in eternal circles.

The shadow pecked at the register again.

Taking a breath, the thief glared at his critic. "I won't; now leave me alone."

"I won't," she echoed mockingly. Pleased with her joke, Mary released a loud giggle, which bore a twinkling sound like chimes that echoed through the store, bouncing off objects that were built to reflect both light and sound. Her giggle harmonized with the merry dinging of the bell at the front door, announcing the entrance of two more shadows.

"Here they come," she whispered as the shadows split from each other and stalked down the aisles of the store. Polter froze yet again, his breath caught in his throat. His gossamer heart drummed against the vase he crouched over. He feared pressing himself too tightly against its surface in case it became an instrument that projected its percussive sound.

"Don't move," Mary warned in a sing-song voice.
He didn't.

The shadows weaved through the grid of shelving, pacing steadily toward him as they perused the wares, looking for something. Perhaps their own vases. Or something they'd misplaced. Or their reflections. But there were none to be found.

"Don't speak."
He didn't.

One smoky mass turned down his aisle and stopped. Polter cautiously lifted his eyes to it. It was staring at the cerulean vase in his arms.

The boy waited with bated breath, praying that the shadow did not investigate more closely. After a few moments, the shadow lost interest, examined another object on a nearby display, and went back the way it came. Another shadow moved in the adjacent aisle, its low churning smoke spreading across the floor like a bridal veil as it moved.

The third shadow departed from the clerk's desk, skipped Polter's aisle, and traveled down the other one adjacent to it. Mary hovered nearby with a smile before following the umbra like it was an oblivious parent that she was playing hide-and-seek with.

But she wasn't the one hiding. "They're going to fiiiind you."

The shadow passed a mirror, but its reflection was vacant. She followed, giving her own reflection a giddy grin. "But not yet." She stopped in front of another mirror, her reflection now gone, abandoning her chosen shadow to wait for another one to catch up to her. "First, they're going to find me."

Polter's heart beat faster. "Mary, don't!" he hissed as quietly and urgently as he could. He was desperate to abandon his vase to stop her, but he couldn't bear to part with it. "Mary, please!" A shadow stopped and turned, searching for the source of his whisper. Polter silenced himself.

Mary waited, smiling up at an ethereal figure as it wandered toward her.

The shadow passed between her and the empty mirror that she faced. It glanced at the missing reflections, then startled. The umber erupted in a black billow of virulent smoke. Toxic clouds plumed from its sudden awareness and was carried through the air by its fear. Fear, of course, was contagious. The smoke multiplied as a chain reaction sparked between all three of the shadows. They rushed to the mirror, coalescing together as Mary skipped away.

She giggled like wind chimes and danced through their pollutant gasses, kicking clouds up into the air as the smoke ate away at her gaunt skin.

"Goodbye, Polter! Maybe we will meet again, in a previous life."

Polter trembled in his aisle as he watched her decay. Parts of the girl dropped to the floor—first her fingers, then her arms, then her eyes, teeth, hair, and finally, her entire head. Her scattered pieces disintegrated as her corpse sank to its eaten knees and slumped to the ground. Blood spilled from her esophagus and greased the linoleum. The black smoke swirled around her remains and then swallowed them whole.

The smoke soon calmed, returning to only one source as the shadows departed from the startled catalyst. The shadows stalked through the antique store as if no such terror had happened. But the umbra that had erupted with fear trembled, volatile and disturbed by what it'd seen in the mirror.

Polter knew he had to leave. Carefully, so they didn't see him. Quickly, so he didn't waste any more precious time. Not that he had a limited amount. He gathered his arms around the vase again. With a great heave, he rose to his feet and shuffled toward the door. He made poor progress. Hefting the vase up higher to hug it against his stomach, he stumbled faster and grunted with the desperate effort. He was nearly to the end of his aisle.

The boy readjusted his grip and hauled the vase forward. But this time, he tripped, just like Mary had vowed. Polter screamed as he fell.

The urn shattered. Dust scattered across the ground. Shards of porcelain went sliding, spinning, and scraping along with it, painting patterns across the floor.

The shadows whirled to him, each startled. Smoke exploded from all three of them and billowed out with a flooding force.

Polter would have screamed again if he could have. The smoke bathed him with the sensation of an unbearable

117

chemical burn. The process of his decomposition was fast, but far from painless.

His ashes were later swept up and deposited in the garbage, along with the ceramic shards used to contain them.

The shadows, who did not know any better, believed in many things—like the existence of God, the kingdom of Heaven, and the threat of Hell—yet they knew nothing of the grim, terrible, reality of the afterlife.

The Fallout

Chris Jorgensen

The raid sirens sent everyone in the Black Swine Pub into a
frenzy. The bomb drops rattled the ground as loud blasts cracked
panes of glass, and bright flashes lit the main room. The pub
hadn't been hit, but the explosions were close.

Oliver Hughes was among those who had gone into
a frenzy, hiding under the table where he'd been drinking. He
knocked over two chairs on his way down, and could scarcely
tell which way was which after the fact. Once the blasts had ended, only a dull ringing remained outside.

Oliver was resting an ice-filled rag against his temple.
He had hit something that left his head spinning in confusion.
He adjusted the cloth and winced at the throbbing pain.

"Keep that on; it will help the swelling go down," said
the barman. Oliver must have pulled the rag away at the pain
without realizing it. He gingerly put it back. Something about
this made him uneasy. It felt familiar.

"Hurts is all," Oliver said. "The kind that makes me
feel every pulse of blood in my head."

"That tends to happen with a mild head injury. I can get you something to tie it around your head if you prefer not to hold it."

Oliver waved him off. "Nah, I'm good. Just twinges. It will go away."

"You came out the worst of us, it seems, which is a good sign."

"Says you, it's not so great for me."

"Suppose that's true," the barman said as he offered his hand. "I'm Tom. I've seen you here a few times."

Oliver shook it once. "Oliver. Coincidentally, I've been here a few times."

"Hey, Cal," Tom called. "Bring that kit over here. I need some of those bandage wraps."

"Really, it's fine."

"Makes life a little easier is all," Tom reassured him. "Makes it so you have two hands to work with; never know, we might need them."

"Place got damaged?"

Tom shook his head. "Nah, not really. A couple of broken windows in the back but nothing terrible. Not sure how the neighbors fared, we might take a look a little later when the sirens go off. For now, it's best we wait and stay undercover. No telling what could happen if there are more. Ah, thanks, Cal."

A tall Irish bloke brought over the bandages and handed them to Tom without a word. He didn't come across like the type who spoke much. Probably works in the forges, Oliver guessed, based on his looks. There were burn scars evident across his forearms and face.

You don't get those by working at a desk.

"Where's David?" Tom asked.

Cal shrugged. "Upstairs," he said.

"Well, get him down here, we need to get things sorted. Maybe take a look outside and see if there's anything in the sky."

Cal nodded once and walked toward the back room door.

"Have the sirens really been going this whole time?" Oliver asked. He had barely noticed. They sounded faint, like a humming in his ear.

"Haven't stopped since they started. But we haven't heard any other blasts since the first few."

120

Everything happened so fast. Oliver felt as though time had stopped during the blasts. And now, things were just catching up.

"Come on now," Tom said. "On your feet, and we can be about getting a plan ready once everyone is here. Sounds like them walking to the stairs now."

Oliver could hear the footsteps above them. That seemed odd. Their footsteps should have been muffled by the commotion outside, but they weren't. He hurried to the nearest window.

"Oi," Tom called. "Don't go getting yourself in a fit. Can't go running about like that with a head injury."

Oliver looked at the street through the window. A heavy blanket of fog and smoke engulfed the outside, making visibility impossible. It was also dark. There were no light sources that he could see. No lamps, torches, and no flicker from candles in windows. Just the fading light of the moon. And near silence.

"Night is all manner of strange," said a new voice that Oliver didn't recognize.

He turned to see the man, another factory worker. He was dressed in dirty work clothes as if he had just come to the bar from the lines. He had dark hair and a short beard.

"What are you on about?" Tom asked the man who was presumably David.

"There's hardly any light outside," Oliver said timidly. "There should be fires and street lamps lit. But there aren't."

David nodded and leaned against the wall. "That's probably the best way to say it. There's light out there, but there's no actual light if you get my meaning. Strangest thing. The whole place is like that. I can't see anything out past that fog, either. Normally, we can see the church tower lights from here, but that fog is too dense. Never seen anything like it before."

Cal nodded along with him. "Nothing," he said.

"Come now, there was just an air raid," Tom said, shrugging it off. "Everyone within half a kilometer would be laying low after that. It's no wonder everything's a bit tense. They will light the lamps soon enough."

Oliver shook his head. That feeling of familiarity echoed in his mind. There was more to this; he knew there was. "Tom, there's no noise either. I should hear people out there, shouldn't I? But there's only just the sirens, and even that is quiet."

Tom gave him a confused look and walked toward Oliver's window. There were long seconds of quiet in the room, broken by the scraping of a chair as David pulled up a place to sit. Oliver felt a steady itch develop behind his ear as he waited in silence.

"That," Tom motioned outside, "is not natural."

"There's some commotion out there," David said. "Can't see it, but you can hear it faintly; sounds like it's on the other side of the street, or perhaps a few buildings down. Hard to tell."

"Really?" Oliver asked. "I can't hear anything other than the sirens."

David shrugged. "Took a while for me to notice, but it's there if you sit upstairs. I opened the window a bit to try and get a sense of things."

Tom turned away, shaking his head. He walked over to the table that David sat at and pulled up his own chair. Oliver copied. Cal remained standing, leaning against the support beam.

"So, what do we do?" Oliver asked.

"I think we might just have to wait it out," Tom said. "Once the city gives the all-clear, they'll turn the sirens off, and people will come back out. We'll just give it some time."

"Perhaps," David said softly.

Cal watched without saying a word. His look made Oliver's shoulders itch. First his ears, now his back. This whole thing was getting him too tense.

"We can set up a watch upstairs overlooking the street while we wait," Tom said. "If anything happens, we'll see it first. We can take shifts for now. No telling how long this could take. Cal, you take the first watch."

Cal nodded and marched up the stairs. Everyone remained silent.

Oliver kept glancing for anything that might hold some secret as to what he should do.

He could feel fear creeping up his spine. His hands fidgeted on his chair, running along the armrests. He was trying to keep his nerves about him.

* * *

David could tell that this Oliver fellow was going to be trouble later. Nervous little man, untrusting of anything he couldn't control. *We'll cross that bridge when we get there,* he thought.

The barkeeper, on the other hand, seemed to be an okay fellow. He had kept his calm right after the raid sirens went off. Perhaps he was some kind of soldier before he found himself minding a bar in a bad part of town.

Cal was a mystery all his own. The man couldn't string more than five words together as far as he could tell. Later he might have to try and break that nut open to see what was going on.

Oliver started scratching at his chair. He was a twitchy one. His eyes were clever, that much David could tell, but they were cautious and always looking around. He was probably the kind of guy who had a sit-down job.

Tom was studious as well but in his own slow way. Definitely a soldier. Perhaps that was a way in. "Where were you stationed?" David asked.

Tom looked up placidly. "How did you know I was in the army?"

David shrugged. "Most everyone I know around these parts did some sort of service. Figured if you work this side of town, you did as well. Not to mention you seemed pretty in line with ordering everyone about when everything went to hell."

There was a very slight change of appearance in Tom. A gentle ease in his shoulders as the tension left him.

"I was in Sudan for a while, but never farther south than Uganda. My time ended years ago."

"How long ago was that?" Oliver asked.

Tom leaned back in his chair. "Twenty years or so. The time really meshes together. Those weren't the best years of my life."

"You've been a bartender ever since?"

Tom shook his head. "Worked farms for a long time after that. But I somehow ended up here. Tell me, what do you do?"

"To be exact, I watch a single line of a belt for broken parts. They build axles in my building. They get carried off and build new auto cars," David replied.

Tom nodded toward Oliver. "What about you?"

"Me?" Oliver sounded surprised at the question. "I keep track of the books for the textile plant down the road. Just work with numbers. It's not bad work, but it's not the best either," he shrugged.

David let their conversation drift from his mind. He got them talking, that was the important part. *Keep people level, that was key.* As soon as too much quiet settled on the place, they would get cautious of each other. David needed them to talk, needed to keep the quiet at bay.

When he had first listened for anything outside, he could hear something. Better to not let them know what he had heard, though. What would they say if he told them he heard whispers calling to him? So long as the room wasn't silent, the whispers seemed to fade away. *Just keep them talking.*

* * *

Something was moving in the mist.

Callum could see the shapes shifting in and out, but he couldn't tell what they were. They didn't move like people. He had considered telling the others when he first saw them, but his curiosity held him. They weren't moving right. He watched, hoping to catch more than a glimpse of a shape in misted swirls. But the heavy fog made it difficult to see. One thing that Callum knew, those figures were moving in places where other buildings should have been.

There were also the voices. Too distinct to be far away, but not close enough to be understood either. Something beckoned him. He heard pleas for help and calls to come outside. Callum remained in his chair, gripping the sides, feeling the grain beneath his fingertips.

"Anything yet?" Tom said, coming up from behind him.

Callum didn't flinch. The calls became more distant.

"Strange things out there," he replied calmly. "No sign of people yet."

Tom was by the stairs. "No one? I'd expect at least a few soldiers going between buildings to investigate."

Callum shook his head. "Something is moving, but it's not people."

124

Tom stepped up and looked at him, quizzically. "Some carts or the fire wagons, perhaps?"

Callum shook his head again. "I don't know, but not people. People would have come over and checked by now; these just stay away."

Tom said nothing.

"Look." Callum pointed toward the window.

They watched the mist for a time.

"Do you hear them?" Callum asked after a minute.

"Hear what?" Tom asked.

Callum gestured out the window again. "Them," he said. "They're calling us."

* * *

"What are you on about?" Oliver asked Tom, who was now going through things behind the bar. The sounds of glass falling and other things tumbling about didn't phase the barman.

David stood up from his chair and walked over to the bar, peering over the counter. "Tom, what's going on? You act like you've seen a ghost."

Tom ignored both of them and came back up with a cudgel, dropping it on the bar before going back to his frantic search. His sudden stiffness put Oliver back on edge, who began wringing his hands. *What could have gotten the man so spooked?*

Tom stood up with another small club in hand. "There might be a problem. Not completely sure, but best to find some way to defend ourselves if need be."

"Defend ourselves?" Oliver asked.

"What kind of problem?" David asked right behind him.

Tom regarded both of them, "Perhaps soldiers, perhaps something else. We didn't get a good look at them. But if it's friendlies, they would have come to check on us already." He looked at Oliver. "Best we make sure that who-ever they are, they don't mean us harm. If they do, we have to be ready."

David walked toward the windows. They were shut-tered tight, but he managed to pry one open. He stared out into the mist. "I don't see anything out there. We haven't heard anything significant since the blasts."

"And I find that odd," Tom said. "You guys were right. We should have heard something by now, but there's nothing. I know it sounds crazy, but there's something supernatural about all of this. I'm not going to be caught unprepared."

David walked back to the bar to pick up the other club. "I'm not happy about it, but Tom's making sense. I want to be ready too."

Cal came down the stairs slowly. His steps resounded in the now quiet drinking hall. "Things are running around outside, keeping distant from us," he said carefully, breaking the silence.

"So, we have to decide what we do," Tom said. "We can go out or stay inside."

"We should go outside and see if we can find anything." David said quickly. "Police or someone. They could help us figure out what's going on."

Cal shook his head. "Stay inside; I don't know what is out there."

"We might be able to find other people to help," Oliver chimed in.

"I'm also not sure what is out there," Tom echoed Cal. "The mist is so thick you can almost lift and stack it. I don't know if it's wise that we go out."

"That's one for staying in, two for going out, and one unsure," David said, looking between them all. "How about we go out a little to look around? Might learn something. If nothing comes of it, we immediately come back."

"If we are going out at all, shouldn't we just try and go home?" Oliver asked. He could think of nowhere else he would rather be right now.

Tom shrugged at the mention of home. "I'm already there, and I don't know how far you would have to go to get there yourselves."

"So we stay close together and only look to see what's around us," David argued. "We keep within a safe distance of the pub and come back if anything goes amiss.

Tom sighed and gripped his cudgel. "Five minutes," he said. "But if there is any sign of trouble, we secure this place without argument."

Everyone agreed.

"We need a sure way to stay close," Cal said. "The fog is too dense to see the other buildings."

"We can use a rope to keep us all together," Tom said. "There are some bundles in the back, just right by that door there. Cal, grab an oil lantern from upstairs. Two of us will stay by the door. The others will check outside." Tom let out a sigh. "I just hope we aren't doing something stupid."

Oliver couldn't agree more.

* * *

The air was chilly. The fog was so dense that David could barely make out the ground three steps ahead of him. He searched for the strange shapes Tom had been talking about. He had heard them earlier when looking out the windows, but he could now hear them much more clearly. Voices of men and women whispering, no, calling to him. His feet itched to move toward them, to follow their summons.

"Alright," Tom said. "Here's the plan, we take a quick walk around the perimeter. David, you go left, I'll go right. Cal, Oliver, you two stay here and keep watch."

Oliver and Cal both nodded.

David started along his side of the building. The damp bricks glistened in the pale light. He couldn't see the building on his right side; surely, it must be there.

Everything about the outside seemed off to him. The air, the cold, and even the alley he was wandering down. He felt around for the other side. His hand found nothing.

"Keep it together," he whispered to himself. "We'll soon turn the corner and meet up with Tom."

"... up with Tom..." came a voice.

David turned quickly behind him. No one was there, but he thought he had heard someone.

"Hello?" David called out cautiously. There was no place where the voice could be coming from. There was only the brick of the pub, the cobblestone beneath his feet, and the endless sea of white fog.

"Who's there?" he called again. The voices of men, women, and children spoke softly. It sounded like they were asking him questions.

"Where are you all?" David asked.

Something moved in the fog. It swirled about and shifted. David put his hand to his head, throbbing. He pressed and shut his eyes, blinking away the sensation.

He felt something grab his shoulder. He scrambled backward, falling to the ground. Tom stood before him, his eyes wide with shock.

"Christ, David, didn't mean to scare you," Tom said. "I was talking to you as I came up. Guess you were really spaced out."

"You were the one talking?" David asked, trying to get his calm back.

"I was just telling you that I found nothing. I was wondering what was taking you so long, so I came to find you. Did you see anything?"

David turned toward the mouth of the alley where he had come. For the first time, the mist was motionless. Not even the breeze seemed to move that dense sheet of white.

"There was," David started, but he let the words tremble and fall. "I thought I heard something—someone calling from a window or somewhere."

Tom swallowed audibly. "Let's get back inside."

Back in the pub, Tom recounted what the expedition turned up. David remained quiet on the matter. When the explanation was over, David volunteered to take the next watch.

* * *

Tom watched him climb the stairs, frowning. Maybe it had been a bad idea to go out so soon after the blasts. Everyone was back on edge. Nerves were all it was. Just their nerves on edge.

Tom shook his head and walked over to the table with the others. "I've been trying to wrap my head around everything, but I also can't shake the feeling that this is all how it should be."

"How it should be?" Oliver asked. "How can anything be as it should?"

"I don't know," Tom said. "But somehow, things feel familiar to me."

Cal looked up at that. "War?" he asked.

Tom shook his head. "No, nothing like that. I can't help but feel like this isn't new. And I can't get rid of this itch in my back when I think about what's going on out there."

"Like we're being watched," Cal said.

"Yes," Tom agreed.

Oliver fidgeted in his chair. "So, we have no real plan?"

"If I had a plan, I'd tell you," Tom said. "But right now, the only thing I can think of is to stay put. From what we could see outside, getting lost would be far too easy."

"Getting lost?" Oliver retorted. "I've walked these streets a thousand times; how could I get lost?"

"That wouldn't be a concern if there had been any 'streets' to speak of. There is nothing out there," Tom emphasized.

This was a street they should know well. But when Tom looked out and saw nothing but fog, he knew this was no longer the city he remembered.

He pressed a thumb into his palm and massaged his hand. Even he was starting to fidget nervously.

Cal's eyes narrowed. He shrugged in his chair and let out a breath. "I'm afraid," he said.

Tom had not heard a more true statement all night. "Me too."

* * *

The cold drifted in slowly as David sat in front of the window. It was supposed to be overlooking the street, but there was only white mist. He found himself in an endless stupor while he waited and watched the constant swirling fog. The others didn't seem to be having the same reaction he was. They didn't hear what he heard.

The window was open, and he let the soft breeze guide the mist to him. There was calm and fear in that fog. No, not fear—hesitation. Yes, that was what he had felt.

And like all the times before, the voices called to him.

"I know," he replied to the empty room. "I can listen."

They continued to speak.

"I can't," he pleaded with a weak voice. "Something's waiting. Something's watching. What's out there? What was coming for me?"

His words caressed and soothed him. "No, no, I don't want to see. I just want to know. I can feel it watching me." David pressed his hands to his eyes. The pressure felt good.

Now he heard cries and whimpers.

"I can feel them watching me. Something watches over them. Why does it want me?"

Then came the screams.

"It's in my head, it's all in my head. I want you gone."

David felt tears rolling down his cheeks. He pressed his eyes shut, closing out the voices. He tried to steady his nerves, tried to calm his emotions. How could someone be feeling so much at one time? Was he afraid? Was he happy? Everything was coming out as he listened to those voices.

"Can't be rid of you," he said weakly. "I need to be myself again. I need to be alone. What do I do?"

The voices spoke to him. Told him what needed to be done. He felt a burden sink in like a weight he had carried a hundred times before. His body craved and loathed it. Still, he listened, and he watched. He sat in his chair and gazed out into the mist, and the mist gazed back.

* * *

Back downstairs, the conversation had turned to more light-hearted things in an attempt to distract themselves from their situation. For the most part, it had worked. Oliver talked about his job, how he was a clerk for a stationary company. Fancy words for someone who keeps track of people who sell paper.

Callum had grown tired of listening to the small man prattle about numbers. He stood and stretched. "I'll go watch. Give David a break."

He walked to the stairs and announced himself. "David," he said as levelly as he could. "I'm here to take a watch, give you a—" Where was he?

There was a creak in the floor and then a blur of motion. A thud. Callum saw darkness, and then he was falling.

* * *

"I'm telling you, there is nothing to gain from going back out there," Tom said. Oliver had been heckling him, and he was growing impatient. He continued, "There isn't another soul as far as we can tell. The mist is too thick. This is the only place with any semblance of safety."

There was a creaking on the stairs. Both Oliver and Tom turned to see David walking sluggishly down. There was something in his stature and mannerisms that made Oliver furrow his brow. "What's wrong?" he asked.

David's head popped up and looked at them, his breathing ragged. "I'm—I'm not sure. It's Cal, he came up to take the watch, and he just fell over. He was too big to carry, so I came down here to get you."

"Bollocks," Tom cursed. "Come on then, let's go see him. David, watch the front, can't be too careful."

David nodded as he passed them. He went to the front of the room, near the window.

Tom and Oliver hurried up the stairs and found Cal on his back. He was still breathing, groaning, and trying to turn his head.

"Looks like he just passed out," Oliver said as they knelt next to him.

Tom leaned over and put a hand on his chest, shaking him gently. "Oi, big guy, you alright?" He shook him again more firmly.

Cal's eyes fluttered open. He looked up at the two of them.

"Awake, at least," Oliver said. "You passed out. Maybe you had a blood rush to your head from the stairs?"

"I—I didn't," Cal started, but Tom hushed him gently.

"Relax," Tom said soothingly. "You had a long day, and it's late, no shame in admitting that you had a bit of a tumble."

Cal shook his head. "David, he…"

"He's downstairs," Oliver told him. "He came to get us when you fell."

"He hit me," Cal finished.

Oliver looked at him, confused. "Hit you?"

Cal nodded in response.

"But, why would David attack you and then come get us to help you?"

Tom frowned. He looked around the room. He quickly spotted the wood plank that must have been used to knock out Cal. His eyes turned to the window, letting the cold fog drift in slowly. He straightened and walked over to it.

"David!" he called. "David, what the hell are you doing?"

Oliver rushed over to see what was happening. David was outside the pub, muttering to himself and frantically trying to tie the rope around his waist.

"David!" Oliver chimed in.

This time he heard them. He looked up to the window and then darted out into the mist.

"Hell, quick, let's get him up," Tom said, motioning to Cal. "On your feet, big lad."

* * *

David was running from the pub. He had to get out there. Whoever the voices belonged to must know a way home.

Something was calling to him. He couldn't remember how he got out here, but he hoped that he hadn't done anything reckless.

He ran across the street toward the lamp on the corner. He had leaned against it every night after drinking. If he could find it, maybe he could get home. He ran through the streets, calling out to the voices. It was possible that they might hear him, guide him.

"Where's that damn lamp?" he grumbled as he felt around in the dark. "Should be here." He stumbled to the ground.

There was a pungent smell that grew worse the further along he ventured. Try as he might, he couldn't get rid of the itch behind his ears that said all of this was too damn familiar.

David scanned where he had come from. He couldn't see a hint of the pub anymore. Not even a glow from the windows or the door that would be wide open. His stomach fell as he looked across that seemingly endless sea of swirling white.

Voices rushed toward him.

"What is it?" David asked quietly. Then louder, "Who's out there?"

There was no one. David turned to make his way back when he saw a shape ahead of him. Was it a person? He couldn't tell.

132

He heard a scream of terror. The silhouette ahead of him approached. It chattered and groaned.

"Who's out there?" David repeated.

The thing quickly morphed into something his mind struggled to comprehend. The mist dissipated behind the creature as it approached.

Haunched legs and gangly arms dragged along the ground as it made its way forward, with a bare, slender body, topped with a canine-like face. Its lower jaw split into mandibles that allowed a tongue to taste the air around it. Tall and lanky tendons and muscles poked out from wet flesh. It had no eyes. It tilted its head left and right as it regarded David.

David stumbled to the ground. The fog had cleared around him and the monster. He could see clearly now. In the distance, he saw an enormous monolithic structure. No, it wasn't a structure. It was another creature, only, this one was enormous, with thousands of tendrils extending in haunting roots upward, clawing the sky, and spreading ever outward.

The massive thing loomed and groaned. He could hear shrieks and wails emanating from it. A million voices cried out in pain and ecstasy. He fell to his knees and clutched at his head, unable to break his gaze from the monolith. The small creature, a pittance beside this hulking god, raised its disjointed arms with long willowy hands and pointed in his direction. The creature sprang forward, and David's scream muffled the gurgling of the monster.

* * *

"Pull!" It was the first thing that had come to Tom's mind when he heard David's screams. It seemed stupid in hindsight, but if something was out there, they had to get him back quickly. "Pull the rope in, I'm going to get him."

Going out was not Tom's best option, but David's cries wouldn't stop. He had to get to him now. So he ran, using the rope to guide him. He could see two shapes in the mist—one on top of the other.

His eyes tried desperately to communicate to his brain what he was seeing, but nothing seemed to click. Whatever it was, it was attacking David. He ran at it as fast as he could, shouldering it off of David.

The creature sprawled out on the ground but recovered quickly. It eyed Tom, then let out a roar that showed rows of teeth in a tri-patterned split.

"Come on, get up!" Tom yelled at David, who was crawling away from the beast. Tom could see cuts and gashes all across David's body. Blood steadily dripped onto the cobblestone. "Run, David, follow the rope." Tom helped him up while trying to keep an eye on the creature as it regained balance.

Tom pushed David forward. David ran along the rope. The others in the pub pulled on it tightly, helping David find his way back. Tom was right behind him, gently pushing him forward, guiding him. The *thing* was now loping after them on long, bent legs.

"This way!" Cal's voice called. The light of the pub was coming into view. The shapes in the doorway solidified into people. The roar of the creature came again. Tom could feel the hairs on his neck prickle at how near it was. Light engulfed him as he and David ran through the doorway.

"Close it, quick!" Tom yelled.

The door slammed shut as Cal pressed his back to it. Oliver stood nearby. "What," he stammered, "What's out there?"

Tom ignored him as he checked on David. David lay on the ground; his breathing was heavy and ragged. There were cuts all along his face and body. Blood slowly pooled from the lacerations across his arms.

"Get the bandages—all of them!" Tom ordered. Oliver nodded and dashed toward the bar in search of a medkit.

"We heard something else," Cal said. He was still holding his back to the door. Thankfully, nothing pushed against it.

Would the creature try to break in?

"Something," Tom said. "Some kind of monster outside, I don't know what."

"Monster?" Cal asked.

Oliver's eyes were as wide as they could be as he gripped the medkit. Tom waved him closer to get him moving.

"I don't know what could do this," Tom indicated to David on the ground, still gasping for air. "Hold on, David, we'll get you patched up."

Tom took the bandages from Oliver and started to wrap some of the massive cuts. Oliver took a rag and held it to David's chest, where he was bleeding the most.

"I saw the mountain," David whispered. "I saw it, the beast, the tower, the sprawling tree." His voice was so quiet that it was hard to catch his mutters. His breath became more and more shallow.

Cal stepped away from the door and leaned to look through the window. The pale white of the night was all they could see.

"Where did it go?" Oliver asked.

"The god, the ever eye, worlds of life at its call," David muttered. "I saw it; it saw me; it knows me. Oh, God, it knows me!"

Tom stood and moved to the back of the bar, looking around for the cudgel they had earlier. He found one resting on a bar stool. He held it firmly as he walked over to Cal. "See anything?" he asked.

Cal shook his head. His eyes never left the window and the fog outside. Tom handed him the cudgel and patted him on the shoulder as he went toward the back room to find the fire ax. As he passed, there was a shift in the air around him.

"David," Oliver said quietly. "David?" Oliver held his hand above the man's mouth. Moved his ear to his chest. The slump in his shoulders spoke a thousand words.

Cal turned to look at David on the floor. "Is he—"

The crash of glass came suddenly, and Callum felt his chest compress as he was pulled through the frame in the wall. He scrambled against whatever held him, but he was now being dragged through the mist. He felt sharp hands around his torso. Their strength was immense.

A dozen or so creatures were pulling him into the mist, grabbing at his arms, legs, and chest. He roared with an effort to break free, but he was caught firmly.

Slowly, Callum started to see more clearly as the mist dissipated. In the distance, there were large, elongated limbs extending over the sky. A figure, a mountain of flesh and tendrils. The creatures carried him toward the monstrosity, ever closer, ever larger.

Callum had always been a quiet man, but now, he howled for all his soul was worth.

* * *

The crash of the glass sent Oliver into a sprawl on the ground. He saw Tom run at the door and push his body to keep it closed. "Get the ax!" Tom cried.

Oliver stood up on shaking legs and went for the back-room door. He opened it. It was dark, save for a small slice of light from the main room. He searched for the ax. His fingers nudged against glasses, cans, and other assorted goods. He was knocking things over in his search, desperate to find the ax. "Where is it?" he yelled.

"Far wall, straight from the door," Tom shouted.

Oliver rushed deeper inside, feeling ahead of him. He found the wooden handle leaning against the wall and grabbed it.

As he returned, Tom called, "Bring that chair too, quick."

Oliver grabbed the nearest table chair and dragged it along with him. As soon as it was within reach, Tom took the chair and shoved it hard against the door and handle, wedging it closed.

Tom took the ax and hefted it, watching the door as it continued to flex and bend. There were crashes against the entrance, like the creatures were throwing themselves at it. "Stay behind me," he told Oliver.

There was the sound of glass falling as one of the creatures jumped through the broken window, knocking jagged pieces to the floor. The creature looked at them. Oliver couldn't find the breath to cry at the sight of it. Leathery taut skin emphasized muscle and sinew, with a face that was elongated and snubbed. The mouth split open, and a tongue lashed out as it roared. The door gave way, and another one of the creatures stumbled into the pub. A third stepped over the second one and walked in to fixate on the two men.

Tom let out a cry as the first of the creatures lunged at him. He swung the ax fiercely. They spaced themselves out, as if to find a way to flank him. Oliver stood behind him, though his feet couldn't help but make some distance between himself and the ax-wielding man.

Soon, the men were surrounded and separated. Two of the creatures leaped at Tom, and a third followed quickly after Oliver. Oliver let out a cry as he fell backward, his head colliding with the solid bar behind him. His eyes rolled back into his head, and he could feel his body falling in slow motion. He heard the roar of the monster as he drifted into darkness.

* * *

The raid sirens sent everyone in the Black Swine Pub into a frenzy. The sirens came out of nowhere, surprising the un-suspecting guests. The bomb drops rattled the ground as loud blasts cracked panes of glass, and bright flashes lit the main room. The pub hadn't been hit, but the explosions were close.

Oliver Hughes was resting an ice-filled rag against his temple. He had hit something that left his head spinning in confusion. He recognized the husky, sandy-haired barkeep. *His name was Tom, wasn't it?* Oliver adjusted the ice rag and winced at the throbbing pain.

"Tom said to keep that on. Otherwise, it's gonna swell terribly," David said. Why did Oliver know his name? Every-thing was still in a daze.

He put the rag back against his head gingerly. He had a terrible feeling in his stomach, a strange sinking that he couldn't explain. Something about this situation made him uneasy. It felt familiar.

Tom, the barman, came from one of the front win-dows. "Nothing but dense mist as far as the eye can see," he said with a sigh. "Might have to go out and look around to see what happened."

Everything felt far too familiar.

The Breathing Wall

Samuel Smith

My research had brought me to the city of Veil at the direction of the officers of the Empyrean Church who kept to their high places in the center of the city, communing with the gods and bathing in ethereal pools. My work was unrestrained as long I kept to what was permitted, and as long as all new findings would be brought to the officers of the church, then given to the Lords Chaotic to be deemed science or Apocrypha.

As I departed Veil, I heard yells and a scuffle in an alleyway. Two men came running out of the alley, one with hands bloodied, shoveling things into pockets as they ran away and out of sight again.

I went to see what they left so quickly and was shocked to find a Maelstrom Major, stabbed in the gut several times, his neck partially slashed, in shock and gasping for air. He was dressed in a dark suit, the pin on his lapel indicating his status. He watched me as I pulled his bag closer to look inside. His head shook as I pulled out a book, vials clinking together as I did so. The book was marked by runes, the pages filled with

cryptic characters and imagery, both familiar and unfamiliar. I
retrieved the vials and put them in my own bag. I looked at the
Maelstrom, who couldn't speak as he shook. He marked out
a symbol in his blood that colored the white bricks. "Hide,"
the sign meant. He struggled to mark another, but his strength
failed him. The shaking stopped, and his eyes went empty. I left
him there and said nothing to anyone about the incident.

I hid the book and vials among my things until I returned home to the city of Hiram. Once there, I resigned myself
to my study until such a time when I had decoded and come
to understand the contents of the book, even going so far as to
postpone the classes and workshops I would normally teach,
claiming sickness. The cipher was not complex, but the actual
contents of the book were further obscured by esoteric state-
ments, words, and symbols. After some time struggling with
this, I resumed my daily tasks, classes, and workshops so as not
to call too much attention to myself. My evenings were dedicated to the unraveling of this mystery.

After a month, I had come to de-riddle the meaning of
the book, and as I saw more of the meaning, the process sped
quicker to the end. The entirety of the book was Apocrypha to
the church. A couple of passages were alchemical formulas for
things that had been expressly forbidden; some were elixirs that
enhanced human functions, and others involved creating things
not understood to the author.

For three months, I devoted my evenings to achieve
further understanding of the contents. Finding the minute
differences in the signs, incantations, and formulas from those I
knew, I tried to puzzle out what the author, or authors, were trying to achieve. There was only one passage that I had difficulty
with for some time, resigned to being unresolvable as it refer-
enced a creature whose own insides were a universe unto itself.
It was not uncommon for mystic literature to speak of such
things. It was on a whim that I allowed myself to experiment
with the idea that this was the end goal of the book—to bring
such a creature into existence. Perhaps even as a means to step
into other worlds.

I had no reason to believe that this would work, and it
wasn't until I noticed a pattern within the book that revealed

which signs, formulas, and processes would produce this supposed being. It took time, and I hid away this research during my usual work hours so as not to arouse questions in my daytime guests and students.

After six months of failed mixture, incorrect incantations, and misdrawn signs, my work came to fruition. In a salt-lined granite bowl, placed on a thin slab of obsidian, that was carved with runes, the mix took form. It was some gray tissue, no bigger than the palm of my hand, with a porous surface. It expanded and contracted as if it were breathing. I needed to keep it out of sight, so it remained in my study where there were no windows. I cleared out the center bookshelf along the northern wall and placed it there. It began to grow, as the book said it would. The edges of the mass that touched the surface showed small but energetic motions. It was after this that I no longer taught in my house, nor did I let anyone in for any reason.

As it grew, I removed the books from the other shelves. Upon my return to my house one evening, after having been gone from sunrise to sunset, the tissue had grown to consume the entire wall of the study. The books that had still been on the shelves were no longer accessible to me. Others that I had laid on the floor were consumed as well. The room, from then on, had a faint smell of smoke. It was now the northern wall, and it was a wall that breathed. This expansion was mentioned in the book, but it was more aggressive and widespread than I had imagined, compared to what the book had accounted for. The borders of the mass showed no movement or indications of liveliness, which led me to believe, at that time, it was done growing.

What lay before me was a growth much like moss on a tree, but fleshy, ashen gray in color, and with a labored breath coming through the pores. Two days later, I began to see a hole form in the center, oval in shape. My imagination led me to think of the mouth of a monolithic tardigrade, an image that gave me an uneasy feeling. The microscopic creature had a look that made me shiver at the thought of something thousands of times larger. It didn't abate my excitement, but my enthusiasm faded into concern, as the hole had grown to be only a few inches in diameter and remained there for several days. I was

141

concerned that this might consume my house, and there would be consequences for that, so I hoped to see something more before I would have to kill the thing.

After two more days, I grew impatient. Peering into the hole, I could see darkness, but not of a shaded area. The darkness like that which you see between stars, but as a viscous substance, undulating. I was curious if it was a tangible thing or just my perception, so I put my right hand in the hole, up to my wrist. The sensation against my skin made me think of diluted, ice-cold honey. I wiggled my fingers inside the dark pool as my middle finger brushed something rough. There was something of a playful nip when I did, like when playing with a small dog. Gasping at the unexpected event, I jerked my hand out.

On my hand was pitch black, rough, leather-like flesh, with pores much like the ones in the breathing wall, but this had hundreds of them, tiny ones, opening and closing. With each opening, the flesh expanded and then contracted until the pores closed, and the process would repeat. The look and feel of the strange flesh on my arm unnerved me to such a point that upon this first glance, I vomited onto the floor of my study.

I tried to cut it from my arm, but it would heal whatever wound I'd create and then grow noticeably further up. I tried to peel it away forcibly, but it squirmed below the surface, creating a burning sensation on my skin, and squeezing my hand so hard it would break the bones if it applied any more pressure. I left it alone, always feeling the very minuscule movements it made to engulf more of my arm. I covered it by wrapping it in fabric, pretending to have cut my hand if anyone in public asked. My sleep became more restless as I woke throughout the night by the ongoing procession.

I had to start covering more of my arm as it slowly progressed, taking extra care that my clothes did not reveal the increasing amount of bandaging cloth. After it had traveled midway up my forearm, I had the sensation of hollowness in my fingertips. The hollowness progressed at the same rate the parasitic flesh moved up my arm. The normal sensations of the bone and muscles working together were gone, but I still had control of my fingers.

The hole in the breathing wall did not grow, but the tissue around it did, to where it consumed half of my study. I moved my personal effects out of the room and all else that wasn't for my alchemy studies. I read through the book again, and the other alchemy books I had left, to see if I could find a way to remove this flesh that was making my whole hand feel hollow. There was nothing written about the behavior of this strange, consuming creature. I could not go into public if this thing consumed my body, yet I could not live as a recluse given my status without arousing suspicion.

A new condition of the foreign flesh became apparent as I was resting on my couch just a day later. I started to feel a warmth on my right side that grew more intense until I saw that the cloth around my arm was smoking. As I hurried to pull the cloth from my arm, it caught fire. I unwound it in a panic, burning my left hand while doing so. The flesh on the right arm looked the same, unburnt and aspiring. I had been in such a fit to remove the wrapping that I had paid no attention to where I had thrown it as I did so. Seeing the burning cloth on the couch, I reached out with my right hand to sweep it off. Everything that I touched with that hand caught fire.

I ran out into the street and requested a passerby's help to put out the small fire in my study. He was quick to help me fill a couple of buckets from the pump behind my house. We doused the flames, and I thanked him for his help when I realized I had made a terrible mistake. He saw my arm with the strange flesh, and from where he stood, he could see something similar along the floor and ceiling in the study. He took off running before I could bribe him into silence.

The days wore on after that. I could not hide my arm anymore. The catalytic flesh was above my elbow. It had caught a shirt I was wearing on fire, and my attempt to replace the shirt was a failure for the same reason. I couldn't tie my shoes since my hand would burn away the laces. I removed the laces with my left hand, but then walking at anything more than a shuffle, the shoes came off. Sleep was becoming more and more scarce. I was worried about the traveling of the hollowness up my arm. The crawling, squirming sensation was now almost constant, and with the strange flesh nearly to my armpit, I could feel the dark membrane against the side of my body, waking me in terror that something was there, touching me.

Someone would arrive within the week. I knew. I could have fled, but my fate would be the same either way. I was not satisfied with what I had seen so far. I wanted to see if the breathing wall would show me something more. I could die there too. I wanted to see what became of this thing I made in a bowl.

A knock came at the door one week after the fire. I was hesitant to open it, until the visitor announced that he was Cyrus, my old friend, now an Arbiter of the Empyrean Church. He was there to determine the veracity, give judgment to those that would come after. I was lucky that it was him. He knew me. Knew my history, my beliefs, and he would know if there was any hope of understanding more of this thing.

He inspected my arm as we caught up. While he studied the wall, I shared with him the book and my notes. As I gave him more and more details, his demeanor went from a warm, concerned friend to grim. He emphasized what I already knew: how under anyone else I would be bound and prepared for execution. He told me that a Furor would be arriving soon in case that judgment was made. I was unprepared for the thought that a Furor was necessary for this thing, that body and spirit would need to be vanquished from me.

"Darkness lies at the boundaries of light," he said, "but light may set its boundaries." He offered me a chance to contain this thing I had brought to life, to set the boundaries for this unearthly corruption. To stop it from spreading. He said I could die by the Furor, or I could put this whole house behind me. Amputate my arm and give it to the Maelstroms Major to deal with. Then I could live the rest of my days in Veil, continuing my work as a prisoner and scholar.

I looked at the breathing wall—my curious hidden endeavor. It was a thrill to do something forbidden again. It had been a long time. I wanted to accept his offer, but the moment I tried to say "yes," the word came out as "no."

No one would ever believe what I felt just before it happened. It was as if something took hold of the inside of my head and made it do something else. Every word I tried to say to align my will with that of Cyrus came out against him instead. He pleaded with me, believing I was irrational; I gave up speaking and wrote what I meant to say with my left hand. The force that took hold of my speech did not have control of my body. At least not yet. I wrote: "Losing speech. Destroy." He was quick to act, heading out the back to prepare a torch.

144

Cyrus spoke an incantation for the fire to change color.
It was white, the emanation of which made the flesh on my arm
shudder. The moment Cyrus put the flame to the wood near
the edges of the gray tissue, there was a scream from within
and one from outside myself. The arm lunged my body at him
to make him stop. Cyrus stepped back, unsheathed a dagger,
and slashed me across the chest. The blade was sharp, cutting
me deep, blood flowing freely from my left side, but my right
side flowed with that same darkness I had reached my hand
into, highly viscous, and emitting a black flame. The wound
from which the flame burst healed quickly and the dark tissue
extended from it. It reached out across my skin to the flesh
that was climbing onto my shoulder. The screaming continued.
It became unbearable, and there was a while of which I lost
memory. As if I shut out any means of observing just to get the
screaming to go away.

It had probably been a few minutes at most when I came
back into my senses. The study was in flames; the white fire
spread in every direction; the gray tissue quietly retreated. In
my right hand was Cyrus's dagger, plunged into his own heart.
I recoiled in shock. I looked down at my body and saw more
of where he had tried to stop me, stabs and slashes, burned and
healed; the dark flesh covered more of my torso. The entirety of
my shoulder was consumed, now extending onto my neck. My
whole arm became hollow. I watched as the last breath left my
friend, shock and regret carved onto his face.

The tissue that covered half the study was dying, curling
up, and turning to ash. I had no reason to remain in this house.
My only advocate would soon be buried in the same fire he started. The Furor would have me, or the encroaching inferno. I wish
I could have died right then in the flames, but the flesh had more
control of my body than I wanted. I couldn't throw myself into
the blaze. I felt thrust to the ground when I tried. My attempts
to resist the pull of the arm were futile. It dragged my body with
such strength that I could not maintain a hold to anything with
my left arm or my legs. I would have to face the Furor instead.

I walked out into the street. Light from the street lanterns reflected from the small pools of rainwater on the cobblestone. The Furor was not far. I could see him down the slight

decline, coming around the soft bend. He was recognizable from afar by his waxed canvas robes, a glowing insignia over the left breast, leather gloves, and a large, broad-brimmed hat tipped down to hide his face until time to act. I knelt down and waited for him. I didn't ask myself at the time why the thing which dragged me away from the fire was so willing to wait for a sword.

The Furor stood in front of me and looked at my house smoking from within, white flame apparent through the front window and the open door. He asked me questions. I looked up to him, my mouth opening to speak, but the words were impossible to form. The harder I tried, the more my throat choked from some invisible force. I was feeling more a prisoner to this consuming entity than I ever was to the Maelstroms or the Lords Chaotic. He looked down at me, showing his face, his brow furrowed. I straightened myself up and extended my neck. I gave a slight nod, then closed my eyes.

The Furor drew the bastard sword. He spoke an incantation and swung into my neck. The sword cut, but stopped halfway through, as if against stone. Black flames exploded from the wound. The Furor let go of the blade and rolled away from the violent flames. He shook his hat and patted his attire to extinguish what fire licked his clothes through the wax.

Death did not greet me. I had fallen to my side, the hit of the blade more a blunt force than an incision. The Furor crouched down beside me, pulling a hooked knife from his belt. After another incantation, his gloves had a glow about them, and he slowly cut into my belly, the flame held back by the barrier around the gloves. I could only feel pressure on the skin, but nothing inside. He inspected within the incision and shook his head. He spoke quietly to me. He said to go to the Maelstrom's Keep in the mountains, that he could not help me in the least; that I should go into the ether pool there.

He got up and started yelling in the street to the citizens to leave their homes and get somewhere safe. Lanterns brightened windows, half-asleep people hearing the Furor's words moved, panicked, fearful, and ran away from the half-beheaded, gutted burning man with strange flesh. I was curious about what he saw in my gut. My neck was still nearly in half, still healing.

I reached my hand into the hole he had created. The flame was hot, but inside it was dry and cold.

Empty.

I tried to see if I could feel anything, but the most I could find was the feeling of the rib cage against the back on my fingers. Even then, the bones felt like they were fading. More and more, I was just a shell, filled with something dark. Dark and dry and empty.

Some time passed. The street cleared, the sound of the crowd faded, and my neck finally healed. My house was engulfed in white and red flames; my old friend buried within; my work materials with him. I got to my feet and began to walk. I knew the path to the Maelstrom's Keep, though I had never been there.

I walked through the streets of Hiram, past the eyes staring out of windows, past the guards of the eastern gate, along the dirt road through the prairie, through the woods, and up into the mountains. The walk took several days, and only because I did not stop. Not for food, not to rest, not for water. I had no stomach, though, in my head, I felt the need to eat; to drink. Unable to satisfy that instinct to consume for survival. My legs should have been tired, but as I walked, the flesh spread down my legs and around my feet. My trousers had burned away as the tissue touched it. It had climbed up my neck and burned away my hair. It had stretched across my face.

When I arrived at Maelstrom's Keep, I was hardly recognizable as the man I once was. The guards at the gate stopped me, ready to attack me, but all I could do was scream and back away. I knew the words I needed to say, but my tongue was not mine anymore. I was even starting to think that the body itself wasn't mine.

After much back and forth, a Maelstrom stepped out into the cold to see what made so much noise. I could see in his eyes that he recognized what was in front of him. He waved me in.

He said no words as he led me through the main hall, down a spiral staircase, and to a set of heavy double doors. Just behind the doors was a glowing white pool. The dark flesh shuddered at the sight of it, yet inside was relief. Confidence. My body moved forward without my intention.

That was when I knew I had only been granted permission to direct the body. It knew we were past being killed by what weapons this world had. We fell into the water, this dark presence and I. The flesh screamed, sizzled, and squeezed what it could, but eventually, it flaked off, and the screams faded. I was not coming back into my own person. What had taken control from within was separate from what had enveloped my body. That which had overrun me had run its course.

Our eyes closed as the water around us steamed. I believe it slept. I didn't. I couldn't sleep. As the strange flesh boiled away, I lost all sensation of anything physical. The hollowness that had eaten my insides was gone too. I was a ghost, an unseen, conscious entity, restrained within the sentience that now possessed my corpse. When it slept, I was here, in darkness. When it woke, I could see.

We stood up, and it looked down at our body, which appeared to be covered in my normal skin, white and very pale, only with deep black veins running underneath it. It was me on the outside, a disguise for whatever this sinister presence was.

When it looked up toward the exit, four beings stood there, so tall their heads nearly touched the ceiling. A growl resonated from my corpse, and I knew I could hear. The last of my senses were somehow intact. This thing tried to run past them, but they caught him and pinned him down. They looked into his eyes, and I looked back into theirs. I knew who they were. These were the Lords Chaotic.

The appearance and behavior of these god-like creatures was rumor and myth among all but the highest in the Empyrean Church. I could say now that at least some of the myths were true. These were humanoid creatures with eyes that made one reflect on how small a matter we are in the universe. The pupils were the abyss. Looking into them was to fall into an endless twilight, time suspending, a desire to scream welling up to never be heard. Their irises stared up into the night sky, with the same scary emptiness, depth, and beauty. Into them, you were thrown, powerless, looking out at all things unreachable. It didn't matter where your eyes searched, you were alone.

There was no way for us mortals to know the soul of these Lords, but they could see into us. Everything about you, your worst secrets and insecurities were there for them to manipulate. In that brief moment, forced to face the incomprehensible immensity that lay behind those eyes, I wondered if they could see me. I prayed they could.

It went dark after that. I don't know where we are, or how long we've been here. You are the first thing I've seen in so long. You, yourself, are something of a myth, but you have those same eyes. You aren't a Lord, are you? I don't even know why I ask. I don't know if you can hear me or see me. I tell you this whole story, but you don't react. My hope fades. If you can hear me, if you do anything for me, please...

Kill me.

Into the Dark

Elizabeth Suggs

Emma stands at the door to the psych ward visitors' center. She holds up an old college photo of her interviewee, one she received from his mother. She had photographs from his court hearing, but it was this photo that his mother forced upon her, told her to see him decent, because that's what he was. This sentence was just a misunderstanding; she was sure. But the old woman was a fool to think Emma can change anything. It's just a story.

She takes another step and spots her target. Sitting in the darkest corner is a man somewhere in his mid-thirties. Once attractive, insanity and sleepless nights have stripped that away. He hides his hideousness under a long brown beard, bespeckled with gray.

"Hello," Emma says, hiding her unease.

She sits in a chair beside him, her overpriced skirt riding up past her knees. She attempts to pull it down, but it rides up again. Ignoring it, she pulls out her notepad. She reaches for a pencil from behind her ear and lets her golden hair flop over. She forces a smile.

"Hello," he says back. His eyes are a shocking bright green. "Please, have a cup of tea."

He gestures to a filled cup and takes a sip of his own.

A smile twitches on his face, then he looks behind them, to a group of individuals huddled in a corner. The group of six entertain themselves with a movie.

A white-haired man in the group glances over and sneers at Clyde. The man was just one of many who detests Clyde, Emma realizes. This man sitting before her is like a plague, a dark spot in the ward, and none are eager to get close.

"You don't seem very popular here."

He glances over to the other residents, then back to her. "Coffee drinkers."

"Oh," she says, and takes the cup. Her notepad crinkles against her bending body. "My name is Emma," she pauses, taking a sip of tea. The bitterness puckers her lips. Tea oozes between her gums. "I'm with the—"

He waves his hand away as his face grows sour. "Who you work for doesn't matter. I'll tell you my story. I like the company." He flashes a look of disgust at the other residents, keeping their distance from him. "You just have to promise not to interrupt."

* * *

It started because of her, my wife. It's funny; when I think back on it, she never did anything different. Whenever I came home, she left the room. If I said hello, her eyes flashed anywhere else. Yet, that day, my mind full of gin and aching, I saw a laugh dance upon her lips. In that moment, she was laughing at me, and I hated her with every fiber of my being, but it was all false—my imagination. If I'd been sober, I wouldn't have seen her joy because it never would have been there. She never smiled.

She had stopped smiling years before...

Stopped laughing

Stopped speaking

I had

no

one for our entire marriage.

She was a block of stone.

So, it was too easy to give in to my desires—

My rage.

When I picked up the knife, she didn't say a word, nor did she look at me. It was just like her to pretend I didn't exist, but that night was different. Neither I nor the horrible pounding in my head would let her forget who I was.

I wanted her to know I was there. I *needed* her to know I was there. I bashed her head in with the handle of the knife to remind her I was there.

I just wanted her to make some sound.

Bash!

One in her temple.

Bash! Bash!

Another in her eye and nose.

Bash!

Blood spilled everywhere. She grunted but never screamed. Never pleaded for me to stop. Just watched me. Took the pain, as if she knew all along where the silence would eventually lead us.

The ugliness of her death wore on me, and rather than feel remorse, I hid her. I needed those all-knowing eyes, gray with death, and lips once so pink turned blue, hidden from my view, though to hide her was almost unnecessary. No one asked me about my wife. No one noticed. Before her death, she never left the house.

She didn't have a job. Her parents were dead. She didn't speak to her siblings. It was too perfect.

No one would have ever found out.

If I hadn't made the call.

Dialed 911.

Listened to the person on the other end ask about my emergency.

Don't even remember speaking.

Telling them anything.

My name...

My address...

Though I must have. Within minutes, there sat a car in my driveway. Blue and red lights flashed up through the front room's window and into the living room.

I ran out the back door. The fear of punishment became the devil's fist clutching my heart, pulsating with each new beat. I sped my legs
faster down the street.

Maybe I was spotted. Maybe police asked my neighbors, and found answers, though I doubted it. The night was dark, not even the moon came out to spy at the ruckus.

I ran until my lungs were about to burst. I bent over my knees to catch my breath. When I looked up, I saw a doorway bathed in blackness, a stark contrast to the brightly lit street and nearby homes. Without hesitation, I slipped inside and slammed the door shut, ensconced by protective darkness.

I pressed my back against the door and drew in a breath. I allowed relief to sweep over me until something touched my arm. That something was sharp and dragged along my skin as if it were a nail. The nail ran up my body and paired with an animal's breath, hot and wet. Both breath and nail danced up to my throat and stopped as light spilled over me.

Blinking away the night blindness, I saw a feeble old man hunched over a doorway leading into a house. I stood in a garage that had been transformed into a room. A thin cot lay invitingly beside a few shelves, some empty, while others held knickknacks.

Growls came from the corner. Somehow I knew whatever thing touched me now stared from those shadows.

"Don't worry," said the old man. "He won't come out in the light."

I dared not to move for fear the lights would break, and the beast would come out again, breathing down my neck.

"And who might you be?" the old man asked.
A wry smile spread between his cheeks. He tried lowering his hands, but as if glued like chicken wings, they remained in their spots. He had just enough reach to wave me in. "Come inside," he continued, his back to me. "Explain yourself over some tea."

* * *

The tea tasted like the salt from my sweat made in the midst of my most fiendish acts.

154

The sweat which dropped off my brow—
Onto my lips—
To kiss her blood.

I looked down at my tea, stray leaves swirled around the cup, and for a moment, I thought I saw myself with my wife reflected inside, but then her angular visage vanished.

"What is in this?" I asked.

"Just a little something extra. Now, tell me, what is it you need?"

"I need to hide." The words leaked out before I had a chance to catch them. "I saw an opened door. Took the opportunity."

We sat at his kitchen table, neighboring the closed garage door. I was across from the old man, watching him. He finished off the remains of his tea, then drew out his old, withered tongue. It traced his mouth and wrinkled flaps of skin.

"You should not always take the first open door you see," he cautioned. "You won't always be lucky."

I swallowed, then looked up to a clock above our heads. It *tick-tick-ticked* away the time I needed more of. How long would it take for the police to show up? To ask questions? Whether or not they'd search the entire neighborhood was beyond me. It was that foreboding fear that drove me to whisper, "Please, help me."

"Why should I help you?" the man asked, near a laugh. Menace played around his eyes. He smiled; a trap had been set, and I fell willingly inside.

"I can't offer much, but I can give you my service. Help me, and I'll clean... I'll fix up your house... I'll—"

He held up a finger before I could finish and swept himself up from the table. His knobbly, little joints jangled together as he walked. He made his way over to a drawer near his fridge and picked out a set of keys. He clanked and cracked his joints back to his seat.

He set the keys in front of me.

"I've needed help in the garage..." he said. "Help me with the beast, and I'll help you hide."

My cheeks flushed; relief struck me dumb. It made me slump in my chair with my head over the still steaming tea. No longer did it smell like sweat from her death, rather, a strange something else. Something mossy. I could not place it.

155

"Tell me, Mr…"

His voice shifted my attention. "Clyde Collins."

Lost in thought, he folded his fingers near his lips and pressed on wisps of facial hair. Frowning, he asked, "Tell me, Clyde Collins, why do you need me to help you hide?"

I straightened in my chair and picked up the set of keys. I ran my fingers along the teeth of an old copper key, then flashed my eyes to his. "The police think I killed my wife."

"Did you?" he asked.

I placed the keys back on the table, my fingers still at the teeth. "Does it matter?" I shot back.

A smile leaked onto the old man's features, carving deep wedges at the corners of his eyes. He laughed. "No, I guess it doesn't. My name is Rolf."

As if the conversation excited the beast, it growled and gnawed at the garage door. Sharp claws tore at corners, broke up boards, but never did they tear through. Never did light pierce between splintered wood, onto his beastly being.

"What do you need me to help with?" I asked, desperate to get the beast out of my mind.

"You'll help with house chores, and get him food," he answered, glancing at the garage door. His eyes flashed to mine as he stood. "You must be tired. Let me get you bedding."

"Where will I be sleeping?"

Smiling, he turned as the gnawing on the door ceased. There was only breathing. Harsh. Peppered with thought. With patience. Rolf turned back to me. Smiling still.

"In the garage, of course. The only other bed is that cot." He made sure to expose his teeth as he spoke. "It's why I gave you those keys. One is to the front door, the other to the garage. I'll be locking the door every night. You'll need those to get back inside."

* * *

I lay in the cot with a flimsy blanket half drawn over me and half pushed against the wall. The pillow reeked of bad breath and old shoes. For that reason, I kept my head turned up toward the ceiling. I stared at the bright orange garage light directly above the cot.

I could hear the beast approach, but it never penetrated the light as if it was caged within the darkness.

The front doorbell rang, echoing softly in the hall. The door opened. People talking. A laughter here, chuckle there. The words were too quiet and became a rumbling noise beneath my thoughts.

The growl rose in the corner. The beast felt my apprehension. Both it and I knew the only sort of people to ring an old man's doorbell at such an odd hour would be police. I kept my muscles tense, tenser than before. The smell of the pillow was almost all forgotten as I strained to understand the rumbles.

Above me, the lights blinked, stealing my thoughts. Growls made from the depths of my damned soul grew in the dark. This sound dominated the room, and then the light went out.

Clyde, came a husky voice inside my head.

I sat up, rolling my legs over the bed. My hands cusped the blanket, pulling it from the wall to my body. I was so cold, colder when the voice spoke. Its words froze my body.

The darkness stole my voice, so I hissed, "Hello?"

Hello, it replied in mid-laugh.

Saying nothing more, my stomach lurched. The voices from the other room had disappeared. I strained to continue listening.

Do you want to know what Hell is like?

The lights above me flickered back on. The monster stole back into the darkness. Those devilish eyes waited, taunted. They grew hard with want, with need, but the light drew away his power. Momentarily, I was safe.

The old man stood at the entrance. Alone. One foot in the garage, another out. His hand still cupped the light switch. His eyes were old and withered, even more so in the light.

"Not quite time for something like that, I'm afraid. Not anymore," he spoke taut and brisk. He motioned me inside. "You just had some visitors. They left, of course." My shoulders relaxed. "I have some questions. I'd like you to join me for more tea. Maybe this time you'll finish yours." He chuckled as we made our way back to the same chairs, hot tea waiting. "Now, I'd like to know if you killed your wife."

My hand touched the already prepared cup of tea. I wasn't in the mood for it, but my throat was tight and sore. The only remedy was hot liquid, so I brought the cup to my lips.

"I thought you said the answer didn't matter."

Inhaling, he closed his eyes. Sipped. Slowly… slowly… tasting something much different than what I tasted—he had to. My memories were getting in the way. Clouding the tea.

He smiled, then set his cup back down. "Things change. I believe I have the right to know if I'm harboring a fugitive or not," he said and took another drink.

I found myself copying him, and tasting the hot, unpleasant liquid. That time it was easier to swallow. I closed my eyes, then took another drink.

"Then you answer me this," I retorted. My eyes burst open, staring hard at his old bloodshot pair, a mirror image of what mine must have looked like. "What is this beast? Where did it come from?"

He held his cup between both hands and replied quickly, "I'm not sure you're ready to hear that."

My hand clenched my cup. Faintly, I hoped to crush the glass. I wanted broken shards to open up my palm and feel my lifeblood leak out,
like
hers
did.

I squeezed harder, but the cup kept its shape. "Is there anything you can tell me?"

He raised both eyebrows, wrinkles exaggerating his long forehead. They bunched over each other. "In due time. I'll tell you everything, but first…" he said, and then his hand came to my cup and pressed it gently to my lips. "Drink up."

I finished my tea, and in no time at all, he poured more of the green liquid. Again, I drank. I looked down at the contents. My wife and I were sitting in the park. She was reading a book while I watched her. Her slender form was hidden beneath a soft blanket, curving around me.

I blinked, and she was gone.

"I did," I whispered. "I—" couldn't say it. Couldn't admit to murder. But he understood. Maybe he always knew.

He gave a single nod as the monster scratched at the door. The old man looked to the sound, then sighed. "You need sleep. Tomorrow I'll have a list of things I'll need you to do." He paused, glanced over at the oversized teapot. "I'll make sure the tea is ready for breakfast."

"You'll have something else made for food, won't you?" I asked.

The corners of his lips twitched. Folding and unfolding his fingers, he looked back my way. He gestured to the kitchen. "There's food. My house is your house."

I stood up and walked over to his fridge. He had some bread, milk, and mayonnaise. The milk was expired, but the bread and mayonnaise were fine. I picked them up and smeared the white goop on the stale bread and ate. It wasn't much, but it was something.

"Do you have anything else?" I asked as I finished.

He laughed. "I'm sorry, but there's nothing. How long do you plan on staying?"

"I'm…"

He waved me off before I could finish and walked up the stairs, leaving me to my isolation.

* * *

"Sleeping at the table?" came a voice.

My eyes peeled open, though I was still exhausted. I dreaded that garage. I was afraid of what would happen the next time the lights were off. That beast, whatever it was and wherever it came from, wasn't natural.

"Maybe I should just sleep on the couch."

"No. The living room is too exposed to the front door. The cot is your best chance at hiding here. I implore you to lay on the cot. If it's the beast you're worried about, then keep the lights on."

"Those lights are unreliable," I said.

He gave a single nod. "There are candles and flash-lights in the garage. Find them. Use them. You have power over the beast. As long as you have light, you hold control." He clapped his hands on his thighs and smiled. "I must get some sleep. If you'll excuse me…"

He walked back upstairs.

I got up from my chair and opened the garage door, switching on the light. My heart was beating hard in my chest. The shadows, though dispersed with the light, tickled across my skin like tiny claws. Intentionally leaving the door open, I walked inside, feeling eyes on me. I turned to the nearby cabinet and grabbed three flashlights, four unused white candles, and matches before returning to the cot.

The combination of the portable lights, the lights from inside the house, and the bulb hanging from the ceiling made the garage gleam and glisten, but it wasn't enough. I clutched one of the flashlights tighter against my chest and closed my eyes. I tried mumbling a lullaby, but the words escaped me. I ended up singing a string of incoherent words until I fell asleep, though sleep didn't last long. Dreams became nightmares, and nightmares became sound.

A crash shocked me awake; the door to the garage slammed shut.

My eyes flew open. The lights flickered as the candles blew out. I clutched a flashlight tighter to my chest as I relit the candles, but no sooner had I done that did the light above me switch off, and the flashlights went black. All I had were the candles and shadows danced violently around their wicks.

Flicker.

One candle blew out.

Flicker.

All candles

flickered out.

Darkness.

The matches were still in my hand. I lit more; they blew out.

I know you want to see it. That's why I'm here.

The words pushed against my skull, splitting the insides of my brain. The sensation spread from my head, into my neck, pulsating with my veins.

Breath exhaled along my skin.

I can see your heart. I know what you desire.

"No," I snapped, spit forming between my lips.

The beast howled with laughter, nipping at my nails. The nails chipped and cracked. The pain was instant; bits of nail fell this way and that. Some of the pieces tapped on the flashlights, and others bumped on my leg.

I cried out in pain, forcing my fingers away. The beast ignored it, and continued on, *You want freedom, but more than that you want to die. I see that in your heart. You feel like you deserve to die.*

"I killed my wife..." I cleared my throat. Tears of pain dried as I spoke. I trailed off, thinking of her.
Those eyes—

I couldn't stop staring at those

gray eyes

as she stared at me,
until they didn't.

I pierced those eyes with our kitchen knife handle, and then cut up dinner with the blade afterward.

"And you're going to kill me."
Silly human. You don't deserve death. You deserve me.

I sat erect; the flashlights clanked in my lap, becoming lead weights and holding me in place. I clutched at the ends of the bed and tried to push myself to move. It didn't work.

Something tapped on the wall, gliding over each board. It *tap, tap, tapped,* impatiently. It stopped at the side door, the one in which I snuck into upon my arrival. On the other side, a new sound made itself known, the sound of growing wind, the warning of a storm to come.

The wind howled against the garage door, yanking and pulling at its old metal chains. The smell of blown-out candles warmed my nose.

The side garage door flung open. Winds blazed in. Cried for attention. Outside light, dimmed to near-complete darkness by the storm. The winds kept the door swinging open, banging against the outside wall. Light trickled in by the chaotic and unpredictable rain.

Leave if you want, but you'll never get either of your desires because now you are mine.

I jumped from the cot and ran into the kitchen. I slammed the garage door shut and drew in a breath. Walking over to the table, I rested my head on it. Too shocked and tired to fight off sleep.

But the garage door sprang open. All the lights in the kitchen were off, and the beast, with all its suffocating glory, breathed against my neck.

"I told you to sleep in the garage," came the old man's voice. "You wouldn't listen to me, and now I've had to bring him in the house. You know how hard it is to get him back where he needs to be? I need to coax him. With you."

"You let it in?" I murmured.

"Yes, of course!" he snapped. "How else will I teach you a lesson?"

The same strange urge I had with my wife rose up in my body, but I pushed it back, like a drunk swallows vomit. And like a drunk, who needs to vomit, I could

only

hold

it

back

so

long.

I watched him walk down the steps and over to the teapot. He picked his cup up and filled it with that hot liquid.

In the moonlight, the pouring tea glistened. I almost smelled it drifting up his nostrils, and like a drug, my body craved—needed—it.

But I wasn't there for tea. I planned something else.

I stood abruptly, and he turned. He watched me approach, letting our eyes speak a thousand words as I picked up the pot and raised it in the air.

"You can kill me. I want you to."

"What?"

"I only have one precious memory left of my daughter, and it's going to be gone soon. All that will remain are the screams."

I stepped away, lowering my weapon. I looked over his shoulder and into his cup. In the liquid, I could have sworn I saw a small girl with long brown hair being pushed in a swing by a younger version of Rolf. The image faded into a cloud of steam, and I knew it was gone forever. And then I understood.

"Please," he whispered. "It'll move on to you now."

In the briefest of moments, a clear thought rose in my head and told me not to kill him, but just like my wife,

I couldn't stop myself.

I struck his skull with the teapot.

The boiling tea flew out, burning the old man and my hand. He cried, so I hit him again, then he fell, withered and broken, to the ground.

* * *

Emma exhales sharply, but she can't stop herself from speaking, "So, the old man's gone. What happened to the beast?"

She fiddles with her notepad and finishes another cup of tea. Her grandmother warned her about too much caffeine, and now she can feel it. Her heart speeds its beat; her breath quickens.

In her cup, she sits beside her grandmother on the porch. They watch the setting sun.

"—Maybe if you didn't interrupt you'd find out."

She sucks in a breath, then attempts to slow the beat of her heart. *That's enough tea.* She places her cup of half-drunk liquid on the table and watches Clyde drop his eyes to the ground.

Emma clears her throat, and again, taps the pencil fiendishly in her hand. *Tap, tap, taps* it against her notepad. She only stops when something shifts behind him in the darkness, a conscious shadow. She catches her breath.

Recognizing what she sees, he smiles. "Don't mind the shadow." With a chuckle, he adds, "Just a little part of me coming out."

* * *

The beast had control of the light. Whenever I switched one on, another would go out. He toyed with me, and I played along. I ran around the old man's house, turning on lights this way and that. I even went so far as to line up flashlights and candles around the halls.

I'm not sure why I didn't leave. It was as if something cemented me into the floor. I was waiting for the justice that I kept running away from.

But I didn't want to find justice with the beast. I wanted the police—prison. I wanted the safety of the known, yet still, I stayed. I made myself tea and thought about my day. I let my mind wander to different, older memories, and then one-by-one, they disappeared. They vanished, like missing scenes in an old movie reel.

And like all lights before this hour, each one went out.

Standing from my spot, I looked up at the light.

Flicker—

Flicker—

Out.

Just a matter of time until—

You think the light will stop me? You keep running, and all I want to do is to talk.

I set my tea down but quickly brought it to my lips. I couldn't answer. I gulped hot sewage as I squinted through the darkness. My eyes locked onto the beastly pair.

You've been bad, haven't you?

The voice echoed between my eardrums, against my skull. It made my brain ache, like a hangover splitting me open. I brought my hands up and covered the pain by covering my ears. I thought if I could squeeze my skull, then maybe I could squeeze his voice out. I wrapped my fingers around themselves, wrapping around my earlobes. When the beast spoke, I squeezed tighter. But still, he continued. So I tightened my grip until even the darkness was light.

You can't hide forever. Not from Hell. Not from me.

Something about those words deflated whatever delusional hope I clung to. My hands fell loosely at my sides. I dropped to my knees to chilled tile.

There was a moment of silent self-loathing, and then the beast breathed in my ear. Its body became a thousand tiny claws, pricking me. Its teeth scraped up my chest, and then a long wet tongue licked along my neck.

* * *

"And you know the rest from the newspapers, I'm sure. The police apprehended me, don't believe my story, and so I've been labeled crazy and put in a madhouse," Clyde concludes.

Emma crisscrosses her legs, then smooths out her skirt. A feeling of discomfort washes over her, and she can't tell whether it's the skirt wrinkles or if it's the way Clyde looks at her in silence.

"I know what the papers say, but I want you to tell me your story," she says.

He smacks his lips, then glances at the other residents. "Well, they said they found both my wife and the old man in a shallow grave behind my house, but I don't remember that."

She straightens. Her left eyebrow flinches. She can't tell whether it's her grandmother or her, but she touches him on the shoulder; he pulls away.

Embarrassed, she leans back and asks, "But you remember it differently?"

He shrugs. "There's no other logical explanation. They don't want to hear my side. I've told the truth countless times, and yet you seem to be the only one remotely moved by it, or by the tea."

Up above them, a clock strikes 7:00 p.m., the end of visiting hours. What few visitors remain, slowly stand and start to leave. Emma finishes another cup of tea, despite herself. The liquid shows a fire. She and her grandmother are camping.

She looks up from her cup. "What do you mean by the tea? This can't be the same stuff you had in your story."

"It is. The beast never lets me go without it."

She doubts this but says nothing. Her grandmother warned her about people like him. An argument is just asking for trouble. Still, it's content for her story. The readers will eat it up.

She rolls her head back. Weariness tenses her shoulders, weighs down the mascara on her eyelashes. She blinks rapidly, then looks back at her notepad. She's been *tap, tap, tapping* on the paper again.

She stops tapping and directs her attention back to the tea, back to the warmth in her throat. Part of her detests it.

Finally, full and fatigued, she decides it's probably best for her to leave as well.

"I think I'm fine with this," she says. "Is there anything you would like to add?"

"Oh, no," he says with a smile. "But before you leave, let's have another cup of tea."

BOOK II
Little Darkness

Ghost Train

K.R. Patterson

There's a ghost that haunts the night train when it rains.

I shrink beneath my hood, trying to ignore him, but I know he's staring at me.

I grasp the yellow, tangy-smelling plastic that shelters my eyes and yank it back. The deluge that the jacket was meant to protect me from runs off my hood and into my hair. It rolls down, chilling my face and nose as I try to be brave and confront him.

He's been following me all day. I saw him at the zoo, and I see him now. Only earlier, he didn't come so close. Earlier, he just stared at my children and I as we traversed the park.

Our children, I suppose I should say, though the man's dead now.

Last year, I sent him out in the rain to buy medicine. The rain. Four-car pileup.

I thought he would never hurt me again.

Last Night's Memory

Elizabeth Suggs

A woman's cries woke me from my slumber. She was yelling at her captor, presumably me. I hadn't remembered grabbing the woman or coming to this dingy spot. Not that it surprised me much. I'd forgotten things more often as of late.

She sat in a chair, blindfolded and tied up. At least I did that right, even being me. I walked over to the woman. She stifled her cries by the sounds of my boots.

"Please," she whimpered. She had a soft voice, even under stress.

By the looks of her and me, and the fact my gallon of water was half gone, I'd guessed we'd been there for a day or so. So, why hadn't I killed her? If I was so good at grabbing a woman on autopilot, why couldn't I finish the job?

"Are you still there?" she whispered.

There was something familiar about her. Something I couldn't place. I turned my back to her and walked over to my bag of goodies. Another thing I did right.

Most of these "events" included a bag, a tied-up victim, and some water. I'd done it for so long and so often that it was ingrained in my memory so deeply that not even whatever disease I had could take that away from me. At least I had that.

I sifted through the bag, searching for a hacksaw or knife or something else to start the process, but my fingers slipped whenever I grasped a weapon. My body shook. I didn't want to kill her; least of all, make her suffer.

I walked over to a chair on the opposite end of the room. I had brought it here a few years ago when I made the abandoned building my prime location. No one came to this place. It was too far off the grid. Forgotten in a city already broken down and starving. There were no funds to bring up these buildings, so I had my pick, though I liked this one best. I was comfortable with it.

Every other time, the job was easy. It should have been the same with this woman, despite my memory loss. Why was she so different? Why wasn't she like the others?

"Please," she begged again. "I want to go home. Can't you please take me home?"

The funny thing was that I probably could have taken her home. If I had bothered with the blindfold, then I would have put it on right before she saw my face or my car. I could bring her home in the same way as I had taken her, and no one would be the wiser. But I liked that solution even less than my first. I didn't like to leave things undone. It wasn't my nature.

"I don't know who you are. I don't have to ever tell anyone about this. I just want to go home. I promise—I promise I won't tell anyone. Please." She broke down in tears.

No matter how many times I did this job, I hated it when they cried. It made the whole thing harder. My mom used to cry when I was a kid when she didn't get her way, which was a common occurrence. Her tears were never real. I could handle fake tears, but real tears? No one ever cried like that. Not even at my parents' funeral. No one shed a tear. That wasn't our way.

"Ple-please! Is anyone there? I ju-just want to go home!" she sobbed louder.

I walked out of the room into a dilapidated hall. There was a broken window overlooking an empty back street. She could cry louder and longer, and the only one who suffered was me.

I paced the length of the hall, checking my watch, trying to ignore her muffled cries. I only needed to wait her out a little longer, and then maybe, I'd have a clear head. I'd finish off the work and be done with it.

Once I was sure she finished crying, I stepped back into the room and closed the door. I did it softly, but her ears were like a dog's. She heard me.

"Who's there? Are you here to help me? Please! I need to go home."

The only other time I had hesitated like this was my first time. My dad had taken me then. He was showing me the ropes, explaining it as medication for our anger. Maybe he'd been right because I never got angry, though I never really felt much of anything, except whenever I saw tears, but that was an occupational hazard.

"I want to go home!" she repeated.

I walked over to her chair, my heavy boots rattling on the floor. She sucked in a breath.

Kneeling in front of her, I said in a low voice, "You're not going anywhere."

Another round of sobs. I shouldn't have talked. "Why not? Why can't I go home? I live on 402 Oakwood Lane. I live there with my cat Sam and boyfriend Kenny. I just want to go home." She went silent; maybe she was waiting for a response. Her forehead wrinkled. She looked so familiar. I couldn't shake it. She started to speak fast, "Do you want money? I can give you money. That's what this is all about, right? You just want money."

Why did they always think it was about money?

"No money," I growled, standing up.

Usually, when they got like this, I would hack off their parts. It was the slow deaths that I enjoyed most. Slow and deliberate, as if their experience could almost be my own. When it was too quick, I still felt nothing. No, it had to be slow. But the pitiful mess before me didn't have my appetite. I didn't want to kill her slowly or otherwise.

My stomach rumbled, pulling me from my thoughts. I stood from my spot and walked over to my supplies. Shuffling past blades, a hammer and nails, and rope, I grabbed a tuna sandwich wrapped in plastic. I unwrapped it and broke it in two, eating the first half carefully, considering my next move. I didn't think I'd figure a solution out to my problem anytime soon, and I wasn't going to let her die in the meantime. So, I gave her the other half of my sandwich. I broke the pieces off with my fingers and set them in her mouth. She resisted at first, but eventually, she ate.

She must have been hungry because she almost bit off my finger when the food ran out. I gave her some water, then drank some myself. At the very least, I wouldn't kill her a coward's way, that much was certain.

"What do you want?" she whispered.

I should have just grabbed the saw and started then, but I couldn't. I stared at her, hoping that whatever caused this reluctance would be answered on her face. It wasn't. It only brought more questions.

The solution was a quick kill. Maybe I needed to chalk it up to bad luck and try again.

I had a gun holstered in my belt. I pulled it out and cocked it. *Gun's a coward's way,* I heard my dad's voice in my head. I pushed the thought out of my mind and raised the pistol.

Coward. My hand shook. I just needed one shot. One shot, and I could start over again.

"Please, don't. My mother's birthday is tomorrow."

How had she heard me? How could she know? I stood inches from her, kneeling back down.

"You're mom's gonna have to miss out," I said.

"No, please. She's dead. I just… I go to her grave on her birthday. I want to do that. I was planning to do that."

"Too bad," I murmured.

"What about you? What about your mother?"

My hand was still shaking. I just needed to get it over with. I went through a list of my upcoming plans. She'd die, I'd clean up the body, get out of here, and take a few days off. Truth be told, my mom's birthday was tomorrow too. Maybe visiting her grave would clear my mind. After that, I'd find someone else, and this time I'd remember doing it.

174

I pushed the gun to her forehead. All I needed to do was a single flick of my finger. Only one, and she'd be done.

"No! No! No!" she cried. "Please, don't you care?"

"Nope. In fact, my mom's birthday is also tomorrow. Maybe I'll wrap up your head with a cute little bow and give it to her as a present."

Childish. I would have done better with silence, but there was something about this lady that kept me talking. It was the same power that paralyzed my true nature.

"No, please, I just want to go home. Can you do that for me?"

"No. You're dead."

I thought she was going to cry, but instead, she drew in a breath and whispered, "Then let me see your face."

"What?"

"I'm already going to die," she said, her voice shaking. "Let me see your face. Let me look at you."

I almost responded to her, but that'd only entice her to speak more, or worse, start up the tears again. I didn't really need to argue with her anyway. She was right; I should let her see me before I killed her. I let the others right at the end. I almost enjoyed seeing the life leave their eyes, a flicker of a candle snuffed out.

But when I removed her blindfold, all I saw were my father's dark blue eyes. Angry eyes. Disapproving. I was a coward. I'd been a coward killing him, and I was a coward now.

"You don't have to do it this way," she whispered. Her eyes changed from anger to fear. "You don't have to do this."

"Your hope went away with that blindfold," I said.

She paled, then nodded. "Make this last death count."

I lowered the gun. "What are you talking about?"

She didn't reply, so I shot her stomach. I had heard somewhere getting shot in the gut was one of the most painful deaths because the stomach acid got loose on the rest of your body. You're eating yourself inside out. Maybe this wasn't such a coward's death. At least here, she'd suffer; we both would.

My hand came to my belly, feeling blood from the bullet. I was in the chair where the woman had sat. Where the woman never was. My memory was getting worse. There had never been another woman.

My dad had been like this near the end. I shot him in the head to put him out of his misery. Even in death, his eyes retained their intensity.

My mom was better. She just pretended to cry because she hadn't really cared whether she lived or died. I saw that in her eyes—that she never felt anything. That's why I knew she and I were too similar for our own good. But then again, maybe we weren't that similar. The cries that shook the building, those had been real tears. My tears.

Backroads

Alex Child

On an especially cold night, I rambled down a two-lane road
in my beat-up red truck. The drive was uneventful until I saw a
disco ball in my headlights. No, not a disco ball. A woman in a
sequin dress. She stood at the peak of a deep culvert overflow-
ing with rancid water, hunched over, sobbing into her hands.

I stopped my truck ten feet from the woman and stepped
out into bitter midnight air, my feet crunching on gravel.

"Excuse me, miss?"

Her back arched, but she continued to cry.

A swift breeze swept cold air across my exposed forearms, causing me to hold myself close. I glanced at the woman
and the filthy river beneath her.

"Ma'am, are you… are you stuck?"

She raised her head, hands still clasped over her face.
My dim headlights reflected off her eyes, exposed only through
small slits between her fingers.

And then something behind her caught my eye.

About twenty feet away, I saw the rough silhouette of a
figure bounding up and down along the ditch's bank.

I switched on my phone's flashlight and pointed it at the crude river bank. The figure transformed into a surly broad-shouldered man, wearing a dark beanie and battered flannel shirt. He held a length of rusted chain.

The light stunned him. He blinked rapidly and then sprinted toward me.

I stumbled toward my truck, but in my panic, my feet slipped off the slick gravel, and I dropped my phone.

I jumped into my truck's cabin and landed with my foot on the gas pedal, speeding off down the road.

I chanced a look in my rearview mirror. The man picked up my phone and waved at me.

My home was close, but I took the long way, through backroads, never letting my speed dip below twenty-five miles per hour.

When I finally arrived, I scanned the vast fields for anything out of the ordinary. Then, with a sudden burst of adrenaline, I sprinted from the truck and inside.

I ran from one window to the other, shoving and locking them just as my sister Sophie stopped me in the hall.

"What the hell, Ryan; why didn't you respond?"

Perplexed, I stared back at her. "What?"

She sighed, "You texted me asking for a location drop, said Google maps wasn't working?"

My eyes widened.

Her Taylor Swift ringtone blared from the bedroom. A chill pulsed down my arms, and I raced to the front window.

The man in the flannel shirt stood across the street, rusty chain in hand, phone illuminated against his ear.

Lonely Hills

Edward Suggs

My fingers wrapped around the steering wheel, the tips of my nails digging into the coarse leather. The car's thick, sweaty air pushed up against my throat. With my left hand, I cranked the window down and took a deep breath. The pungent aroma of strawberry tingled in my nose.

   Something inside me told me to smile. The smell was nostalgic, and apparently, that was enough to make one feel happy. But alas, I'd stopped smiling a week ago. I stopped. I stopped smiling. A week ago.

   A week ago?

Oh—
Yeah.
Then I slipped,
mud stuck to every idea,
sliding down now.
Thin folds of my thoughts,
gray and wet with mud.

Simple things which weren't important before
a week ago,
a simple week
trivial gray thoughts spinning;

I tried to focus on the colors as they vanished beneath me. The yellow street lines dashed under my car as I switched lanes. I couldn't bear to look up from the road. Everything was now a

reminder
of who
I'd lost.

The numbness couldn't stop my migraine.

My fingernails dug deeper into the wheel as I pulled up to my sister's house. I looked up for a moment, unluckily locking eyes with her. She was sitting patiently on her porch, just like every other time I visited her. I bit my tongue and wished it was just a visit this time as well.

I put the car into park at the edge of her driveway. Grinding my teeth together, I slowly rolled the window back up and unbuckled my seatbelt.

My sister, Sera, walked down the porch steps, and though there was a door between us, I could still hear the prissy clip-clop of her heels.

Clip.

She poofed up her perm.

Clop.

It bounced back down to where it was before.

Clip.

The cycle repeated.

Clop.

Until she stopped in front of the car.

I hesitantly opened the door.

"Penny," she said from behind a smile. "I'm glad to see you're doing alright."

I pushed her aside, stepping onto the pavement, fumbling for balance. She insisted on standing uncomfortably close; I could taste the eggs she had for breakfast. I shut the door and walked toward the house.

"Now hold on—wait, Penny, let's get your stuff." She looked into the trunk and arched her brow. "Where's… well, basically everything? I see, like, two suitcases."

"I don't need much," I lied. Truth be told, everything else in the house was

his.

But she didn't need to know that. Neither of us wanted to talk about it anyway.

Sera grabbed my shoulder and swung me around to face her. She gave me a cold glare. I avoided her piercing eyes, holding a staring contest with her faded red lipstick.

"Look, I know that your husband just… I know that you've been dealing with a lot, but you gotta keep it together. We can pack your things into the guest room. It's yours now."

I didn't say anything. I just nodded. We gathered my two suitcases and went inside. The lights were off, which helped my migraine at least.

"Take off your shoes," she muttered as she did so herself.

As I untied my shoes, something caught my eye. A dark thing crouched behind an archway in front of me. I looked up, my jaw hanging from my skull.

I slipped the shoes off and tilted my head to Sera.

"Do you have a dog?" I asked.

"What?"

"Oh, I just saw something, and I…" she still seemed to be confused. I decided to drop it. "Never mind."

"Alrighty then," Sera said awkwardly. "Here, I'll bring your things upstairs. You can wait here, I guess."

I watched her struggle with my bags, scaling the stairs until the ceiling enveloped her figure. Once gone, I stood and glanced back over to where I saw the shadow. There was nothing, of course. Yet, a chill crawled over my skin.

My attention was drawn to the portraits lining her plain white walls. I brushed my fingertips over the dusty frames and avoided each repressed family photo. Until, unfortunately,

I saw   his face   again.

I was afraid I'd see   him. But I knew I'd see   him.

My shaking hand dropped to my side and closed my eyes. But it was of no use. I could see it with my eyes shut.

His stoic
features.
I violently shook my thumping head.
His inquisitive
eyes.
I tried to shout, but my palm held my mouth closed.
Thunk!

Something hit the ground in the other room and rolled my way. Startled, I stumbled backward, facing the shrouded object as I fled into the living room. The rolling sound grew soft as it toppled over the fluffy carpet and into the light.

I leaned over to pick it up, but my fingers reached out and clamped over nothing. My lip twitched, my hands scraping the floor. *Nothing, nothing, nothing, nothing, nothing, nothing.*

I refrained from the urge to panic.

My spine straightened like an old, bent straw. I clenched my teeth together, pulling my attention from the missing object and looked up. Out from behind my caged teeth, I let out a scream. A tall shadow of a man stood no more than a foot away from me. His clothes
smelled so familiar.

But despite being horrified, I couldn't move.

It was him. Will. It had to be him.

He was dead. It wasn't him. He was dead. He was dead. He was dead.

He was—

He was something else.

"Penny?" Sera's voice interrupted our reunion as she tumbled down the stairs, clutching the rails.

Will—or whatever it was—glided over to the closed bathroom door on my left and vanished. I saw the lights flicker on through the crack.

"Penny, you okay? Did you hurt yourself?" Sera rushed over to me and grabbed my clammy hands. Her Estée Lauder perfume overpowered my senses, making me lose track of Will's musk. It certainly didn't help my head either.

"It… it was my husband. He's here." I stole my hand from her pushy grasp, pointing to the bathroom. "H-he's in there."

Sera's face drooped. She wrapped her arms around my waist and squeezed me. My nose dug into her striped shirt, the flowery stench making me sneeze. "Oh, honey, it's okay. Let's get you to bed."

"Don't touch me!" I cried, pushing her away. "I need to see him. He never even said goodbye."

Sera scratched her head. Her fingers combed through her curls and separated knots in her hair. She bit her lip, and looking off into space, she said, "Alright, look, just wait here while I get some coffee started. Then we can talk. Maybe it'll help you."

And without waiting for a response, Sera left me alone.

I used the time to my advantage, rushing over to the bathroom and trying the knob. It was locked. Though I could hear the

faintest whisper from inside.

He was   calling

my name.

I twisted the knob harder. I shook it aggressively and tugged with all my strength.

A gentle *tap, tap* resounded on my shoulder. I let go of the handle as I turned my body around slowly. I was met with two open arms.

Blood dripped out of his coat sleeves,
congealing at his fingertips

and blessing my skin with its touch.

Blessing my flesh to remember every
soft
word which pooled out of his
mouth.

I stood on my tippy-toes to kiss him, holding his cold cheeks against my warm hands. He dipped his head lower to meet with my chapstick-glossed lips.

Glass shattered against the hardwood flooring. I blissfully craned my neck to gaze upon Sera's flabbergasted expression. Her jaw fell down, almost as low as her collarbone. Two mugs of hot coffee now shattered at her feet. I stared at her, my eyes unblinking.

"I know. I'm excited to see him too." I smiled.

"Who are you—what are you talking about? Are you having an episode or something?" Sera moved toward us warily.

"No! Stay there!" I snapped. "I don't want him to disappear again. He'll disappear if you come close."

"Penny, you're holding the air. There's no one there," she said. "You… we need to just calm down here." She walked closer, her arms outstretched to me.

"If you come any closer, I'm gonna hurt you. I'm sorry," I hissed. She stood still for a half-second, her eyes batting in disbelief. "Yeah, I'll hurt you real bad."

She stepped backward. While still looking at me, she snatched a phone clinging to the wall and dialed. She spoke into it, hand over mouth. She finished the call and stumbled into the dimly lit kitchen. Her silhouette shook anxiously at the table, facing toward me. She was silent, which came as a surprise.

All three of us stood still for almost ten minutes. I held my lover, and he held me, as my sister simply observed. It didn't seem long until the wails of a siren rang from outside.

My heart dropped.

* * *

It was strange at the institution, but I had found a brooding spot at a moldy window. It was away from the lunatics which surrounded me, staring like I was hot, juicy meat. At this window I could see much of the city, one mostly made of trees.

Most of the days were obscured. I remembered snippets, deals with twitching psychos and something about me sending out a letter. Or perhaps I hadn't sent it yet?

To pass the time, I hummed old tunes which used to play on the radio. But whenever I'd start, someone joined me in harmony until one day the hum came over my shoulder.

I turned around. I was alone, yet the humming kept going. Not in harmony with me, but on its own. I followed the musical trail into a bathroom.

I was sure it couldn't be him, but there was a faint glow of excitement in my mind.

I went inside, but I could not find Will.

Disappointed, I sat near the sink with my blossoming migraine in my hands. But when all seemed lost, an envelope slid under the door. The paper was old and brown, and stained with what was probably blood. To my great surprise, it was addressed to me. From Will.

184

I tore it open and shook the contents out.

Two shiny razorblades slipped out and clattered onto the porcelain.

I picked one up and looked into the mirror.

Will overshaowed my small frame, donning the second blade.

The Call of the Sea

Austin Slade Perry

It had been a gray and dreary day out on the bay. The green
ocean water splashed, warning of a storm to come. It was starting
to get late. Mr. Wallace and I had been out fishing most of the
day with only empty nets to show for it.

"Alright, Malcolm, my boy," Mr. Wallace sighed, "pull
in the net and we'll head ashore."

I did as I was told without hesitation. I never liked being
out on the water after dark. As a child, my grandfather would tell
me stories of the dangers lurking beneath the sea. Even now, in
my young adult life, that fear remained.

An eerie stillness had fallen over the waves. The wind
had slowed, and I could hear a faint whistling. I moved closer
to the edge of the boat only to catch a glimpse of something
white bobbing under the surface.

"Lad, have you finished with the net?" Mr. Wallace
called out to me.

"Aye, sir!"

"Then take us ashore."

Brushing off what I had seen as a trick of the eye, I made my way to the helm. Mr. Wallace sat at the bow of the ship, looking out over the water as he lit his pipe. I went to turn on the engine, but it wouldn't start. I kept trying but with no luck.

"Sir, the ship won't start." I called out to the captain but there was no response, "Sir?"

The faint whistling on the wind had turned into a gentle hum. It was growing louder. The sound was so familiar, like a song I had heard in my childhood. I could feel my body being drawn to it. Then I remembered my grandfather's stories, warning of a song from the sea. I quickly covered my ears.

"Sir, cover your ears!" I shouted, but Mr. Wallace didn't budge.

He stared out over the water, unblinking. I moved to follow but tripped over the net. I caught myself on the taffrail, absorbed by the horrors glowing below.

A woman tredded, revealing only her head and shoulders. Her flawless skin was so pale and transluscent that I could make out green veins running across her body.

She erupted in song, exposing long, sharp fangs. I pressed my fingers into my ears as Mr. Wallace leaned over the edge. She raised her arms, pulling herself up by the gunwale.

"Don't listen!" I cried out.

The creature perched upon the bow. Green fins lined the sides of her white tale and down the side of her forearms. She reached out a hand with long claws, caressing Mr. Wallace's beard.

Her seranade ended as Mr. Wallace pressed his lips to hers. The heated kiss did not last. His eyes shot open in panic as he fought against her hold. He broke free, his mouth stained with his own blood. He cried out, "Malcolm, get out of here!"

She dragged him off the ship, while I reached in vain.

I staggered back to the helm to start the motor.

Then the cruel melody started again.

Eyes

Becca Rose

I watched her daily routine endlessly.

The girl prepared herself every day in the hopes that she would leave her apartment. Dalia. It had taken me three days to learn her name. She never spoke it aloud, so I had to wait for someone to address her. She'd been completely alone for those three days, locked away from the world.

Dalia was obsessed with appearing her best. She would bathe in the morning, taking her time. The warm waters soothed her. I loved the little smile she got when she laid her head back in the water, allowing her blond hair to float freely.

It wouldn't be until her bedtime shower that she'd cry.

I watched without the ability to comfort her. I watched her dry her hair, apply a light layer of makeup, and choose an outfit. She had a closet of looks to choose from, much like the closet of an actor. The clothing ranged from childish to scandalous. She could freely change her appearance with makeup to match her chosen outfit. I'd seen her do it.

This morning she chose a simple look: a jean skirt and tight shirt. She walked the apartment barefoot, snacking on almonds. Dalia was thin and weak. She didn't have enough food in her cupboards, though it wasn't her choice.

It wasn't her choice to be locked in a basement apartment either.

She fell asleep reading on the couch. With her love of books, Dalia had to be smart. She should have been in college. I would make sure that she had that chance.

The lock on the door rattled, disturbing her rest. She sat up, plastering a fake smile on her face. When Sam's large frame entered the apartment, Dalia's rage filled me.

"You're dressed," Sam noted. He held a brown grocery bag and set it on the coffee table.

"Am I going out today?" Dalia asked, her voice frail.

I hated how she cowed beneath Sam, but Dalia was a third the size of the man. There was nothing she could do, or rather, nothing she could risk doing.

"We'll go for a walk," Sam agreed. "Just around the neighborhood. Put on a shorter skirt."

I watched her choose more revealing clothing. She tied up her hair to show off her long, lean neck. Back in the living room, Sam nodded his approval before opening the door.

Dalia hadn't been outside in the week I'd been with her. The sun was too bright for her eyes, making them water.

Unable to see, she stumbled in her heels. Sam gripped her wrist tightly, dragging her along without a care. They walked the neighborhood slowly. Sam would point things out as they walked, making her reach up or bend over to show off her curves. I could see her dull eyes during the process.

Dalia was tuning it all out. She would shut down her feelings until her nightly shower. Then I'd watch her cry.

Sam returned Dalia to her apartment, locking her back inside. She opened the bag he'd left her. Instant noodles. I didn't know much about nutrition, but I did know that instant noodles were cheap and empty. Dalia didn't care. She boiled water and ate.

Sam was back an hour later. He unlocked the door to let a man inside. Dalia had been on the couch reading again.

190

The new man was older, gray in his hair. He'd been in the neighborhood for one purpose; it was clear by his suit that he wasn't from around here. His eyes burned with hunger.

I wanted to throw him right back out the door.

"What would you like, sir?" Dalia purred. She set down her book to stretch out on the couch. The man's eyes drifted over her body. "I can be whoever you want me to be."

This man had no special requests. I had seen one other customer in the seven days, and that man had wanted Dalia dressed like a doll. He'd stayed for over an hour, paying Sam handsomely when he'd left. Dalia had sat in the shower crying until the stream of water erased her makeup.

This man was all action, not even taking Dalia to the bedroom. He was rough. I could see Dalia's discomfort even as she yelled words of encouragement. He took her twice. Sam collected money on the way out and shut Dalia inside again.

She retreated to the bathroom and undressed. She looked at herself in the mirror, sneering. Dalia never gave that look to the men who came. She didn't even frown at Sam. She played her part well because what choice did she have?

She broke down in the shower. If I had a heart, it would break for her. Instead, I held onto her deep-rooted fury, letting it inspire me to act. She pulled on a large shirt before climbing into bed. I watched as she slept, fitfully in the night.

I listened for the sound of the lock.

Sam frequently visited at night. I'd foolishly thought he was checking in on his property. No. Turned out he liked to sample the merchandise. Sam didn't sleep with her. He'd spirit in when she was most vulnerable and fondle her while she slept.

When I heard the lock, I was ready.

I reached into Dalia's mind and bade her to grab a sliver of glass hidden beneath her pillow. We kept still in the bed, like we were sleeping.

Sam crept in, setting the keys on the bedside table. He wasn't a pleasant-looking man. He was large, but most of his bulk was fat. His beady eyes and long nose gave him a rat-like appearance. I'd seen Dalia look at his teeth a few times. They were crooked and plaque-ridden. I hated to imagine what his breath smelled like.

Sam unbuckled his pants.

Now.

Dalia's eyes open. She pulled out the glass and slashed Sam's jugular, rolling to avoid the spillage.

Sam's hands went to his throat.

Dalia was disgusted, shocked, and scared at what she had done, but there was a glimmer of triumph.

We watched as Sam fell onto the bed. When he was done twitching, no longer breathing, Dalia went through Sam's pockets for cash. She'd be long gone before people found the body.

Dalia showed how smart she was, taking control. I watched as she tore the pages from her beloved books. She grabbed a jar of Vaseline, and coated the body, bed, clothes, and furniture in the goop. Then she used a bundle of pages she lit on fire with the stove to burn everything before walking out the door.

I would give her the strength to carry on if she needed it, protecting her when I could.

Dalia never knew I was there, but the rage that fueled her actions had been hers alone.

I knew she'd be safe now without me.

Wronged women were warriors.

Limbo

Samuel Smith

When we looked on the shores of paradise, we saw a heaven
that roared angrily. The waves were the island's hands, and they
smashed us against the rocks. We were stranded in an alluring
land that did not want us.

The produce made us see, made us realize too much.
We turned on each other, hunted and killed, in the hopes of
sparing them from their new reality. The flowers in their soft
simplicity glowed brightly in the night, their light revealing the
souls of the dead. They warned me, advised me, screamed at
me, demanding answers. The entire crew were in a deafening
uproar for a resolution that I could not bring myself to do, for
closure that their apparitions could not hear.

We had come for the spring, that fountain of youth that
was rumored to be at the island's peak. It is but a stone's throw
away from me. Morning breaks. Its skinny, pale yellow fingers
worming their way into my haggard shelter. The birds begin their
oblivion chorus, and the cool sea air beckons to me. I see the sun
for its lies, know the cunning of the birds, and the tempting inti-

macy of the wind. They… it… the island knows I grow thirsty;
I cannot drink and live with what I know, but I refuse to die and
haunt the inevitable expeditions that will follow us.

The God Tree

Brandon Prows

Old folk in the town sometimes spoke of a ghostly tree that bore the face of God. It was said that whoever gazed upon its face could find their way to heaven. It seemed without a doubt that if there was such a tree, Richter was looking at it now. But staring into the gnarled visage didn't bring heaven to Richter's mind. The only thing he could see in its gaze was death.

The wind crashed against the forest clearing. It shook between the cracks of the tree, making it moan. The loose bark shifted with the breeze. It looked like the face was moving.

Combined with the dead chiming of the branches, Richter heard whispered words, "Come... to... me..."

The voice filled Richter with dread. He tripped before breaking into a sprint back the way he came. Before he could leave the clearing, a flare of scarlet light burst in his path. He fell back, shielding his eyes. Coldness overtook him as he uncovered his face.

Before him, stood a willowing creature lit by a crimson glow, with the body of a man and the breasts of a woman, naked save for a tattered loincloth. Enormous antlers crowned its half-rotted mule deer skull, dripping red with blood. It carried a staff decorated with rotting human faces. Some still had their eyes.

Richter recognized the faces of the Wagners, his neighbors from a few farms down. The youngest daughter, Johana, stared lifelessly at him from the top of the pole.

"Richter, where dost thou go?" the creature asked with the voice of a child. Its mouth did not move.

"I…" Richter stammered. His voice was weak.

The creature lifted its staff and the eyes of Richter's neighbors glowed crimson. Their mouths opened and out came a terrible utterance, "Join us in the God Tree."

"The God Tree is hungry," shrilled the mother.

"Salvation is at hand," mumbled the father's head.

Richter cried out. He scrambled to his feet and turned to run. But there was no path. He was blocked by naked villagers with white eyes that lacked pupils. They reached for him.

"Richter, where dost thou go?" repeated the creature.

"God! Save me!" Richter screamed. He struggled, but the strength of the crowd outweighed his own.

"There is no God. Only the God Tree," it said.

The crowd dragged Richter backward. A fierce gust blew through the clearing, shaking the abominable tree before him as the wood warped and opened its maw.

Richter could see inside the tree, into a portal to another world—one with a dead landscape under a cold sun, buried in a blackened winter. A thick miasma coated the air, draining all life. At the center of the world was an enormous tower, and on top of it, stood a shadowed figure with wide wings and many writhing arms. Its eyes glowed, and when it opened its mouth, tongues of fire flew. Richter now knew the truth. There was no heaven beyond the tree.

It was a gate to Hell.

The Piper's Song

Jonathan Reddoch

This boy is deserving
Of a fate unnerving
Echoing the walls
Is the death that crawls

The lad will not fail
To face tooth and nail
Of the mad piper's rats
That devour whole cats

The deadly throng
Was reined by my song
And so paid at last!
The rats end their fast

Do you not fear
The last sound you'll hear?
Is my tune too weak
Under that deafening squeak?

BOOK III
The Darkness Between

In the Shadows

D.A. Butcher

Its claws caught in my corpse
Cut like unsuspecting paws
Its sweat stuck to my skin
Stunk of festered body parts
Its fur flush with my flesh
Felt as soft as rotting peach—

A heathen breathing heavily
In the shadows of my dreams.

Forest dwellers hanged
From ropes and choke
With pantyhose from mothers drawers
To decorate the darkest routes, sticks
Crack and bow like brittle bone
A campfire casts a cozy glare
Where my sadist often plays
In the shadows of my dreams.

I preached at its command until
My cheeks were numb, face afloat
On blood, beating buried hunger
Unsuccessfully.
But time ticked by on tilted-clocks,
Fearful-pixels cross and focused
On the sins our father warns of

The devil delving deftly
In the shadows of my dreams

Its hypnotizing eyes
Reveal my reflection
It grins with grim complexion as
I inhale your passing gasp,
Oh!
Death is my climax
It hides its
Tongues inside my sacrifice.

Crush the cords, conceal the cries
Bind the limbs, affix the knots
Bag the skulls, pull the plastic—
Ties tightly about your throats

The monster meets its maker
In the shadows of your dreams.

The Green Window

Sophie Queen

At the top of Sarah's rickety stairs was a window that let out
an eerie green glow. This glow did not spread a far distance;
in fact, it was only strong enough to light up the pale, chipped
window frame. Upon closer inspection, the glass was not tinted
green. Rather, it seemed that the light emanated from within.
Stranger still that it only appeared as the sun's light set below
the tall city buildings.

At first, I speculated that a green light from the street
cast the odd gleam. I was satisfied with this on my first night in
Sarah's apartment. We laughed and drowned in the pleasure of
warm contact. Her toothy smile had enamored me so. She was
so sweet, so much of what I wanted in a partner.

It's funny how all that changed, and how quickly.
For when her breath evened out and her lashes fluttered, my
thoughts returned to that ethereal emerald glow. Even as sleep
pressed itself upon my weary body, the image of the window
kept appearing in my mind.

The Darkness Between

My second visit to her apartment was much different. In but a week's time, I had grown more curious about the cause of the green light. The answer I had satisfied myself with no longer quelled my curiosity. Instead, new questions filled my mind. I wondered why she had not mentioned the window. If I had such a strange window in my home, I think I would point it out. Wasn't that the normal thing to do? On further recollection, it became clear to me that she hadn't even glanced at it, or acknowledged it in the slightest. *She must be used to it*, was my first thought; so used to it that it was like it wasn't even there.

Then a curious thought crept into the depths of my mind. Like an itch. An irritation. Perhaps... she couldn't see it? I'm not sure why that thought even came about. But I found myself disturbed by it, and perhaps that fear was the source of my reluctance to question her. So instead, before entering her place, I peeked momentarily down the alley, separating her apartment building from her neighbors. There didn't seem to be any outside source of the green light. And for a moment, I questioned if I had been mistaken. Maybe there had never been a light at all.

Yet, there it was. As I walked up the stairs, more luminous than it had been before. I found myself so transfixed, I could barely feel her hand grab hold of mine and pull me inside. Her kiss felt distant. Her smile failed to capture my attention. As the night progressed, all my thoughts were on that window. It wasn't possible—it was inconceivable. I longed to understand how the glow came about. But I could not ask her; for if she said there was no glow, I felt I would go mad.

That following week, between classes and work, I met up with my friend Mark at one of the local dives. A ritual, something we had done since we met in our first week of grad school. I told him about the window. He commented about how strange that was. But his eyes and body language conveyed his disinterest.

I don't know why, but I felt I had to explain just how peculiar the window was. "It's like she didn't see it. Like it didn't exist! Wouldn't you, if you had a window like this, tell people about it? Explain it?"

He looked at me funny, and changed the subject, asking how things were progressing with Sarah.

204

I felt frustrated. With him or myself, I wasn't sure. But I allowed the conversation to change and decided then not to bring up the window to anyone. The glow would be mine and just mine. Because no one else got it. No one but me could understand its majesty.

I continued visiting her apartment regularly. Upon every viewing of the window, the glow grew more vibrant, brilliant. It felt otherworldly, the way the color radiated its brilliant shades of jade. Sometimes it looked like shimmering rainforest leaves or the soothing color of grass out of freshly melted snow. So pure, so beautiful. I dreamed of it. I longed for it—to touch it—feel it.

Nothing else mattered. Not even the apartment's resident. I could barely distinguish her face from any other. No longer could I taste her skin or smell the scent of her hair. By the end, I couldn't even remember the hue of her eyes. Our days together became a blur. In the depth of my haze, the only thing I distinctly remember her saying was, "I'm going to move." Her thin lips spread in a sad smile. "Will you still visit me?"

She left a month later. And I rented the apartment immediately, discarding my home and my friends without a second thought. All memories of her dissipated into the shadows of a dream.

In a few days, I was completely moved in. Yet that evening, the glow… it was not there.

Throughout the night, I sat, waiting for the glow to return. But it did not. The disappointment was overpowering. I couldn't understand it. What had become of the luminous green?

As the late hours ticked away, anger grew in my chest, *how could it just disappear? Had it ever really been there at all? No, it had to have been! I wasn't mad!* I spent every evening for a week, no… two, maybe three, sitting on that step, waiting for its return.

My friends and family no longer bothered to call or text me. I was lost and helpless. But as the weeks turned into months, my hope of seeing the green glow faded. Slowly, I was able to begin my life again. It wasn't easy. There was no one there to push me. I just moved on, as one does after the loss of a loved one.

I found work at a small shop around the corner; with ample apologies, most of the people I had once felt great affection for forgave my negligence. They dismissed it as sort of a pre-midlife crisis. They did not know, nor did I care to explain, the reason behind my temporary madness. And slowly, I allowed the memory of the glow to retract into the depths of my mind.

After a year, I was made manager and even found myself lucky enough to find Laura. A sweet lady, who really seemed to genuinely care for me.

Then one night I had a dream. A dream about the window. The glow had returned. I walked up, reaching out and touching the warm glass with delicate fingers. I moved closer. Until my face was engulfed within the swirling light. Deep within the color, beyond the glass… no, perhaps, within it, was a figure. I could make out no features. But I knew it was looking at me. I was over-whelmed with a desire to enter it. To be embraced by it. But as I pushed against the glass, the figure shook its head slowly. And then I awoke.

I looked next to me, finding the bed cold and empty. I walked out into the hall, and a feeling of dread tugged at my heart. I knew what was to come as I walked toward the stair-well—I just knew.

There I found Laura, captivated by that window, which still looked to me like ordinary dull glass. I sat next to her, watching her wide, mesmerized eyes. I could see, though faint, that same glint of green.

Though I don't know whether she knew I was there, still I asked, "If I moved, would you still visit me?"

Inky Sea

Elizabeth Suggs

I am a ball of blackness
which starts from the
center of my belly and
explodes outward.

My innocence evaporates
into a cloud of sin.

I run my fingers along the depth of these transgressions,
and it pours out of me, infecting anyone who enters my space.

Exhale.
Let go.
Breeeeeeeeeeeeeeeeeeeathe.

I do as it bids, and tiny white dots peek out through the sea of
ink, like eyes staring down at me. Below them, black concaves,
and the voice speaks again.

The Darkness Between

You promised it would be for us.
Monster tendrils reach out to grab me, but I pull away.
You're not letting go.
You're not letting me out.
You said you would let me outtttttt.

This blackness was supposed to be my escape, yet it only
drenches and suffocates.
Come back!

But I ignore its calls
and wiggle free
of the ocean made of my absent promises.
I don't get very far.
I'm pulled back
into
the clutches of my self-made sea.

I thrash my arms and legs in hopes of evading, but those, too,
fail me.
Before my very eyes,
My limbs wrinkle
and
dry,
like raisins.

My bones dissolve, and I fall helpless into the black.
I cry out, but ink chokes my mouth;
my eyes are blind;
my nose and
ears muffle.

I am the monsters inside me
Until a pool of what I wanted to forget drowns the world.
And then I am nothing.

Only Darkness Remains

Jonathan Reddoch

A blind woman straddled the wall, clumsily searching for the entrance to the soup kitchen. I stopped and turned back to offer my assistance. "Ma'am," I said, realizing she could not see the operating hours. I took her by the elbow, "the kitchen is closed for the night."

"Oh, I see," she said. Her eyes had been sealed shut by yellowed crust. "Thank you, dearest. I am so hungered." When she spoke, I thought I saw a phantom eyeball protruding from her throat.

"Yes, I can see that." She was nothing but skin and bones draped in tattered rags. I panged with guilt. "Can I feed you something?"

She took me by the hand, smiling. "Why yes, I think you can. I appreciate the invitation to sup."

Then her eyelids burst open as flames of lightning and chaos penetrated my retinas. I stood erect, unable to move, as she sucked my sight away as a mosquito drains blood.

The Darkness Between

I was overcome by sudden midnight. Her laughter was cruel, as all vision was purged of me until I finally collapsed into a mass of formless void.

And when I was awakened, the thief was gone, but the darkness remains.

And a new hunger forms in the back of my throat.

Selena's Eyes

Alex Child

Tony hadn't bothered bringing his equipment to investigate what he assumed was just another false alarm. His baton, flashlight, and walkie-talkie were all sitting safely in his desk, while he quivered in the hotel kitchen's cupboard.

He could hear it slurp across the floor, slow and steady, though he knew it could move much faster. It nearly got the jump on him in the dimly lit storage room, but even in the dark, the liquid mass shimmered gloriously, allowing him to narrowly escape.

He shifted uncomfortably as he caught a whiff of burning rubber. He examined his shoe. Some of the residue had stuck to his heel when fleeing the storage room. His sole was starting to smoke. Before it ate through, he removed it and tossed it across the kitchen, where it collided with a stack of dirty pots and pans.

The gelatinous blob flowed toward the collapsed cookware, pausing as Tony's hiding place fell into view. He saw it clearly for the first time: a grotesque mass of eyeballs oozing through the door. In unison, its thousand eyes turned to him.

Tony leaped from the cupboard, but he tripped over an extension cord, forcing him to the floor chin first.

Scrambling to his feet, he grabbed a knife and swiped furiously at the creature. It moved forward and swallowed his leg, eating through his polyester pants.

He slashed at it, causing one eye to explode with a green and blue gush. The splatter struck his own pupil, partially blinding him.

Tony screamed, flailing his arms and toppling a salt shaker. The contents poured onto the living liquid, forming violent bubbles. The mass recoiled and retreated toward the pantry.

Numbed from the pain, Tony grabbed two more salt shakers, limping on his melted limb in pursuit. From there, he hobbled over to an industrial-sized container of table salt. Victory was near. He looked back and smiled viciously.

And then he saw them: Selena's unmistakable brown eyes. So gentle and pure. Suddenly, he was transported back to a hundred summer nights.

He gingerly placed the weaponized seasoning on the counter and lay down on the sticky tile.

A wave of slime washed over him until he was eye to eye with his beloved. His screams were muffled by acidic sludge. And when it passed, all was dissolved, save his eyes, for those belong to Selena.

They

Jess Rougeau

In the small hours,
Forest animals freeze
The underground rises
As eyes in the trees

They do not belong here
They want to feel closer
Curled fingers, amorphic in
Black tar water

They mimic, irk
Provoke, over and
Over
A trauma simulator
Pushed
But worse,
To warp us, dysmorphic
They spill from our heads

The Darkness Between

Serene and sour
They sip our fear
They strip our power

The Mortician's Daughter

Jo Birdwell

Cordelia, my sweet love! It was a little over two years ago when my dull excuse for a life was restored. Yet, sometimes I feel like it was just yesterday when I first saw her.

I had just finished placing purple, wilted clematis on my mother's grave, when I looked up and saw her standing there, the mortician's daughter.

It was a cool autumn night beneath the stars, stars that dimmed and failed in comparison to her beauty. She stood there, atop a freshly dug grave, unknowingly bringing meaning to my, formerly bleak, existence. I was gripped with an inexplicable urge to be a part, any part, no matter how insignificant, of her world. How I longed to be the ground upon which this other-worldly creature walked, the pillow on which she would rest her head at night, the darkness that blinds her when she closes her eyes. I would devote my entire life to her if only she let me.

Long blonde locks fell past her shoulders, curling just beneath her small round breasts. Her skin shone like alabaster in the night, putting the full moon to shame. All I had never

known I desired was gliding my way, hips swaying beneath a
loose lavender dress, fluttering in the light breeze. She had a
soft smile on her face and sadness in her blue-gray eyes. Her
icy gaze caught mine, as a sense of foreboding set in. I knew
in that moment, although I was not worthy, that she would be
mine. And for better or for worse, I would never be the same.

She bade me walk her home to her family's mortuary,
and I obliged. We moved silently, arm-in-arm, toward the edge
of town, her soft skin touching mine, her despondency sending
chills my way. As dead leaves crunched beneath our steps, I
told her I could, that I would, be her everything. Her piercing
eyes revealed that she did not think me up to the challenge.

We reached her ancestral home, exterior paint crackling, shingles and shutters missing. The twisted, gnarled trees
bore no autumn leaves, and the ground was but dirt and rocks,
even in the spring. Cordelia kept the garden just less than alive,
with the flowers wilting and the greenery sparse.

Before leaving me at her doorstep, she leaned close,
lightly pressing her lips against my cheek. Her bosom pressed
against my chest. The sensation that had been building up
inside me had reached its peak, and I longed for her. I took her
for the first time in her garden.

I threw her to the ground, and a faint blush rose in
her cheeks. She grabbed my hands and wrapped them tightly around her thin neck as we writhed on the ground, worms
crawling in the soil beneath us. To see her gasping for air took
my breath away. My hands slowly released as the moment
came and went, and then we lay for hours in the dirt, gazing at
the stars. I was no longer master of myself. I was taken. And
Cordelia was my captor.

Over the next few weeks, our mysterious connection
deepened, and traversing the depths of our hidden sorrows, we
grew to know one another on a level that few before had been able
to reach. My life before her was nothing but a faded, grim memory, unrecognizable to even myself.

Cordelia came from a strange family. Her father was
a haggard, tired man who rarely spoke and always avoided
eye contact. It was as if his work had taken over his body,
and he was nothing more than a hollow corpse himself.

216

Her father found the aged, dilapidated home perfect for his occupation. He worked on the bodies in the basement, frequently having around half a dozen down there at one time. The ever-present scent of formaldehyde lingered in the air; it was a subtle reminder of his dedication to his craft, which made him the best mortician in three counties.

The more time I spent in their home, the more darkness and despair I observed. Mourning families, clothed in black, routinely came and went. I then understood the melancholy in Cordelia's eyes.

Cordelia and I spent hours, days, in her bedroom attic, conversing about life, love, death. As the wind whistled outside her window, we read Poe by candlelight, the shadow of the flames dancing on the wall. His words portrayed us perfectly. We were only eighteen, "but our love it was stronger by far than the love of those who were older than we, of many far wiser than we." She was my life, my love, my paramour, my own *Annabel Lee*.

While her father was away, we would steal into the basement and embrace among the corpses. It was so cold, but she was so warm. Lying on the concrete floor, our bodies intertwined, we struggled to keep quiet, lest we should wake the dead.

Afterward, we would admire the deceased's dark beauty. The cadavers looked like freshly polished dolls, like angelic mannequins, waiting to be put on display. Cordelia and I would invent tales about them, to make them come alive, draping ourselves and the bodies in old clothes from the attic. At times, Cordelia would lay motionless on the stony block and pretend to be her father's next client. She even taught me how to care for her corpse, explaining the steps of preserving her after death, calling me a natural.

Sometimes, in the middle of the night, when she was still sleeping, I would get up and walk around the homemade mortuary, further admiring the bodies and my sleeping beauty. Her father knew how to bring a corpse to life. And, although his work was extraordinary, I couldn't help but feel a sadness when I saw the bodies of the elderly. My gut wrenched at the thought that my Cordelia could one day end up this way: wrinkled, sagging skin, gray hair—*if only there was a way to preserve her beauty for eternity!*

217

When her father was in town, we would lie in the cemetery beneath the moon, the cold, freshly dug earth lying submissively beneath our naked bodies.

One night, I saw it. As I was pressed up against her beneath the night sky, a glimpse of an elderly woman took the place of Cordelia's face. Then, I knew what must be done. This time, as she placed my hands around her thin neck, I bore down more than ever before and did not let go. She tried to fight. But her frail frame was no match for my desire.

Her body was found the following morning in the woods, bordering the graveyard. I feigned despair in the presence of others, knowing that it was I who actually saved her life. She would never grow old, never suffer life's ills, never experience sadness or pain again, and she would stay pristine forevermore.

Now, she lays peacefully on the stony slab in her father's basement. I see her there, her empty eyes, her marble skin whiter than ever before, and I realized how Poe's words that we had recited so many times before were written about us. Our love was too strong to withstand life. "Neither the angels in heaven above, nor the demons down under the sea, could ever dissever my soul from the soul of the beautiful Annabel Lee."

I brush her long fair hair, dust powder across her face, rouge her cheeks, and add color to her blue lips. She looks more alive in death than when living. I run my hands along her body, feeling stiff, lifeless flesh beneath my fingertips.

Soon she will be home with me, and we can remain together eternally, as "the angels, not half so happy in heaven, went envying her and me." I hold her in my arms, resting warm beneath the covers of my bed, the moon shining through the crack of my curtains. *Cordelia, my sweet love!*

Confessions

Ali Blanco

Pay no attention to the scratching at the floorboards.

There's a devil that I keep
In my closet.
A secret,
Of sorts,
That I cannot unveil.
A deeply rooted ghost that resides,
Forever gnawing,
Crawling.

Pay no attention to the scuttling in the shadows.

There's a monster that dwells
Out of sight.
But beware his outstretched fingers,
Reaching,

The Darkness Between

Casting shadowed puppets in my mind.

Pay no attention to the silent darkness that oozes beneath the door.

A familiar beast lives in my belly,
Who feasts on every fear that I harbor.
He consumes every treachery,
Grows stronger,
And spews more sickly sin.
I swallow it down,
Trying to ignore,
To hide the constant tingles beneath my skin,
But he's
Itching,
Alive,
Drawing rasping breaths within.

Pay no attention to the whispers drawing near.

There's an unseen foe that lingers and stirs,
One that I cannot address,
Cannot fight,
Cannot evict.

Pay no attention to the demon beneath my fingernails.

He scribbles upon the walls,
A story,
Of sorts,
Seething,
Well-hidden.
Mirrors reflecting
Blood-stained lips,
Teeth biting back harsh
Confessions.

The Roost

E.C. Hanson

Christmas was the perfect day for a full-fledged takeover.
Three ginger siblings sat around three square presents that had
the same red wrapping, green strings, and white bows. All of
them were perplexed why Gladys, their new stepmother, ordered them to the living room at six in the morning, wearing
a sequin dress, matching heels, and Runway Red lipstick. She
looked ready for a hot night on the town instead of the moder-
ator of gift-giving.

"Where's our daddy?" the youngest one asked.

"That doesn't concern you. Choose a present," said Gladys.

"Whose is whose?" the eldest son asked.

"First come, first served," replied Gladys.

The eldest grabbed his present; his sister and brother, aged
eleven and nine, wrestled over a substantial gift next to the tree.

"Freeze!" yelled Gladys.

"We'll freeze when you tell us where our dad is," coun-
tered the eldest.

"Open your gifts, then I'll tell you about daddy."

The siblings tore into their presents like vicious animals. Their freckled faces displayed utter confusion.

"A glove?" asked the youngest son.

"To cover your missing hand."

"A mask?" asked the daughter.

"To cover your missing nose."

"A patch?" asked the eldest.

"To cover your missing eye."

The eldest snickered at her responses. His siblings erupted into laughter. Gladys allowed it because she held all the cards now. When they composed themselves, she withdrew a cleaver for the youngest son's hand, a saw for the daughter's nose, and a scalpel for the eldest son's eye.

"Your days of running this show are over. Daddy is dead. I rule this roost."

Miller Drive

E.S. Danon

Innately I knew the concrete under my tattered shoes
would cause me horror, and thus ensues:
I was a kid with keen senses beyond the fifth,
but Miller Drive made me no more than nature's filth.

The move from town, at first, made me excited to explore
my new home surrounded by trees and fields filled with folklore.
But when I first left the car, fright was my woe:
from the tall prairie grass, death's eyes smiled with glow.

A man stopped me from his grassy abode,
as I walked my dog down the concrete road.
"Be warned, it's almost time for Samhain's repayment—
taken every fifty years—the moon's accruement."

"Since the Civil War, ghosts have been seeking
an innocent life for nature's taking—
their bodies were forgotten by all they loved:
rotting in the stones, faces forever gloved.

The Darkness Between

At my glassy stare and dog's ceaseless bark, he said:
"Girl, this Halloween Eve, you must stay in your bed."
I thanked him, and left in disarray,
for I too sensed that I'd soon fall prey.

I shook at home, causing my parents great concern,
and left for my room, leaving their questions to burn.
From outside and to my shock, bright eyes shined through my room,
whispering, "soon you will be inside my rocky tomb."

Shoving fear away, I pretended it was make-believe:
But that was a mistake my mind did gravely misconceive.
For on the eve of Samhain, midnight beckoned my name,
and those glowing eyes shined above my bed all the same.

Now I rest in a stream, hidden and spellbound:
Fifty years between my bodily impound,
waiting for the next soul to be forgotten with us,
the innocent spirits, for whom justice is no must.

A New Life

K.R. Patterson

A stream of sunlight cuts across my face, yanking me from the dregs of sleep enough to discern a permeating, metallic scent. I am barely able to open my eyes, but when I do, I notice that there is a crack in the heavy hotel curtains where I failed to pull them completely shut.

I turn the other direction. *How much did I drink last night?*

I feel something clutched in my hand. Hard, either a smooth wood or a firm plastic. Narrow, like a handle. Ominously wet and sticky.

The disgusting, pungent scent intensifies as I grow more alert. The rock in my gut grows into a boulder.

Minutes pass as I inch my other hand to pull down the white sheet.

What. The. Fuck.

My fragmented mind tries to comprehend that I'm holding exactly what it feels like: a bloody knife.

Releasing the blade, I sit up with a jolt. A surge of nausea hits me. My brain whirls like a roulette wheel, blurring my eyes. I blink a few times to focus... and see something else.

On the floor beside my bed is a body. Face-down, multiple knife-wounds in his back.

Blood everywhere.

A surge of bile rises in my throat, and I stumble to the toilet just in time to wretch.

After puking, arms still draped on the seat of the toilet, I rack my brain. I have no memory of this. I wouldn't do this. Someone must have set me up.

No, that can't be. I moved here just two days ago.

I tighten a shaking hand on a fistful of my hair as I scan through memories of the day before.

I'd unpacked a few things, then I meandered down the beachfront and entered Ripley's Believe It or Not! There were a lot unbelieveable odities, but it was the Maya box that had caught my eye.

"Start life anew!" promised the placard in front of the creepy stone box. A jagged, rectangular hole had been cut in its top, and a stack of papers sat next to it. The inscription read:

> *Archeologists believe Maya priests used stone boxes, like the enchanted box of the k'ul ahau to change their fates. The k'ul ahau bequeathed transformative power to a chosen few, allowing them to become anything they imagined. This ordinance was accompanied by an unknown sacrifice. However, it is often said that to find oneself, one first has to lose oneself. Don't believe it?*
>
> *What would you sacrifice? Give it a try!*

I wrote, "I want to be in movies" and placed it in the box.

Later that night, I found an old theater. One of the titles caught my eye: *Night of Evil.* Sounded like a B movie, my favorite.

Just as I entered the lobby, a woman bumped into me. She glanced to apologize, then did a double-take. Her eyes widened and her face paled to near-white. She took two steps back, swaying.

I wondered if I should prepare to catch her, but then her color returned and she laughed at herself.

"I'm sorry," she said. Her eyes wandered, avoiding my face. During a quick look, she stepped back, then forced a small giggle. "You look like the guy from *Night of Evil*."

I'll have to get a good look at my doppelganger as I watch the movie.

Enjoying my popcorn and soda, I leaned forward in my seat. The stupid protagonist, as always, ignored every damn clue that something wasn't right. They got a good slashing in front of a red phone booth. When the hooded killer turned from his grisly task, the Night Slayer pulled his hood down.

You rarely recognize your own likeness, even if others do, but he looked nothing like me! His hair was blonde and mine was dark brown. The only resemblance was our height.

After the show, I meandered through the lobby's thick, butter-charged air. I breathed it in, intoxicated.

Did I normally come out of slasher movies feeling giddy and—I'd searched for the right word—*accomplished*?

Even when I exited the building, things seemed different. Colors were brighter. My footfalls made the most pleasant *click-tap* in time with my steps. I wanted something. More of something, but I didn't know what.

I passed a glimmering red phone booth and was overcome with a perception that didn't seem to belong to me, but maybe it was only the deep, delicious darkness.

Back in my bed, I'm only just remembering that last bit now. *What else happened?* I inhale a deep, ragged breath and wipe my bloodstained hands on my jeans.

What was that peaceful, yet unsettling, feeling? What made me forget everything after that?

It was the wish: *I want to be in movies.*

And there was something else: a phrase, somewhere on the plaque: *What would* you *sacrifice?*

I catch a small glimpse of mussed blonde hair and twist away from my reflection, refusing to see more.

An inner, delighted voice chortles. It attempts to take control of my mind, but I resist.

I return to the body and place my foot beneath it, flipping it over.

Horror grips me with his dark tendrils, entering my mind now, turning, twisting, twirling through my body as I stare into the face of... my old self.

Immolated

P. Vincent Horta

I think someone said a pandemic was starting.
But I know enough not to trust what I know.
So, is this what it feels like?
Strung up like a slow roast, stake in the ground, sticks piled
around.
Spirits are silent; onlookers, ambivalent.

How odd to receive the cold shoulder when mine holds fire's
weight.
Light dances. Smoke tastes like strep throat
and feels like forever.
Wrapped in heat like a blanket—
like being two again and crying at night.
Tears dance on the griddle.
Time has escaped—
fled—
and still I wonder—
Is this twist, this bite on my wrist…

The Darkness Between

Is this what it feels like? I should have called in sick.

The throb in my wrist, in my head, in my fist.
      Bite them off; kill the pain that licks.
That caresses and cuts, one and the same,
My breath ragged, catch and cough and black:
Once, twice, snap.
A stick, an arm, a rib.
Is this what it feels like? A cough and a hack. With a rasp and a
saw?

Dread
Fever pitch is not just a saying.
Dancing is for people, not for flames. But flames are licking,
I am curling, and if it's inside or out or inside-out, it's all me or
worse.

Screams? Not sure who they're for any more.
Dreams and other things feel like another place, not mine.
Flesh and walls separate, curl.
Squeeze out the soul, the sweat, blood, sweat, flesh, sweat,
Tears, and steam.
All that I know is this immobile, dark heat.
So is this what it feels like?

Is there no one to help someone burning alive?

Little Red

Austin Slade Perry

"Due to the recent string of animal attacks, authorities are re-questing that citizens remain vigilant and avoid Cardinal Forest at this time," the newscaster warned. "Attempts to capture the animal responsible have been called off due to the storm ex-pected to roll in later this evening."

I poured myself another cup of strong, black coffee. A misty rain had started to fall outside, casting a dark haze over the town of Willowbrooke. A full moon peeked through the clouds, illuminating the carmine treetops just north of the small coastal village.

"Does the sun ever shine here?" I asked.

"Roisin, my boy," my grandfather interjected from the kitchen, "In this town, we have four seasons: overcast, rain, snow, and mist. Now that you and your mom are living here, you're gonna have to get used to it."

I rolled my eyes, "Whatever you say, gramps."

Ding!

The front door opened, and frigid air swept over me as I zipped my red jacket up.

A rugged hunk with a dark beard and black aviator sunglasses stepped inside. He eyed the empty diner, fixing the collar of his fur-lined leather jacket, and proceeded to an empty booth.

I straightened up and walked over.

"Welcome to Granny Ruby's. What can I get you?"

He glanced up at me. I could feel his gaze pierce through the lenses and it sent a chill down my spine.

He curled his lips into a slight smile. "Water," he growled, "and the ribeye. Extra rare."

I returned behind the counter, avoiding the customer's penetrating look. Normally, I wouldn't mind the attention from a handsome stranger, but this was different. I could feel it under my skin.

"Order up!"

I'd never seen a steak cook so fast, which was a relief. The sooner he had his food, the sooner he would leave.

I forced a smile and set the plate down in front of him.

"Roisin, is it?" He studied me, taking note of my every detail.

"Yes, sir," I answered, averting my eyes from him. The way he growled my name made my cheeks flush.

"Take a seat," he gestured to the empty spot across from him. "I'm sure your grandparents wouldn't mind."

His words caught me off guard. I opened my mouth to respond, but he raised his hand to stop me.

"It's a small town," he said, "the people gossip, and I've got large ears." He chuckled, "Now, please, take a seat."

I had work to do, but something about him enticed me, so I slid into the opposite seat.

"It's not every day someone new comes to town," he said, digging into his steak. "What brings you here?"

My stomach churned as I watched the meaty liquid flow over his plate and into his fries. He picked up one especially bloody fry and bit into it.

"Just needed a change of scenery, is all," I explained.

"Liar," he snickered, inhaling the air. "I've got a nose for bullshit." He leaned in and whispered, "No one comes here on a whim, so what's the deal, Little Red?"

I turned away from him, but I could still feel his eyes burning into me.

"Let me guess: nowhere else to go?" he remarked playfully. "Is Little Red lost in the woods?"

My fingers dug into the leather seat, "Maybe you should keep those 'large ears' out of other people's business."

The newscaster's shrill voice pulled my attention away from the man, "This just in, a new unidentified victim of a gruesome animal mauling has been found near Mountain Grove Hiking Trail. This is the third such attack in recent months."

That hiking trail was only two miles up the road from the diner.

"These attacks are getting closer to town," I muttered, swallowing down the panic in my voice.

The man took another large bite of his steak, the juice dripping down his chin. "A wolf has to eat."

"How do you know it's a wolf?"

"These woods are full of them," he explained, "Only a fool would dare wander out there alone."

A faint howl took my attention to the now wet and blurry window. The rain was falling faster. My eyes focused on the edge of the dark forest, where a set of glowing yellow eyes watched from the trees. I shuddered and looked back at the man.

"Is Little Red afraid of a big bad wolf?" he teased.

"No," I whispered.

"Don't lie to me," he leaned in again. His lips curled back into a wry smile. He lowered his glasses, exposing two bright yellow eyes. "I can see it in you."

I shook my head sheepishly, "Wh-what are you?"

His grin widened, displaying blood-stained canines.

A crack of lightning flashed across the sky, illuminating the window just long enough to reveal the customer's reflection: a snarling lupine figure, baring jagged teeth. It was covered in matted fur, and its long claws scratched across the table.

I fell to the floor, striking my tailbone. Ignoring the pain, I scrambled across the linoleum to the counter, daring not to look back.

"Something wrong, Little Red?"

The Darkness Between

I glanced over as he finished his meal. He dabbed the edge of a smile with his napkin. His reflection shifted back.

I froze, searching for words stuck in my throat.

A loud crash broke through the diner. My attention shot to the kitchen, where my grandfather screamed, "Roisin!"

I found my feet and ran to him. A trail of bloody paw prints lead to the back door.

I stepped outside and saw my grandfather's body crumpled beneath the dumpster. His stomach was ripped open, and a pool of rain and blood formed around his body. He opened his mouth to speak, but his words were muted by gurgling blood.

Tears burned behind my eyes as I dialed 911. Another howl broke through the storm.

Ding!

The front door opened. I rushed into the kitchen and peered into the empty diner. All that remained of the mysterious guest was a large tip and a handwritten note on a napkin.

"See you soon, Little Red."

Scared Straight

Michael J. Moore

I couldn't breathe, let alone climb a six-foot-wooden fence, but the red and blue lights flashing in the night sky were growing brighter. The sirens echoed inside my head, mixing with the beat of my racing heart and a dog's bark. My shadow appeared then vanished, repeatedly against the wood. In that moment, I found a will that existed somewhere between what was impossible and what was necessary.

Straightening my body, I reached up, grabbed the ledge of the fence, and felt splinters dig into my hands as I hoisted myself over. I dropped on damp grass, nearly slipping.

The lights grew brighter, and the sirens louder, and then they passed. Car prowling was a misdemeanor in California. I had never been to jail, and at twenty-two, the thought of it scared the shit out of me.

I examined the blue, two-story, home with a balcony atop a wooden staircase. I exhaled, finally relaxing when I saw the lights were off and there was no doghouse.

Reaching into my pocket, I fished out the stolen iPhone and checked the time: 12:22 a.m.

I looked up. A small tin shed caught my eye. Just what I needed.

I pried open the shed doors; the scraping metal-on-metal was obnoxiously loud as I squeezed my thin body through.

The second I was inside, the doors slammed shut so hard the impact echoed like a gunshot. The smell of mold and motor oil choked my lungs. I grappled with the doors, but they wouldn't budge.

I feared that the homeowner had padlocked me in until the police could arrive. I spun on my heels, broken glass crunching under my feet, and became entangled in a spider's web. I swiped frantically, tumbling backward into a stack of cardboard boxes and plastic bins. One fell, barely missing me, and crashed on the concrete floor, spilling metal pieces that clinked like silverware.

I needed to move, to get the hell out of there, because somebody was still outside, and the police would be here any second. I wasn't halfway through this thought, when the walls began to shake violently like a giant was outside rattling the entire structure.

"I'm just gonna leave!" I called out. "I don't want any problems. I'm not here to steal from you!"

"Really?" the smooth voice of a twenty-something woman rang out from right behind me.

I jumped, startled, and the pile of storage came down like an avalanche, right on top of me. A power tool crashed on my collarbone, but I ignored the pain. The woman laughed, and she was so close I could feel her breath on the back of my neck. An electric chill rushed from the bottom of my tailbone to the tips of my hair, but nobody was there.

At this, she laughed even harder. "Good night to be out prowling, eh?"

"Oh, holy—" My voice shook.

"What's your story, man?" Her own voice became as tranquil and indifferent as a cashier at the checkout counter. "Robbing houses? Mugging? What are you, twenty-one? Twenty-two? Wait—did you shoot someone?"

I hated myself for trying the doors again, and even more so when I heard the word, "Please," spill from my mouth, like it was on autopilot.

"What is it?" she asked. "Drugs? Are you on drugs, dude? Is that your issue?"

And because I was more horrified than I had ever been in my life, I cried, "Yeah! Yes! Yes, I'm a meth addict! I'm sorry!"

"You don't have to be sorry to me. It's your life. Lemme tell you a story, about a woman around your age who made some dumbass decisions and found herself living in a shed, shooting heroin. It was one of those sheds they keep on display in the parking lot at the hardware store. Well, that's where she overdosed and died, and eventually, the shed was sold and put in a yard where some idiot kid broke into it. I guess it's fitting he should die in it too, don't you think?"

Once she'd uttered the last word, a chainsaw revved to life, and exhaust fumes filled the room. She laughed as the doors flew open.

I didn't think—I just sprinted through the yard, hopped the fence, and jogged all the way home, where I vowed to check myself into rehab as soon as the sun came up.

Z

J. Paré

I bought an elegant old house in Connecticut, right along the border of Rhode Island. Shortly after settling in, I spotted a large oak tree in the middle of my backyard that I was sure hadn't been there the night before. The bulky mass had thick, long branches with narrow, twisted ends, towering unnaturally over the house.

Its lumbering mass posed a hazard to my home if it ever fell, so I set aside the weekend to remove it. The tree fought back with hidden hands, bleeding a thick and syrupy sap. But after six hours, I cut it down, and my chainsaw hated me for it.

After it finally toppled over, I went to bed exhausted and dreamed of children screaming.

* * *

The next morning, I took coffee to my back porch and dropped my mug. As tall as the night before, stood the mighty oak. The only evidence of my cutting was thick bark around its middle, like a scab over skin.

I touched its trunk, and the bark tightened around my fingers. I tried to remove my hand, but the sap held me like glue. Sensing the malevolence inside the tree, I pulled my hand away and wiped the residue on my pants.

I heard a voice whisper in the leaves, "Won't you join us? We are Z; we are Omega."

I broke free of its trance and ran back into the house, locking the door. Perhaps if I avoided looking at it, things would be fine.

* * *

Weeks went by, and the incident dropped from my mind until I noticed my lawn had overgrown. I began to mow the grass when I bumped into the loathsome tree. I froze, feeling unseeing eyes on me.

"We're hungry, David. Won't you feed us?"

I cupped my hands over my ears, though it was of no use. Z spoke again, "Come on, David, give us a hug."

I tried to block it out of my thoughts, though no matter where I went, the blasted thing was inescapable. The more I thought about it, the more it called me to it. "Join us."

The tree became my one and only obsession. I was determined to destroy it at any cost. This time I would have to remove it root and all, leaving no stump to regrow.

I found a spade in the garage and dug deep into its roots, shaped like long, twisted, wooden fingers. I did my best to ignore its taunts, but no matter how deep I dug, there were always deeper roots.

I grew despondent at my failure as the laughing tendrils closed around me.

I whispered, "I need a hug."

Umbrilus

Edward Suggs

I come to my senses. Blotchy, squirmy, cowardly spots flick
away from my pupils. My fingers dig into the soil and my
thighs work me off of the earth. Small roots entangle my torso
and snag me back to the ground.
Oh yes,
this young wood is trying to eat me alive.
It was about time some life grew into the moors. And by God,
it grew! Grew like mold in some discarded wet clothes. Such
an appetite it has, having no respect for my world. I beg for the
townsfolk to join my side, but I see them petting the trees at
night. I'm simply surprised something like this hasn't happened
until now. After all, there's opportunity in this wetland.
I tug off my wooden parasites.
Their spiteful roots crumble away.
They are worms writhing like tobacco-stained fingernails.
Struggling to steal an easy way out.
My fingers are caked in dirt.
Funny enough,

It's the dirt the sleepers eat too.
But they aren't writhers;
Not for tobacco or anything.
No, they sleep.
Why I like 'em.

I haven't been outta the graveyard for... A few... Well, it's been a few days, I suppose. My bones long for my bed, they sure do. I'm growing rather tired of the company of these dirt sleepers, despite our common interests.

I look to the sparse forest outside the perimeter of the church. The trees don't know me much, but I'd wager this swamp does—and this town does, too.

... And they know that I'm going back home.

Those newly placed church windows wink when the sun sees me through the other side. What a good young devil that fat old sun is! I keep well away from the chapel, for I don't want history to repeat itself. And that pastor of ours has a real jittery trigger finger, I'll tell you what.

I step over the cluttered gravestones, gripping the tongue-tip of the hewn rocks.

My fleshy fingers erode away the infinite moss and roots.
A parade of dirt crescendos around my back.

I say farewell to my new friends! I, admittedly, grew too comfortable there. I'll be sure to keep my head turned well away from it.

My eyes follow the hugging ring of cottages praying to the church.

My queasy frame slips between Victorian-style houses, leading to an old shanty.

I am a moth clinging to the light.
I close my eyes and feel the warmth.
I am not man enough to face the spectacle with my best sense.
There is so much shame inside of me!
I unsheathe a key from my pocket.
Unlocked.

The door opens, and an overwhelming stench fills my nostrils.

"Nikolla?"

I feel... No, I hear a dizzying low hum.

No...

I open my eyes.

God!

The forest has reclaimed my home. Thick and mutilated branches breach the walls and greenery sprouts from the cracks in the floor. Splinters form a nest in the center of the room. Items from the house are weaved into its design in a combination of two worlds.

My Nikolla...

Her pale, slimy body is curled cozily into the nest. She... clutches something to her chest. I peer into her arms, and the hum rattles my vision. She holds a vaguely translucent egg to her heart. It drips a residual discharge onto her bosom.

Out of guilt—or fear—I dare not behold her face, but I cannot tell if she is awake or asleep.

And how I   Wish,   in this moment,

I had stayed back in the graveyard!

Instead, I found a putrid noise making my ears itch.

There is a fresh stream dribbling out of them... Blood.

Oh, dear! I feel as though this isn't fair. I was given silent ignorance, but this pries open my head and shovels into me a gurgling pain. I did not know there could exist something so unrelentless. I can bear the sound no more.

As I think of this, the invading branches slither up my torso for an embrace. Alarmed, I try to shake myself free.

My feet fumble over the vines as I stumble through the door.

Rooftop squatting leaves drip onto the narrow path— and It's just my luck, too. Oh, how I despise the decaying leaves that dance their mournful piece.

I am running from the trees' grasp, away from my dilapidated village.

Suddenly, I notice, the deeper I dive into the swamp, the deeper the roots grow.

I trudge into this quagmire.

The woods open up, revealing a peculiar, frowning tree.

The tree perceives me with its first eye

and comes to know me.

In that twinkling moment,

> it suckers me with its great maw.
> I'm unable to struggle;
> I am the flesh of the great deceiving tree.

* * *

The village is now in consort with the forest,
whose many new limbs sway in the wind.

To the Condemned

Cory DeAn Cowley

Condemned Lover
#7 Circle
The Dark Pit, Outer Darkness

To the Condemned,

There is no greater pleasure than watching the life in your eyes slip into the nether regions of darkness, the subterranean caverns that wind into endless mazes.

     I watch, and I wait, and I feast my eyes on the prey. Such a pitiful sight to see arrogance wither like a rotted piece of meat. But that's all you are: a rotted piece of meat. I live to serve a master so content in watching the haphazard struggle of human life.

     The desperation, the sweat that pours from every pore—it's a joy, a delight even.

     Do you know what it feels like to crush someone's soul between your fists like a dried orange? I do. I know what it's like because I've watched bare hands sever the windpipe and choke the last vestige of innocence from my body. I hated watching the capillaries in your eyes bulge from watching me suffer, and in turn, watching you struggle is a suitable punishment.

And now we are here. Oh, but a sweet, little nugget you are. So ripe in your fear and so absentminded in your confidence. You know, I used to think I would always be a little girl who played with her dolls. But then Ken wasn't so pretty, and Malibu wasn't real.

But it's okay because now, who is the one clawing at life when life has come to cycle back around? Snakes aren't so sly when their heads are cut off, and scales look very pretty on clothes. Oh, what a shame; you're being hunted. Pity, here everyone was thinking how tragic you are. A martyr unto us all and the thief that hung with Jesus on his cross. No, you're just prey now. A slave of karma and a servant to the lord who stamps on those with cloven hooves. And I smile every time you moan out of pain. Your misery is my drug injecting into my soul, like black tar heroin.

It's not so fun, is it, darling?

The agony is something you'll never forget like I never forgot.

Oh, but you did forget something. Vengeance is kind to the woman of scorn. And his mercy upon thee is the crown upon her head.

No Longer Yours Truly,

C

The Monster Within

Jen Ellwyn

A gravel pathway churned beneath the 1987 station wagon, sharp and rocky under its tires. The car passed through a thin corridor of trees, which opened up to a clearing. In the center of it, a cabin stood erect, shrouded in navy hues of twilight.

The cabin was crooked and ghastly. The shingles were peeling from the roof like old skin from an unsuccessful reptile shed—so black they almost appeared burnt. A fungus grew in the crevices of the cabin's facade and one shutter hung from a second-floor window by a single rusty nail on a single rusty hinge.

The station wagon crept to a halt in front of the porch, its brakes squeaking in agony. A man stepped out of the vehicle, followed by an eight-year-old boy. "We made it," the man sighed. "Just before dark."

The child rubbed his eyes, tired from the long day of hiking with his dad. He was looking forward to getting a full night's rest in preparation for their fishing expedition.

After they unpacked the station wagon, it was time to settle in for the night. Inside the cabin, a few landscape paintings adorned the bruised and battered walls. A dusty grandfather clock ticked in the corner, though it was a complete mystery how it still functioned considering the condition it was in.

"Tell me a story," the boy asked as he climbed into bed, "about a Norse giant... or a Greek god." He shifted down further under the covers, bunching the loose edge of the sheets around his chin.

"How about I tell you a story... about an Eldritch monster?" his father enticed, sitting on the edge of the mattress.

"An Eldritch monster?" Thomas echoed, intrigued by the new word.

"Mhmm," his father hummed with a nod. "A very scary monster that lives in the woods."

"What does it look like?" Thomas whispered.

"Nobody knows," his father whispered back.

"How come?"

"Nobody's ever seen it," his father explained. "Except for the people it kills, but they don't live to tell the tale."

"Nobody?" Thomas emphasized.

"Nobody," his father confirmed. "It lives in the shadows, and the shadows make it strong." He continued, "It sneaks up behind people when they're not looking. It snatches them, when they least expect it."

"What does it do to them?" Thomas worried.

"No one knows. All they know is it makes people... disappear," his father breathed. "One by one. Gone without a trace. It hides inside people." The father's finger came to rest over the boy's chest, then it moved to his own. "Like you and me."

Thomas didn't like the thought of that.

The father's finger settled over the child again, lightly poking into the boy's ribs. "It buries itself deep, deep down within us."

Thomas focused on the feeling of pressure upon his chest. His father's finger was like a penetrating harpoon. He imagined it being the monster, trying to embed itself in his heart.

His father released his finger and rested his hand upon the boy's chest, relaxed and harmless. "It's very good at hiding," the man continued. "One moment, you're lying in bed, looking up at your glow stars..." He tilted his head to look up at the green galaxy above them.

248

Thomas followed his gaze upward. He loved his glow stars. They made the cabin feel a bit more like home.

"And the next thing you know… you're gone!"

The loose edge of Thomas' bedsheet whisked over his head.

Thomas unleashed a muffled scream and struggled, but his father's hand kept the material pinned tightly over him.

A moment later, Thomas was allowed to thrash free. The child's gasp instantly morphed into laughter.

Beside him, his father chuckled too. As he stood up to leave, he murmured, "Sweet dreams, son."

"Goodnight, Dad."

Left in the company of his own thoughts, Thomas' smile faded away.

He couldn't sleep.

He knew he shouldn't be afraid of monsters, yet as the hours slowly ticked by, something nagged at him. Something buried itself deep, deep inside his head. It was that irrational, childish fear of a certain Eldritch monster that the shadows supposedly strengthened. He reminded himself it was nothing but a silly story his father had concocted to scare him.

The child stared up at the dull green radiance of his glow-in-the-dark stars and tried his best to doze off into some sort of sleep.

Then, he heard a scream. It sliced the air in two, resonating from a near distance.

Thomas snapped awake, his heart pounding in his chest. Every muscle in his body was frozen with a paralyzing terror. His glow stars were dim, their chemical reservoirs empty of borrowed light. As fear slowly ebbed through his veins, a sense of dire curiosity tangled with his confusion.

Another scream echoed in the night, wretched and ragged—tapered by a dwindling sob.

Thomas' discomfort level skyrocketed beyond what he could tolerate, and he slipped out of bed to approach the window. Outside, the night sky was endlessly dark, like a gaping black hole midway through the process of swallowing the Earth. He pressed his forehead to the cold glass, watching the petrified forest for any sign of life as his breath fogged up his view. The car was still parked where they'd left it, in front of the porch. Thomas scanned the treeline. The pines were so still, they seemed frozen. The world felt frozen, trapped in an eternal night.

Thomas bundled himself in a coat, fetched his pocket knife from his camping bag, and snuck out of his room.

Despite his best efforts to move quietly, his steps *creak, creak, creaked* down the feeble wooden staircase. He extended his knife in front of him with both hands. It was usually reserved for whittling driftwood, but now it acted more as a comfort item than anything.

Downstairs, one dusty lightbulb dangled from the exposed ribs of the ceiling slats, fighting valiantly to combat the night. But like his glow stars, it succumbed to darkness. A taunting breeze batted at its corpse like an invisible housecat.

His father was gone. Thomas couldn't find him anywhere in the house, and he grew sick with an overwhelming sense of abandonment. Had his father left to investigate the screams, only to fall victim to whatever made them? He must have, for the back door was open.

Not only was it open, it was gaping—like the maw of a beast. It was a void that perpetually inhaled, intent on consuming him. It reeled him in as if he were a hooked minnow, its ominous attraction irresistible. The longer he stood there thinking about all of the terrible things that he couldn't see out there in the woods— all of the terrible things that fed off the darkness—the faster his heart pounded against his chest. He couldn't help but imagine an Eldritch creature made of nebulous black smoke, who would either kill him or bury itself deep within him. Either way, the next thing he'd know... he'd be gone.

Thomas carefully stepped out into the chilled night air—moving sluggishly, as if he was sleepwalking. He kept moving, desperate to find his father. The forest was soaking wet and aromatic, as if the sky had wept. The boy ventured further and further into the woods, debating whether it would be wise or moronic to call out for his dad.

Then, he saw it. The source of the screams.

It wasn't a monster. It was a woman, bound to the trunk of an oak. Nylon ropes dug into her wrists as she tried to pull and twist her limbs free, but the knots did not budge or give way. Her lips were bleeding profusely, frothing with white foam, and haphazardly sutured shut like a ragdoll. She saw him and began hyperventilating through her closed orifice. Soon her whimpers and whines escalated to muffled cries of hysteria.

Thomas stared at her. His orbs were wide and full, as if he'd forever forgotten how to blink.

She continued sputtering through the sutures and bile, the foam turning pink with blood—the same pastel shade as her nightgown. She seemed to be whimpering and nodding to the knife in his hands.

Thomas snapped out of his trance, rushed forward, and put the blade up to the nylon to begin sawing at it. It severed each thread in the tight, twisted rope with a small *snap, snap, snap.*

He asked the lady some questions, but she didn't answer him, only wildly glanced at the gaps of darkness between the trees as if she expected something to descend upon them at any second, bringing their death with it.

"Is there a monster out here?" he whispered.

She nodded profusely and began to weep when the *snap, snap, snap* of the nylon rope became drowned out by the *snap, snap, snap* of twigs being crushed in the nearby underbrush. The monster was coming.

Thomas sawed through the bindings faster, though every instinct within him screamed for him to leave her and run.

A final snap of the nylon, and she was free.

The released woman collapsed to the ground.

Thomas yelled for her to run with him back to the cabin, but she couldn't. Something was wrong with her legs. They were twisted and broken. Thomas hesitated to leave her behind, wishing there was something he could—

"Thomas."

The child whirled around.

"I see you've found Delilah," his father smiled.

The woman screamed through her sewn lips.

The boy looked between them, demanding, "What's going on?!"

The man smirked as he took a step forward. "It's alright, son."

Delilah writhed on the ground, choking on the foam spilling from her stitched mouth. She propped herself on her arms and started to crawl away.

The boy watched her nervously eyeing his father. In a hoarse whisper, he said, "What's wrong with her? Why is she out here?"

"She's sick," his father answered, taking another step toward him. "I'm helping her."

Thomas backed up against the tree. With tears in his eyes, he gripped his knife with both hands.

"She's in a lot of pain, Thomas," the man murmured without looking at Delilah. He held out one hand. "Will you give that to me?"

The boy struggled to breathe, glancing down at his knife. "What are you gonna do?" he croaked.

"There's only one thing I can do for her," his father answered. He knelt in front of the boy, his palm still upturned and waiting to receive the tool he asked for. "Remember when your friend took his terrier to the veterinarian when it was very, very sick? The vet said that the creature was in too much pain and that it would be cruel to keep him alive."

Thomas blinked and tried to piece everything together. "He killed it," the boy translated, his heart clenching in agony.

"Yes," his father answered softly. "But… he killed it because he didn't want it to suffer anymore." His tone changed from kind to hollow. "Now, give me the knife."

Thomas's heart drummed, fear immobilizing him.

"It's the only thing we can do for her, Thomas. You don't want her to keep suffering, do you?"

Thomas couldn't answer him. He could only stand there and stare as his father reached forward and gently took the blade from his tight fist, peeling his small fingers away like they were flower petals.

Then, he stood and walked over to where the woman had crawled, a trail of pink, bloody foam snaking behind her to mark where she'd dragged herself across the ground. The man readied the tool over the woman's trembling body.

At the last second, Thomas managed to squeeze his eyes shut to spare himself from watching the murder. But he still heard it. He heard the chink, shink, squelch, smock, and splatter.

He heard Delilah wail, choke, garble, and finally exhale a deflating wheeze.

252

He heard his father suggest, "Now, why don't you go back to bed?"

Thomas was too stunned to speak, having trouble discerning if this was a nightmare or reality. He dared to open his eyes, and did well to stare down at his feet where he knew he wouldn't be greeted with a gory sight.

"Go ahead, son. I'll be right behind you."

Caught in a debilitating trance, Thomas slowly turned to go. His steps were dragging and sullen. Part of him wanted to run. Part of him wanted to scream. But another part of him warned him to move very slowly, and not make a single sound, lest he provoke the monster within.

His sense of self-preservation conquered his panic. He walked toward the cabin calmly and obediently. But as soon as he was free of the trees, oh, how he was going to run. He'd run straight past the cabin and straight down the gravel road toward the highway. He'd run far, far away, and he would not fear the darkness of the night. It couldn't be as terrible as that within his own father.

He dragged his gaze upward, toward the stars. They twinkled encouragingly at him, oh so far away. A blue hue was starting to permeate the horizon, promising the eventual light of day. Promising freedom.

But the next thing he knew...

Elizabeth

Sara Brunner

The fiery moon shines upon the blood soaked shoreline. Streaks
of scarlet tinged droplets are splattered throughout the pearl-white
sand. For a battle raged on here. Not just for the body but for the
mind and soul also. Elizabeth had won the war, but at what cost?
Her soul is decimated and her mind is shattered and broken.

Her legacy would forever be tainted, skewed, and destroyed. Washed away in a crimson tide of madness. Made out to
be the monster that she was forced to become.

Backed into a corner until the beast came out. Tearing
her enemies limb by limb. Eviscerating them till there was
nothing left but the pools of blood at her feet. Ruby red remind-
ers that there is no turning back now.

She must embrace who she has become. Let the monster wrap its vines around her now blackened heart. Let the
thorns penetrate her decaying soul. Let the flames of tragedy
consume her in a feverish rage. Only to be reborn in the blood-
soaked waters, the dark entity that this world had created.

Elizabeth

Sara Brunner

Birdie's Journal

Angeli Castellanos

Evidence
Trial Exhibit: ST:0090

8/8/10
So basically im writing in the dumb diary because of my
counselor. She says that I'm "too distant" and have "behavior-
al problems". Like what am i supposed to do, talk to people i
don't like and don't care for... HELL NO!! She's trippin.

But my mom says that the best way to fix something is from
the beginning. Even writing in a stupid diary. Nope nevermind,
journal. Well to start off, my name is Birdie Goldn. And yes I
heard all the birdie golf puns so save it will ya. I like "collecting" bottle caps, buttons, coins, rings, cards, hair pins, anything
I can get my hands on really. Sounds pretty weird but once it
catches my eye, I just can't help but take it.

The Darkness Between

8/10/10

Believe it or not i don't have a lot of friends. Well I got Moses and Tedo but they're ok half of the time. Mostly they talk about cars and girls that won't even look at them. And I wouldn't blame em, we all have achy and scrawny bodies. Well except Moses, he's the biggest in the grade. But together all of us really dont give a fuck. Which makes people say we are "too quiet".

8/11/10

Today I realized I ALMOST like one of my classes. Well, I liked part of the lesson Mr.Mcvay taught today. He might actually teach some interesting stuff this year. Well, at least I thought it was interesting. Other kids said it was "morbid" or whatever, but knowing how a murder detective does their job is extremely useful. Especially so you know how NOT to kill someone and get rid of the evidence. You'd have to be an idiot not to think of it that way. Gotta think like a detective to dupe a detective, obviously. I mean, not that I would kill anyone and have to hide their dead body or anything. But IF I was, don't you think I'd want to be good at it?

8/21/10

School once again has proven to be the most boring thing on this planet that I'm living in. It has only been a month in this abominable school year. There's only two things that's been keeping me from dying now and actually surviving this apoc-alypse. Lunch, and the dark haired girl that just transferred to school last week. Her name is Sorina. Every school day is a hell hole, but every class with her makes it seem like heaven. Hopefully I'll get guts to talk to her before I'm 50.

8/22/10

"Give me envy, give me malice, give me your attention"-panic at the disco

9/11/10

As Moses, Tedo, and I were eating lunch, Moses had the "Bright" idea to try and get Alexas digits, (AKA Moe's monster crush) so Tedo and I hype him up saying stuff like "ok big guy" and "go on then loverboy". Moses walked up to her and started

258

chatting her up. I bust out laughing and Tedo had milk coming out his nose. But lo and behold here comes the NSYNC wannabes (Seth, Maliki, and Duncan. All different but equally as douchey). They walk up to Moses and start tossing him around like a fish in shark infested waters. They were being assholes and called him "fatboy", "tubby", and " little dick".

THESE BOYS REALLY THINK THEY CAN MESS WITH MY FRIEND LIKE I WON'T BEAT THEM TO A PULP!!!

I got up, ran towards the crowd of people and clocked Seth right in his jaw. Once the other two held him up straight, he grabbed my arm and put me in a choke hold. I thought I was actually gonna DIE. "

BREAKING NEWS: TEEN BOY GETS CHOKED OUT DURING CAFETERIA FIGHT"
But thankfully before I passed out Mrs.Wilton and the principle broke up the fight. I mean, I could have taken him but I lost my footing that's all. But before escorting us to the office, Seth said something that made my stomach drop "YOUR NEXT BIRD SHIT"

9/11/10
I hate people who think that they can be the boss of everyone. I hate the way they talk and I especially hate the way they talk to me. They act like I'm the weird one, when they have no clue what they look like.

9/12/10
I MESSED UP!!!
I REALLY FUCKED SHIT UP THIS TIME!!!

WHY AM I SUCH AN IDIOT!!!

WELL WHAT WAS I SUPPOSED TO DO, IT WAS EITHER ME OR HIM!!!

Listen after Seth said "YOUR NEXT" I literally couldn't stop shitting myself. BUT I REALLY DID IT THIS TIME.

Let me start from the beginning. After fifth period Seth and
his douchey lap-dogs came up to me, grabbed my shirt and
said "Hey faggot, meet me after school behind the old church
off of Carr Ave. Come alone, AND DON'T BE LATE!!!"

After that he spat in my face and pushed me to the ground.
On the outside I shrugged it off to look cool, but on the inside
I was having a full on panic attack. What was I gonna do? I
had to fight him. I'm not a punk. So after school I went home,
changed, and started heading to the spot. The walk was 3
miles away but it felt like 10.

I made it to the church praying that I couldn't get any broken
bones and just have a few cuts and bruises during this. I saw
Seth sitting alone on a tree stomp. In an intimidating grin he
says "Oh wow you really came, you must really be ok with
dying" I take a deep breath and say "The only person that's
gonna be laid out on this grass is you". The second those
words escaped my mouth, I regretted it.

We start throwing punches, I went for his groin and head while
he got my stomach. Blow after blow I get weaker and
weaker but the rage in me gets stronger and stronger. Nearing the end he punches me in the face knocking out one of
my teeth. Angry as hell I grab his neck tightly, crushing his
throat with my finger tips. I let go after he kicked my shin.
Then I shoved him on to the ground.

"YOU HAD ENOUGH YET!!!" I yell as he slams his head
against a cinder block. But he just lays there, not talking,
not moving, not...breathing. I shake him trying to get him
awake, but I'm too late. Blood covers the back of his head
and the cinder block. I try not freak myself out and think
what i have to do do i call the police? no. go to the hospital? no. especially when i have his blood on my hands there
will be lots of questions. Freaking out I drag his body to the
stream behind the abandoned church. Then I realize that the
stream is shallow and if he did float the steam covers most of
the town.

Then I got an idea. I break into the church window then drag and pull him through the window. It was dark from the inside and out so nobody saw me. But it was a small church so there weren't a lot of places to hide him. As I walked around I tripped on a plank of wood covered in moss and stickers. I lifted up the floorboard and found a hole that could probably fit a person. I push him into the floorboard one leg bent and the other over his head.

After that I crawled out the window, went back to the stream, dug a hole, and buried the cinderblock so nothing could be traced back to me. But before I left I saw Seth's watch laying in the ground, so I took it just for safe keepings. I ran home, ran up stairs, put my clothes in the trash, and took a shower. But however long or hard or much I wash my skin I still feel… dirty…

9/13/10
"Seth?" echoed through the classroom as the teacher called out attendance."Maybe he's sick" said a boy with a blonde bowl cut. "He's probably late again" said an annoying girl. Just act like everything is normal…I didn't do anything, he just fell and hit his head. And I had to hide him because the blame would be put on all me that's all. Just keep it cool and twiddle your thumbs.

9/14/10
Can I just be a little kid again?
No stress, no worries, just…fun. I guess it's too late for that.

9/15/10
I met with my counselor and she asked me how I was doing. I lied and said i was happy but i just feel dark inside and i kinda like it. Maybe i should do it again.

Stars and Carpet

Abishek Parapuzha

Glistening through the sky, beams of light enter and reenter the atmosphere. There was a woman who lived nearby. She sat in her apartment, lost and alone, despite being surrounded by busy city. Alacrity seemed like a faraway feeling.

She stood, moving like molasses. She snuffled. No tears were evident, and no remorse was to be found. She clutched the knife loosely. And rose it to her neck. Someone had once said her neck was a beautiful landscape.

She sliced horizontally. Her veins oozed.

The knife dropped to the floor, hitting the carpet with a soft thud. The carpet wasn't ready for this today. The blue tones started to weep. The red tones started to laugh. The pattern was swirling slowly as the woman sat down on the carpet. Her knees buckled and her hips slowly flopped down. She smiled and her eyes glistened like stars. Alacrity!

Run

Christopher M. Fink

The dark, endless highway rolled under the headlights. Darlene had lost track of the miles she covered since leaving behind everything she knew. The thought of her husband's disloyalty—the destruction of a life they'd spent more than a decade building was too much to bear. Escape was all she wanted, but it did little to console her. After three hours of driving along the east coast, from Vermont to northwest Massachusetts, her mind raced with scenarios, guided by the memory of questionable phone conversations she had with Lucas over the last few weeks.

Darlene was in dire need of a stretch. There was no traffic, which gave her plenty of time to pull over and get out without the threat of a speeding car or truck rushing by. It was that very isolation she hoped would settle her mind.

She stepped out of the car and made her way around to the front, in plain view of the headlights.

Darlene rested a leg on the guard rail, the blood rushing back to her extremities.

She tried to enjoy the calm breeze and the clean air, but thoughts of Lucas stirred inside her. *What was he doing right now?* She convinced herself it didn't matter; this was her time to get her bearings.

How could you betray me?

In the midst of her sorrow, something stamped behind her. She turned to the noise, but saw nothing. She remembered seeing a sign a while back that warned of wolves in the area. Not wanting to risk it, she rushed back to her car.

The car began to roll forward as something wet slapped against the rear passenger side window. Darlene spun in time to see a tentacle hand brush the length of the rear window. She stifled a scream, and started the car, not daring to look back.

Having lost sight of it now for several minutes, she let off the accelerator a bit, but the fear and shock remained. Darlene caught sight of the blinking gas icon on the dashboard. As much as she tried to ignore the warning, it had to be addressed.

Her salvation lay ahead in the prominent LED lights advertising gas prices, the red beams of light cutting through the trees. Darlene parked under the oppressive fluorescent white lights above.

She closed her eyes. *You're being crazy; nothing's chasing you.*

She stepped out of the car, fumbling with the nozzle, cursing herself, before finally getting the pump started. *Get the gas, and get the hell out of here.*

The road, the station, the surrounding woods—they were deserted. Darlene scanned the windows of the gas station, but couldn't see a clerk or customers. She was alone, and the silence was closing in on her.

She focused on the sound of gas pumping. The flow of liquid momentarily eased her mind before she heard it again. The same faint stamping of a being approached her from the dark.

A hand came to her shoulder, and she nearly collapsed onto the ground, "Need any help?"

It was the gas station clerk.

She choked out a "no" and replaced the nozzle. She started to say something else, but a loud crash came from the back of the gas station.

She and the clerk exchanged astonished looks. As he ran off to investigate, Darlene clambered into her car, speeding off down the road.

After a few miles, her gas light came on again, and this time she was caught between stations, stranded on the side of the road.

She got out and checked under the car. A pool of gas formed under the tank. She could call someone, but there was only one person who would help her this late.

She heard the stamping again.

The wet, slapping steps of the figure grew closer, and before Darlene could decide, her body snapped into a sprint in the other direction. Checking over her shoulder, she caught a glimpse of its sweeping elongated limbs.

Darlene's lungs burned as she faced an increasing incline. Tears flowed as her knees buckled under the strain. She could hear her hunter closing the distance.

In a final effort, almost in defiance, Darlene stopped, and turned to face her pursuer.

She found herself facing only the night. Was it gone for good, or had she merely imagined the whole thing? Not waiting for the answer, she continued on toward the next town.

No matter the cost, she'd keep running.

On a Dark Road

C.M. Forest

Alison got out of her car, the engine still on, and started walking down the road. Blood soaked through the front of her dress. It looked black—like a growing oil spill—under the haze of the street lights. A smattering trail of circles on the pavement marked her route as she stumbled away. Her underwear, torn and soiled, hung limply around one ankle.

   She did not want to look back at the car, but a deep, primal urge overrode her wants and desires. Even as her body trembled, she found herself peeking over her shoulder. Tendrils of mist, seeping from the nearby dark fields, gave her vehicle a ghostly appearance—a three-thousand-pound wraith waiting to lunge. The headlights, blazing through the fog, stared back at her. The fender, a taunting grin. Specks of blood dotted the windshield from the inside; gory handprints stained the seats.

   Something moved within the car. An arm, a face, briefly—horribly—illuminated by the interior lights. A shifting figure, covered in a blanket of shining viscera. It was already bigger than it should be. It was growing fast.

"Oh, God, please help me." The prayer fell past her trembling lips. "I didn't know." The tears came soon after. A small, distant corner of her mind commended her on keeping up for so long—on showing the fortitude to hold back the fear, the pain. But she could do so no longer.

Her body sundered, her mind flayed, she could no more stop the tears as she could keep the sun from rising the next day.

"Maaawwwrr." The cry, which issued from the back of the car, caused Alison to stop. Even her trembling, tormented muscles stilled. Helplessly, all she could do was stare at the car as it rocked slightly.

She remembered the night it all began. It was seared into her brain: the scent of the candles, all black, dripping wax, and angry orange flame. The sound of the witnesses; their robes brushing the floor like a chorus of whispers. The dais, with its arcane engravings hard against her bare back. She recalled the chanting and the singing. And then… Then, it came. Not a man, but rather the absence of one. A void. A walking oblivion.

Time ceased to exist. All light collapsed in on itself. She was taken to the threshold, to the event horizon of madness. And then it was over. Something new, undefinable, left inside her.

Alison had pledged herself to the cause. But as the months went by, and her stomach grew, she realized she had to get away. To try and find salvation.

Now, watching the back door of the car swing open, she knew she had made a terrible mistake. She should have thrown herself into the river. Or jumped in front of a transport truck. She should have done anything, everything, in her power to stop the child from being born.

She willed her legs to move, but she had nothing left. The thing she had birthed fell from the backseat. The sound of its tender body hitting the asphalt like rotten meat falling to the floor. It mewled and whined, before rising on unnaturally strong legs. Horrible arms raised, it cried for its mother again before starting toward her.

BONUS STORIES

Ghost in My Soul

Elizabeth Suggs

There's a ghost in my soul who haunts me at night. His shadowed form drifts just out of reach, ready to pounce. He stares at me while I sleep and trails me when I walk through unlit halls.

I feel his fingers up my spine, his breath at my neck. In the dark, I convince myself he isn't real, yet I know he's there. Some nights, I hardly notice, but others, he is the clamp on my chest—the reason my lungs squeeze tight.

And he will never let go.

Maelstrom

Jonathan Reddoch

Two unlucky men break into a fine townhouse. They plan not, they think not, they heed not.

As they rummage through random cabinets and overturn furniture, Mother Mariona hides in the closet with Daughter Providence.

The younger of the two reprobates, Clarence, spots a twitching slipper under the closet door. He yanks it open and his accomplice, Davine, drags the cowering pair out, laughing. They plan to make vile sport of their captives.

Knives shine brightest just before dawn.

Mariona shakes her captors loose, "Take what you will. We care not for treasures on earth."

The intruders repent not from their unrighteous path. "Your trinkets are an afterthought. It is your heads we were hired to collect." Their loud laughter and mocking jeers only intensify.

"No, you worldly fools," testifies Providence, dark eyes growing molten. With the strength of ten unshaven men, she sends them flying across the room. "Mother hid me not for my sake, but for yours." She raises her cupped hands nigh and unholy water the color red runneth over, baptizing the floor in fire and brimstone, preparing the way.

A new voice speaks, looming with powers great and ancient, "I, Maelstrom now cometh, to baptize all wicked men with my dark spirit." Providence had summoned the agent of chaotic evil to devour the prostrate wretches before them.

Maelstrom, the spirit of doomed deliverance, swallows them up, bone, liver, and greasy tendon. But leaving the eyes, nose, and ears intact. For every eye shall see, every nose shall smell, and every ear shall hear their own damnation.

As Maelstrom finishes his gruesome sup, Father Tomas returns to hearth and home, stupefied by the presence of the master of dark lights and unearthly delights. "I believe it not," he utters in disgust.

Maelstrom palms Tomas' head like a tiny plumb to be plucked.

"No, not daddy," cries Providence, "only the bad men."

Maelstrom snickers, "Your daddy this mortal is not." He looks at Mariona, who nods knowingly. He nods back and feasts on the pretender's head. Slurping up the entrails, he chortles, "Only the bad men," and disappears back into the sulphuric depths below.

All that remains alive of Tomas is his impure black heart, forever pumping within the family vault. It rests beside the unclaimed life insurance policy on Mariona and Providence purchased by the paterfamilias before he hired the two lowlife assassins.

AUTHOR BIOS

Elizabeth Suggs
Elizabeth Suggs is co-owner of the indie publisher Collective Tales Publishing, owner of Editing Mee, and is the author of a growing number of published stories, two of which were in a podcast and poetry journal. She is the president of two writing groups, one being part of the LUW. She's a book reviewer (www.EditingMee. com) and popular bookstagramer (@elizabethsuggsauthor). When she's not writing or reading, she's playing video/board games or making cookies.

Jonathan Reddoch
*Jonathan Reddoch is co-owner of Collective Tales Publishing. He is a father, writer, editor, and publisher. He writes sci-fi, fantasy, romance, and especially horror. He has been working on his enormous sci-fi novel for over a decade and would like to finish it in this lifetime if possible. Find him on Instagram: Allusions_of_Grandeur_*

Author Bios

Chris Jorgensen

Chris has often been described as an amalgamation of too many things for his own good. Writer, musician, academic, book collector, scavenger, builder, drinker, shiny object enthusiast. Horror is the gateway to the truly primal, the unknown void, and the creative outlet that can be explored without fear. He has written for online publications and short story collections for Utah Valley University. Currently, he reads far too much to have a singular favorite author, but is often inspired by: Patrick Rothfuss, Robert Jordan, H.P. Lovecraft, Stephen King, Brandon Sanderson, and Joe Abercrombie. One day he will be hopefully as well read as that list.

Jen Ellwyn

Jen is an emerging writer specializing in horror and fantasy with a background in theatre and film. In addition to being the author of the short story "Polter Geist" and "Monster Within." Jen also engineered the Collective Darkness *audiobook.*

B. Todd Orgill

B. Todd Orgill is a warehouse manager, avid outdoorsman, fitness enthusiast, and devourer of knowledge. His experience with horror has largely been relegated to personal experience, most of which was, luckily, non-Lovecraftian. He knows an unnatural number of digits of pi for no good reason at all. He's published several rather dreadful pieces of poetry and the odd short story. His favorite authors are Orson Scott Card, Brandon Sanderson, John Scalzi, Jim Butcher, and Patrick Rothfuss. He once read a book and thought, "I could do that" and has struggled to "do that" ever since, realizing that, in fact, writing is quite difficult. He loves mashed potatoes and sleeping through his alarm.

Austin Slade Perry

As a child, Austin was always told he had an overactive imagination. When he grew up, that imagination transformed into storytelling and his passion for writing. He also finds joy in other creative outlets, such as drawing, event organizing, and supporting his friends with their artistic passions. Writing has always been an important part of his life, and this project re-

minded him that it is always important to find happiness in the things you enjoy doing.

K.R. Patterson

K.R. is, first and foremost, a human, though a few of her psychiatric patients have told her she is not. She has been called a vampire, an alien, a mixed breed of cat/dog/dinosaur, and a mermaid—and is unable to rule out any of those possibilities. She is lured to studying psychopaths and writing horror because she is a curious cat (dog/dinosaur), and attracted to the occasional adrenaline rush. Besides the short story in this anthology, she has been published in Writer's Digest, *written and published a pirate novel titled* A Dead Man's Tale, *and has won various writing contests when she was able to satisfactorily use her vampire compelling spells. She also has a novella, "Snow White and the Blood Curse," which is in a fairy tale boxed set titled* Fractured Snow. *She enjoyed cracking the mirror, and the princess, a little too much.*

Brandon Prows

Brandon has a passion for fantasy that he gained at a young age after reading JRR Tolkien's The Lord of the Rings. *He also loves the horror genre thanks to the works of HP Lovecraft and Stephen King. He leisurely reads and enjoys playing video games and composing music in his free time. He is the copy editor of the anthology.*

Becca Rose

Customer service by day, killing characters off by night. Every story needs a little darkness to make it more complex and interesting. She listens to music while writing, either classical, alternative, or 90s punk, and reads her work aloud to her three pets. They give excellent feedback. Check out her other works at beccarosewriter.com.

Alex Child

Writing has a unique power, and Alex Child is just smart enough to know that he's nowhere near smart enough to accurately describe it. Between working half as hard as he should and twice as hard as required at his day job, he continues pursuing that indescribable emotional swell from relating to a literary character and sharing their experiences. He hopes his stories bring you even just a portion of that rush.

Edward Suggs

He is an award-winning author, included in all three Darkness *anthologies. He loves to write strange little things, which he hopes will urge you to look deeper. He also loves to make music and tries to convey feelings and concepts that he couldn't explain with words. Edward hopes to lead you to think in a way you may not have before.*

Samuel Smith

A Marine Corps veteran who currently works in the IT field. He spends some of his off-time writing, focused mostly on short humorous fiction which he sometimes posts on his blog, natterbanquet. He enjoys watching comedies and action/adventure shows, playing video games, disc golf, reading, and spending time with friends and family. He grew up in the midwest, but lives in Utah, longing to be back out east where the good thunderstorms are.

Michael J. Moore

His books include Highway Twenty, *which appeared on the Preliminary Ballot for the 2019 Bram Stoker Award, the best-selling post-apocalyptic novel,* After the Change, *which is used as curriculum at the University of Washington, the psychological thriller, Secret Harbor and the middle grade horror story,* Nightmares in Aston - Wicker Village. *His work has received awards, has appeared in various anthologies, journals, newspapers, magazines, on television and has been adapted for theater and radio. Follow him at twitter.com/MichaelJMoore20 or https://instagram.com/michaeljmoorewriting.*

E. C. Hanson

He earned his MFA in Dramatic Writing from NYU and was the recipient of an "Outstanding Writing For The Screen" certificate. He has been published Smith & Kraus and Applause Books in eight play anthologies. More than 35 of his ten-minute plays have been developed and produced in the United States. He's also been published with Trembling With Fear, Ghost Orchid Press,

*and The Parliament House. D&T Publishing will release his first
collection,* All Things Deadly *(Salem Stories), in August 2021.
As an educator, Hanson has taught undergraduate and gradu-
ate-level English courses at Sacred Heart University.*

J. Paré
*He has lived most of his life in Coventry, Rhode Island. He
lives with his wife, Patricia and his two children, Mikaela
and Tyler. He has been self-published with such titles as,*
Cycle of the Beast *and* Look Behind You. *His short fiction
has also appeared in* All Roads Magazine.

D.A. Butcher
Also known as *Dylan Alfredo Giovanni Butcher, he is half Brit-
ish, half Italian, and grew up in London, England. He worked
as a comic and movie journalist for three years, voluntarily, to
refine his writing skills. He has won writing competitions for
his short-stories and poetry, and been shortlisted for others
in leading writing magazines. He recently had a short-story
placed in a digital anthology. He now lives in the Midlands,
UK, with his wife and three children. Dylan is studying toward
his Master's Degree in English Literature and Creative Writing
with the Open University, and dreams of becoming a commer-
cially successful author. He recently self-published his debut
novel,* Eyes of Sleeping Children, *which is available to buy on
Amazon.*

Cory DeAn Cowley
*Cory DeAn Cowley was born and raised in Hendersonville, TN.
Growing up, Cowley always had curious interest in spirituality
and the occult. With an extensive background of theatre, she
has shot a multitude of videos, as well as acted, wrote, and produced plays. It was her dream to pursue writing and bringing
life to the words she has written. Cowley's primary goal is to
maintain the art of literature, and keep authenticity alive. Her
dark works are a testament to the meaning of soul. As a child
she spent many years becoming fascinated with underground
horror and becoming immersed in the dark culture surrounding
it. Cowley is currently a practicing esoteric/ Luciferian witch;*

with her personal knowledge, she gives her art and work a dark spin—allowing the reader or viewer to become lost in the worlds she creates.

Jess Rougeau
Jess is a horror writer living in New Orleans. Her book, Witch Doctor, *a horror poetry collection, is pretty cool too. You can check out www.thisiswitchdoctor.com for more info. She is currently working on a collection of scary short stories called Invisible Spells.*

C.M. Forest
C.M. Forest lives in LaSalle, Ontario with his wife and two children. His works include the short horror collection, The Space Between Houses, *a science fiction collection (co-authored),* No Light Tomorrow, *and a crime thriller novella titled* Sugar's Last Dance, *found in the anthology,* All These Crooked Streets. *His writing has also been published in a number of anthologies and short story collections. When not writing, he spends an exorbitant amount of time watching horror movies and playing video games. For more on C.M., head over to ChristianLaforet.com.*

E.S. Danon
E.S. Danon is the author of Moon In Bastet, the first book in The Battle of the Mystics *series. She has also written articles for magazines like* Hey Alma *and received an honorable mention by the* Writer's Digest *for her short story, "The Roku." In regard to horror, she used to see ghosts frequently as a kid, having lived in multiple haunted houses. Miller Drive is based off one experience that she had while living in Pennsylvania: she saw the apparition of a Union soldier standing behind her in the reflection of a window.*

Christopher M. Fink
Christopher M Fink is an up and coming horror author looking to give new life to the genre with all the chills, thrills, and savage kills you can handle. With his first anthology Sacrifices Incarnate, *and debut novel,* KyN, *coming soon, there will be nowhere to hide and nowhere to RUN.*

Abishek Parapuzha
Abishek Parapuzha is a first-time author. He practices writing by reading and watching films. While writing is not his professional occupation, he enjoys the art and is slowly developing his skill.

P. Vincent Horta
Peter lives with his longsuffering spouse and rambunctious young family in the Cincinnati metro area, where writing provides an enjoyable (and sometimes necessary!) reprieve from his professional career. Although working as a business lawyer finds him crunching numbers as often as crafting words, ages past have seen him published in print periodicals and as a digital marketing writer, and he is a onetime prizewinning poet. More recently he published the fantasy epic A King for Ravens, his first novel, which is the beginning of an anticipated trilogy.

Ali Blanco
Ali Blanco is a Latinx mother, writer and performer. She is a founder of Poets House Common Room, a community building poetry platform. Ali hosts various artistic events and shows, and aims to be a supportive, hype-womxn extraordinaire. She is also the genre editor of her college's literary magazine, The American River Review. *Her most recent work,* If Words Could Talk, *is a collection of poetry with themes in mental health, and identity. When she's not scribbling song lyrics at the piano, she can be found enjoying California life, lounging beneath the trees, brewing teas, and discussing Earth-saving solutions with anyone who will listen.*

Sara Brunner
Sara Brunner's a writer with a love for the avant garde, gothic, mysterious, and darker side of life. Bleeding melancholia nostalgia through onyx ink. Always being fascinated by what lurks in the shadows. None of this would've come to fruition without Anna, the only person in this life who means the world to her.

Author Bios

Jo Birdwell

Jo Birdwell hails from Texas and has been working full time as nurse since 2015. However, she has always been a writer at heart, spending her spare time working on short stories. Her genres of interest are horror and gothic short stories. "The Mortician's Daughter" is her first published work. Her hobbies include daily watching of horror films and collecting horror figures and memorabilia. She spends all her time at home with her husband, her new baby, and her fur baby. New on the writer scene, she is one to keep your eye on for further works.

Sophie Queen

Author of the Riley's Excellent and Not-At-All Fake Exorcism Service *Series. Sophie Queen has been telling fantastical stories from the time she was a little girl. A ravenous reader of classic gothic novels and has an unhealthy obsession with cheesy horror flicks. She has written a collection of unique short stories and even a poem or two. She lives with her husband, cat, dog, and sixty-five fish in an old (haunted) Victorian home.*

WANT MORE?

Check out current and future anthologies at
www.CTPFiction.com